She blew her nose again. It was not an elegant gesture. Nor did she look very appealing with her eyes all puffy, her lashes stuck together, and her nose a bright pink. A half-drowned rat was possibly more attractive. And Lesley found her irresistible. So he kissed her.

He'd been wanting to do it almost since he'd met the woman, so prim and proper he was challenged to see if he could melt her icy disdain. Then, when he'd seen her hair down, he'd wanted to taste her lips, to prove to himself that he was right, that a real woman lived inside the shell of sanctity she wore like a chastity belt. Recently, however, having come to know her sweetness and humor and intelligence, he'd simply wanted her.

Carissa did not struggle, did not kick him or slap him or stab him with her hatpin, wherever the thing had gone. She did not even take a step away, full knowing that he would release her at the first sign of resistance. No, she kissed him back. She'd been wanting to do that almost since she'd met the viscount, to see if a rake's kisses really were more proficient, more pleasing, more profound. They were. . . .

By *Barbara Metzger:*

Published by Fawcett Books

LORD
HEARTLESS

Barbara Metzger

FAWCETT CREST • NEW YORK

A Fawcett Crest Book
Published by The Ballantine Publishing Group
Copyright © 1998 by Barbara Metzger

All rights reserved under International and Pan-American Copyright Conventions. Published in the United States by The Ballantine Publishing Group, a division of Random House, Inc., New York, and simultaneously in Canada by Random House of Canada Limited, Toronto.

www.randomhouse.com/BB/

Library of Congress Catalog Card Number: 98-92930

ISBN 0-449-00171-7

Manufactured in the United States of America

First Edition: December 1998

10 9 8 7 6 5 4 3 2 1

To a very grandnephew indeed!
Joshua Collin Siegal
March 6, 1998
Welcome

Chapter One

*H*igh living was well nigh killing him. Lesley Hammond, Viscount Hartleigh, staggered out of the hired hackney in front of the narrow four-story brownstone in Kensington that he maintained for just such occasions. The occasions were occurring with such remarkable regularity, he hadn't stepped foot in the family pile in Grosvenor Square in months.

His head was splitting, his stomach was roiling, and he stank of spirits, cigars, and scent, but he had a roll of flimsies with which to pay the jarvey. He must, therefore, have had a lovely evening. In actuality, he'd had more of a full night, since rosy-fingered dawn was plucking at London's sooty skirts. Either that or he was seeing the world through bloodshot eyes.

As the quiet neighborhood prepared to face the new day, Viscount Hartleigh prepared to traverse the front yard of his pied-à-terre. The grounds were as big as his handkerchief, he knew, yet the front door seemed miles away to his bleary eyes, and up a flight of seven steps. Steps, by Zeus. At least this wasn't lofty Hammond House, home of his stepmother, her stepsisters, and more steps than the stairway to heaven. These seven seemed insurmountable enough. Lesley fumbled at the gate and then lurched forward, while his legs still remembered how to hold him upright. He immediately fell into a freshly dug hole. His forehead hit the brass stair rail before his cheek hit the bottom step. "I am going to murder that dog," he muttered, tasting blood from a cut lip.

As he lay there in the dirt, the viscount thought that he really ought to take control of his life one of these days. Take back Hammond House from the harpy and her half-witted stepsisters, take a wife, take his proper place in London Society. Right now he thought he'd take a nap.

No, Lesley told himself, this would never do, not at all. The sedate neighborhood of merchants and retired schoolmistresses was shocked enough by his comings and goings—and the company that came and went with him. The Applegate sisters next door were like to have apoplexy to find Viscount Hartleigh in his supine position, half in a hole, half draped over the riser, half conscious. He owed it to his name, his class, his pride, to at least go inside before passing out.

By dint of the dogged determination that made him such a renowned sportsman, gambler, and carouser, Lord Hartleigh dragged himself up the stairs and through the unlocked door. Such purpose and perseverance would have made him an admirable officer, if he'd been permitted to join the war effort. But Lesley was a viscount, heir to a dukedom. He was expected to provide the country with gossip, glamour, and another generation of overbred, overdressed, and underwhelming fribbles. He did what he could, sailing his yacht to bring home casualties. And he didn't drink French wine. The swill he did swallow was perhaps responsible for his current condition, but a fellow had to have the strength of his convictions.

He did not have the strength for the flight of stairs to his bedroom, however. "Bloody hell, who needs a bed anyway?" The sofa in his study would do, as it had for the past few nights, or weeks. He stumbled into the room, which would have fit into the butler's pantry at Hammond House, and tripped over the large hound that was asleep in the middle of the room, the same hound that hadn't sounded an alarm when someone entered the house at dawn and hadn't bothered to greet his own master. Luckily the viscount fell onto the couch. "I am definitely going to murder that dog," he vowed. "As soon as I wake up."

Awareness returned a great deal sooner than his lordship expected, desired, or was prepared for. After a deal of rattling crockery, a tray was slammed down next to his nose. Curtains were opened to let in enough light to pierce his closed eyelids, nay, to pierce his very brain. And someone was shaking his shoulder. Lesley groaned. "The house better be on fire, Byrd, or you're a dead man."

"It's worse'n a fire, Cap'n. You have to get up." Byrd was the viscount's sailing mate, majordomo, and longtime, long-suffering valet. "I brung coffee."

"Coffee isn't going to help. Get a pistol and put me out of my misery. You'd do as much for a lame horse." Hartleigh rolled over, moaning from the activity.

"Devil take it, Cap'n, this ain't no time for your gammon." Byrd hauled his employer to an upright position, propping his limp form in the corner of the couch.

Lesley tried to fix his eyes on the man—both of him. Byrd was a huge fellow who'd been a prizefighter or a pirate, or both. He never said, and Hartleigh never asked too closely. The bloke was useful to have around, except for times like these. With trembling hand, the viscount accepted the steaming mug from Byrd's massive mitt. "So what is it, Byrdie?" he asked with a sigh of resignation, knowing he'd get no peace until the man had his say. "Have the French invaded Kensington?"

"The Frogs we could handle, Cap'n. This, I'm not so sure about." Byrd shook his bald head, making the viscount's head spin even worse. "A package came this morning."

"A package? You disturbed a perfectly good hangover to tell me a package has been delivered?" The viscount would have shouted, but his tongue was stuck to the top of his mouth. He sipped at the scalding coffee and succeeded in scorching his esophagus. "Bloody hell!"

"It's not just any package," Byrd said, with a jerk of his head toward a large hamper that reposed near the fireplace. "And this came with it." He held out a folded note.

Lesley reached for the letter. It was on heavy, expensive paper, with his name scrawled across the front. Even if he hadn't recognized the handwriting, or the scent that perfumed the letter, he would have known the seal on the back. How could anyone not recognize the lions and crowns and mountains of Ziftswieg, Austria? His lips twitched in an effort at a smile. "Ah, Princess Fredericka Haffkesprinke. Find out where she is staying, Byrdie, and I'll call later. Much later." His eyes drifted shut.

"Ain't you going to see what she wants?" Byrd demanded.

Now Lesley smiled in truth, a soft, sensual grin. "Oh, I can guess what she wants. Not even for a command performance could I perform right now. Her Excellency will have to wait."

"There ain't no waiting, I tell you!" the big man almost whined. "Read the blasted letter!"

The viscount broke the seal, after much tooth-gnashing and hand-wringing from his servant, and fixed his eyes on the awkward script. " '*Liebchen* Lesley,' " he read aloud. " 'Here is a souvenir of our interlude in Vienna. *Salut.*' " He tossed the note aside. "She sent me a gift, is all. Nothing to get your britches in a bumblebroth. I'll look at it later and compose a very proper thank-you." He shut his eyes. When he did not hear the sounds of his heavy servant lumbering out of the room, the viscount added, "You're excused."

Instead, the wicker hamper was slammed into his lap.

"Just what my stomach needed, a bit of jostling. At least the princess's gift will be useful if I decide to cast up my accounts."

Byrd snatched the basket away. "Please, Lord Hartleigh, just look."

The use of his title finally roused the viscount. Poor Byrd must be more upset than he'd thought. So Lesley sat up straighter and nodded. After Byrd carefully laid the large hamper on the sofa next to him, the viscount reached out and gingerly raised the lid. All he saw was blankets. He raised an eyebrow in Byrd's direction, but the man just kept staring at the basket. "Damn if you don't think the princess is sending me Austrian adders, if they have such there. I swear I left the lady with a smile on her face, Byrdie."

Byrdie must have lost his sense of humor along with two of his teeth, Lesley decided. Gold caps were no substitute, none at all. He shrugged and folded back the top layer of soft wool. "I still don't see why this couldn't have waited until— Bloody hell, it's a baby!"

"That's the first thing you've got right today, Cap'n."

4

Lesley was gulping the coffee, burnt tongue bedamned. He held the cup out for more. A man needed his wits about him at a time like this. "A baby, by George!"

"By you, is more like it! What are you going to do about it?"

The viscount was doing some mental calculations. "Do you think he's about three months old?"

"How the bloody hell should I know how old the nipper is? I do know that foundling hospital is right across the square. Want I should take it there?"

Lesley was staring at the sleeping child, all pink and rosebud-lipped. He hadn't been the princess's first lover, he knew, and probably not her last, but the timing seemed right that this was, indeed, his child. The pale fuzz on its head could have been a match to his own blond curls—or Byrd's bald pate. He touched the infant's cheek with the tip of his finger, and sky-blue eyes opened, eyes with the same distinctive black rim of Lesley's own eyes. "My son."

The babe stared up at him, yawned, and went back to sleep, obviously not as impressed by what it saw as the viscount was. "My very own son."

"How do you know?" Byrd asked.

"Did you see those eyes? There can't be any question."

"There never was. Even a princess can count on her fingers. But how do you know it's a boy?"

The viscount reread the note. And again.

Byrd shook his bald head. "It don't say."

"It has to be a boy, is all. You check."

Byrd jumped back. "Not me. I weren't laying with no high-born bird of paradise. And I weren't hired on to be no wet nurse, neither, so you better figure how to get rid of the little bugger. I'll take it to the foundling home, but that's all."

His son, in an orphanage? "I don't think those places are very healthful. I'm sure I can find a decent family to take him in. That must be why Fredericka left him here."

"She sure as Satan couldn't think you'd make the bantling a proper da," Byrd said, laughing.

The viscount frowned. "She could have left him at a church. Isn't that what women always do in novels?"

Byrd hadn't read many novels. "What's a bishop to do with a bastard? I'm sure he's got enough of his own. And even that popish church is tended by women what never wanted infants of their own. They'd all just take it to St. Cecilia's Home."

Where every whore dumped her unwanted get. Where mill owners and chimney sweeps came to buy likely workers. Where there wasn't enough food or heat or money to go around. No education, no name, no affection. "No, not my son."

Byrd cursed through his gold teeth. "Tarnation, Cap'n, you still don't even know if it is a lad or a lass. And if you're thinking of keeping the mite here, I'll be off to start my packing."

"You can't leave me, Byrdie. Not now." He gingerly peeled back two more layers of blankets to reveal a lace-trimmed infant gown and soft white woolen booties. "Look at how tiny those feet are," he marveled.

"Just find out what else he's got tiny, Cap'n, and get rid of him."

Lesley placed one finger under the skirt's hem and lifted, while Byrd leaned over the basket. The manservant jumped back, waving one hand in front of his nose.

The dog got up and left the room.

"My friend," the viscount said, "we are in deep . . . trouble."

Chapter Two

"*W*e need help."

Byrd backed up another step. "What do you mean, 'we'? I weren't the one cuddling in castles, Cap'n."

Hartleigh ignored his man. He couldn't ignore the pounding in his head half so well. He dragged unsteady hands through his fair curls. "Dash it, I've got to think."

"There's naught to think on, Cap'n. We've just got to get the young'un over to that home afore anyone sees your butter stamp. It's not like we're taking it out to drown or anything, like a litter of stray pups. Hell, half the men in your crew came out of orphanages."

Did Lesley want his son growing up to be a half-savage sailor? This son could never grow to be viscount, of course, but a solicitor, a land steward, a scholar? Any of those were within reason.

Byrd was going on: "And we've got to do it afore the whelp wakes up."

The viscount looked down at the sleeping infant, noting the bluish veins on his eyelids, the curl to his perfect ears. This tiny cherub was his—and was going to wake up hungry. Hartleigh looked at his man in stark terror. The viscount had sailed his yacht through fleets of French warships to bring messages to Wellesley and help transport wounded officers back home; he'd been out twice on the field of honor; he'd even told Sally Jersey to give her tongue a rest. But this? This was beyond him. "Oh, my Lord. What'll we do?"

"What I've been telling you, Cap'n. And soon, by the look

of it." The child was beginning to make soft whimpering noises and sucking sounds.

Lesley gulped more of the coffee. "Lud, the sprat's entire life depends on my decision. I ought to make it sober, at least."

Byrd wisely refrained from noting that the viscount rarely did anything while sober. "What's to decide? You can't take the cub to your stepmama, can you?"

Agatha, Lesley's father's widow, was but ten years older than her stepson, and disapproved of everything about him except for his title and wealth, which she firmly intended to ensnare for one of her bran-faced stepsisters. She was also vaporish, viperish, and as ugly as a vole. "Jupiter, can you imagine the uproar if I asked her to look after a baseborn brat? Burnt feathers and sal volatile and laudanum drops—and that's before I told her it was mine. Besides, the female has less maternal instinct than an andiron. If my father thought he was going to get his spare heir off her, he was sorely disappointed. Chances are, once she had his ring on her finger, she had nothing but headaches and excuses for him." He shuddered at the idea of anyone willingly bedding Agatha Crumwell.

"I never understood why he married her in the first place. Wasn't like your father needed her da's blunt. And the governor could have had any chit from the ton iffen he wanted a young bride, without taking on some mine owner's daughter."

"Trapped, he was, in an inn and a snowstorm and a room with no lock on the door. Rolled up, horse, boot, and rifle. He was a downy bird, but no match for the scheming jade, who was set on getting a title one way or the other. No, I wouldn't inflict the shrew on any innocent babe."

"Then take the nipper to one of your friends' houses. Some of your cronies have to have legshackles, I'd guess."

"And promising families, but I can promise you that no lady is going to take in a bastard. Highborn females are taught to ignore the very existence of such unfortunate creatures. They'd all go off in strong hysterics like Lady Hartleigh, and then their husbands would be calling me out. But you know, I believe you have given me an idea. . . ."

Byrd muttered, "I should of given you a kick in the—"

"An excellent idea! Nothing is more likely to get me out of the Marriage Mart than an illegitimate issue. What woman would agree to rear another female's love child? What papa would let his daughter near such a loose screw? Why, Agatha might even send her sisters back to Yorkshire rather than let the gruesome twosome be contaminated by my wicked ways. I'd be free, Byrdie, free of all those females twisting their ankles on my doorstep, free of the chits trying to sneak into my bedroom at house parties, free of those man-eating mothers of marriageable misses."

"You wouldn't be free. You'd have a baby." A baby whose fists were starting to wave in the air and whose lower lip was starting to tremble.

"But only for a while. Just long enough to make a stir and give everyone a disgust of me."

Byrd was disgusted already. "I'll be handing in my notice, then."

The viscount ignored him. "Meanwhile I'll be having my solicitor look out for a nice family to raise the infant. Perhaps in the country. There must be some childless couple who'd jump at the chance, especially if I agree to pay for his expenses and education."

"And while this search is going on, are you going to feed the nipper and change its nappies?"

The viscount's complexion turned from gray to green. "Of course not. I'll, ah, hire a nursemaid. Find me a newspaper. There's bound to be an advertisement or two."

Byrd shook his head, but went to see if, in addition to this morning's catastrophe, the morning paper had been delivered.

Lesley decided he needed another cup of coffee, at least, so reached for the pot on the table next to him. Just then the baby awoke entirely, hungry, soiled, frightened, and loud. Mostly loud. The pot landed on the floor; the hot coffee landed in the viscount's lap. "Byrd!" he shouted. "Get in here!" The infant screamed louder. Lesley's insides tied themselves in knots, and his brains—what few he had left—tried to escape the din by drilling on his skull. "How far away is that foundling hospital?"

"I'll get the carriage," Byrd said, tossing down the papers.

"No, get some milk."

"But you always drink your coffee black, Cap'n. What you don't pour on your pantaloons."

"Not for me, nodcock. For the infant."

Byrd groaned, which was barely audible over the squalling. "I think we had some cream t'other day, iffen it ain't curdled."

"No, go get some fresh. There's always a dairymaid around the streets this time of day." He knew that from coming home so many times after daybreak. "Do you think he can drink from a cup?" he asked as an afterthought.

"How the bloody hell should I know? I never had a baby, never touched a baby, and, far as I know, never was a baby. You're the one as got all goo-ga over your get, so you figure it out. And figure how to shut the brat up meantime, else you'll have the Watch here for disturbing the peace. The tyke likely misses his mum. Whyn't you pick him up or something?"

"I doubt he ever saw the princess after he was born. And pick him up? But he's all wet and . . ."

Byrd shrugged and went to find a milkmaid, leaving his lordship alone with the bawling bairn. That ought to knock some sense into the viscount, Byrd thought. Lord Heartless tending an infant? Hah! Not for long, he wouldn't.

When Byrd returned, though, having taken his own sweet time about fetching the milk, all was quiet in the little room. The viscount was rocking the wicker basket with his left hand, and dribbling brandy—laid down in his father's time, long before the embargo—off his finger into the baby's open mouth with his right. Occasionally he paused in one activity or the other to lift the decanter to his own lips for a hefty swallow. "There, this isn't so hard."

They tried dripping milk into the gummy mouth from the viscount's handkerchief, then they tried spooning it, pouring it, soaking a sponge with it for the sprout to suck on. The milk was on the baby, on the viscount, on the floor. The dog belched. And the baby's blue eyes, staring up so trustingly at the viscount, started to fill with tears.

"We need help."

"We need a blooming miracle."

The viscount cudgeled his already battered brains for the name of a temporary angel of mercy—and motherhood. He needed someone with knowledge of the infantry, not too high in the instep to look after a nameless brat; someone who lived in the immediate neighborhood. Junior's face was beginning to turn red, a sight more frightening to the viscount and his servant than any French cannons. Lesley did a mental tour of Gibsonia Street. Surely in this little corner of Kensington resided someone whom he could bribe or browbeat or beg into coming to his aid.

A family with hordes of ragged children lived around the corner. The viscount was always threatening to horsewhip the urchins for playing in the street, disturbing his daytime rest. The mother, a drink-sodden, slovenly creature, was forever threatening to take her rolling pin to him. No, she knew less about tender infants than Lesley did. And she'd likely laugh in his face, to boot.

According to Byrd, the two children who lived behind them never stopped sniffling and wheezing. That wouldn't do. The young couple next door were childless, and she had a racking cough besides. The schoolteachers on his other side were dried old prunes, and the elderly couple across the street were high sticklers. A solicitor and his grown son resided next to them.

Which left Sir Gilliam Parkhurst's housekeeper, two doors down across the street. Lesley shivered at the thought. The female was a prig. She dressed like a crow in shapeless black, with her hair scraped back under a hideous mobcap. Worse, her lips were always pursed in disapproval and her spine was as stiff as a poker. She crossed to the other side of the street when she saw the viscount coming, lest she be turned into a toad by his proximity, he supposed. Heaven knew it would take more than the viscount's vaunted powers as a rake to turn her into a warm and willing woman. Granted, Sir Gilliam's housekeeper only saw him infrequently, and when he was not quite at his best. Like the unfortunate time he was relieving himself in the bushes, or when he was escorting that bit o' muslin to the carriage. How was he supposed to know he had silk stockings draped over his shoulder? He did allow as how the widow had seen him arrive home in his evening clothes on more than a few instances, when she was returning after her morning grocery shopping. What business was it of hers, though, that she should raise her chin in the air and turn her back? After all, Hartleigh never paid heed to Byrd's speculations that Mrs. Kane was not really a widow, and was not, in fact, Sir Gilliam's housekeeper. He pitied the old knight if she was anything more, but doubted the redoubtable female was warming the banker's bed. She wore her mantle of respectability with such a vengeance, 'twas more likely she'd sent Mr. Kane to an early grave so she could be rid of him and his baser instincts. Lesley shuddered again. Kane was probably happy to stick his spoon in the wall.

None of which made a ha'penny's worth of difference to Lord Hartleigh. A proper upper servant or a prodigious actress, Mrs. Kane had a daughter. The child wasn't in leading strings, but was small, solemn-eyed, and quiet, and the widow took her everywhere with her. While Mrs. Kane was marching to the rhythm of respectability, the little girl skipped at her side. She seemed happy and healthy and devoted to her mother. That was enough recommendation for the desperate peer.

"Mrs. Kane it will have to be. You'd better go ask her to stop over," he told Byrd. "The woman hates me."

"Well, she plumb terrifies me. I ain't going."

Not for the first time, Viscount Hartleigh regretted being on such familiar terms with his employee. They'd been through too much together, however, for him to come the lord and master at this point, so he pushed himself up off the sofa and tugged at his mud-and-milk-spattered waistcoat. His neckcloth hung in limp folds down his filthy shirtfront, and his trousers were still damp with coffee. His cheek was scraped raw, and a purplish bruise was forming on his chin, just visible under the blond stubble. He sighed, thinking of the widow's likely reaction. There was no hope for it, though, no time for a bath or a change of clothes, not from the sounds coming from the basket. "Very well, I'll go across the street. You stay with the baby."

The infant was starting to wail again. Byrd was already at the door. "You don't pay me enough."

"I'll double your salary, by George!"

"Fine, and you can send it on to me in Dover. Moral morts and infants is two things I can't stomach. I won't even be asking for a reference, Cap'n, for no one'd hire me on your say-so anyway. Not as a valet, leastways."

Chapter Three

*L*oyalty was everything; money was more. They both went. Hartleigh carried the basket as far from him as he could; Byrd carried the hopes of his own pub a little closer to his heart. The exhausted infant slept again, thank goodness.

The viscount rapped on the front door of the dwelling that resembled his own in shape and matching brownstone, naught else. This building's lawn appeared manicured, with carefully trimmed shrubbery and a border garden of bright spring flowers. The steps were swept, the railing was polished, the knocker gleamed. Curtains hung in all the windows and the shutters were newly painted. Whatever else she might be, Lesley considered, Mrs. Kane kept a neat house. He rapped again. Someone had to be awake, at such a respectable domicile. The hour might be early by his standards—hell, it was the middle of the night, by his standards—but the rest of Kensington was surely stirring.

A very proper butler finally answered the door, with immaculate white gloves and powdered wig. The man was short, thin, and sharp-featured, and the nostrils on his pointed nose flared at the sight that met his close-set, beady eyes. He looked like an indignant weasel, Lesley noted in the half second before the door slammed in his face.

"I told you we should of used the servants' entry," Byrd said, adding to the unraveling of the viscount's already frayed temper.

"I," his lordship pronounced, "am not a servant." Lesley squared his shoulders to their not inconsiderable width, raised his square chin, and hit the door squarely in the middle with his

14

fist. The door shook. This time, when the stiff-rumped rodent opened the door, the viscount pushed it in and stepped inside before the butler could slam it again. From his greater height and greater arrogance, Lesley announced: "I am Hartleigh and I have come to see your Mrs. Kane."

If anything, the butler's demeanor grew more contemptuous. He couldn't look down his pointed nose, but he could thin his lips into a smirk. "Mrs. Kane is an employee here. She does not receive, ahem, gentlemen callers."

Lesley would have stuffed that "ahem" down the dastard's throat, except Byrd's cough reminded him of the urgency of their mission. "This is not a social visit, my good man, so please be so kind as to fetch the woman."

The butler announced, with equal pomp and satisfaction, "Tradesmen may call at the delivery gate."

The viscount supposed that his appearance was off-putting enough to justify the man's lack of deference, and his reputation might have preceded him. An unfortunate aroma certainly did. Still, such a decided lack of cordiality rankled. Lesley could easily have gone around to the back gate. Lud knew he'd used the kitchen entrance or the servants' door or the second-floor window, even, to reach a lover's bedroom, but not today, and not at this rat-faced rudesby's direction. So he didn't look bang up to the mark, and his companions didn't smell so sweet; he was still a peer of the realm. "Viscounts use the front door, sirrah."

The butler sneered and stood his ground, looking from Hartleigh's scuffed boots to his bedraggled neckcloth.

"Want I should darken his daylights, Cap'n?" Byrd asked.

"That will not be necessary, gentlemen. What seems to be the problem, Mason?"

They all looked toward the stairs, where an elderly, silver-haired gentleman was descending on the arm of a young footman. Lesley had been introduced to the wealthy cit, now a knight, on a few occasions at Carlton House, so before the butler could open his mouth, Lesley bowed. "Forgive the disturbance, Sir Gilliam, but we have a bit of an emergency," he understated.

"More like a calamity," Byrd was muttering from behind him, as Sir Gilliam made his slow way across the entry hall.

Sir Gilliam adjusted his spectacles and surveyed his callers. "Yes, I can see that you do, my lord." The old man's eyes widened at the sight of the basket which now rested near the viscount's foot. "Indeed." He coughed, and took a moment to catch his breath. "How may I, ah, be of assistance?"

"It's your housekeeper I've come to ask for help, actually. I was hoping she might be of temporary aid, until I can make other arrangements, of course. Your Mrs., uh—Kane, is it?— seemed the likeliest, nearest source of advice in this quandary."

"Yes, Mrs. Kane is quite the most competent female and an excellent mother. I am sure she will be happy to render what service she can." He coughed again. "Mason, why don't you show his lordship to Mrs. Kane's sitting room?" His nose twitched. "Pardon me if I do not invite you gentlemen to share my breakfast parlor."

Mason turned his back and stalked out of the entry, down the central corridor, his rigid spine bespeaking silent reproof. Lesley shrugged and, with another bow toward his host, gathered up the straw basket and followed. Mason showed them into a neat parlor at the rear of the house, jerked his head in barest obeisance, and left.

They waited, and waited. "The gent didn't tell that Mason fellow to fetch the woman, only to show us here," Byrd said, unnecessarily, in Lesley's opinion.

The viscount had been pacing the tiny room, checking his watch against the plain wooden clock on the mantel. Other than the timepiece, the shelf was bare except for a small vase of flowers and a miniature of a man in uniform. He felt like an intruder. "I know that, you clunch. And the cur must have known she'd be about her duties somewhere. We'll just have to find her."

"Like as not, they know where she is—in the kitchen. Told you we should of used the service entrance."

Lesley gritted his teeth and followed another uppity servant—this one his own—down another well-lighted, well-maintained corridor.

Mrs. Carissa Kane was indeed in the kitchen, fixing Sir Gilliam's breakfast plate just the way he liked it: two eggs, two slices of toast, two rashers of bacon. He wouldn't eat more; she wouldn't offer him less. Carissa also made sure her employer's favorite jam was on the tray, and some fresh butter, with a rose stamped into each pat. While she waited for the bell from Mason to indicate that Sir Gilliam was seated, with his coffee and his newspaper, Mrs. Kane arranged some tulips from the front border garden into a jasperware vase. She kept glancing over to the corner of the kitchen, where her daughter, Philippa, was eating her porridge. The four-year-old sat with her bare feet tucked under her stool, carefully out of the way of Cook, who was kneading dough for the tea cakes, and Bonnie, the maid, who was cleaning the already spotless kitchen.

"If you are very good this morning, Pippa," Mrs. Kane told the brown-haired child, "perhaps Cook will make an extra raspberry tart. Should you like that?"

The little girl nodded solemnly and kept spooning up her breakfast.

Cook smiled and said, "Our Pippa is always an angel, isn't that the Lord's own— Oh, my stars and Scriptures!" She dropped the bowl she was holding with a clatter, the spoon falling to the floor. Bonnie shrieked and raised her apron over her head. Pippa kept eating her porridge.

Frowning, Carissa looked toward the doorway, where everyone's eyes seemed to be fixed, and she almost dropped the expensive vase. "Good heavens," she whispered. There in the entry of her orderly kitchen, a place where even Mason seldom intruded, stood two of the most disreputable characters she could imagine. Carissa couldn't decide if she ought to grab up her daughter and run, or reach for Cook's meat cleaver to defend them all. What such brigands were doing invading Sir Gilliam's quiet kitchen she could not imagine, but there they were, bigger than life.

The younger, shorter of the men, the one wearing the remains of a fashionable ensemble, with the remains of his breakfast, bowed slightly and stepped farther into the room. "Mrs. Kane?"

Now Carissa recognized the callers—and they were still her worst nightmares, both of them, the pirate and the profligate peer. The gentleman, and she used the term loosely, was the rake who staggered home nearly every morning in his evening clothes. He lived in that derelict house across the street, although he definitely belonged across town with the other pleasure-seeking patricians. Bonnie and Cook had speculated endlessly as to why such a wellborn, well-heeled toff would choose to reside in Kensington when he had a perfectly splendid mansion in Mayfair. They had also made sure Carissa knew that he was Lesley Hammond, Lord Hartleigh, the viscount the *on dits* columns labeled Lord Heartless. They dubbed him thus, Carissa was given to understand, not because he was unkind, but because he was unattainable. London's premier matrimonial prize wasn't brutal; he'd just left a broad swath of bruised hearts behind him. He hadn't yet succumbed to the beau monde's beauties or the demimonde's dashers. Nary a woman in all his four-and-thirty years had held his affection for more than a brief—albeit joyful, by repute—affair. Lord Heartless was as fickle as a flea, and as hard to catch. The women were the ones who were left heartsore and sad, which never stopped a single ninnyhammer from vying for his attention, to Cook's glee and Carissa's disgust.

"I am Hartleigh, ma'am," he was saying now, as if there were a female in all of London unaware of his name, "and Sir Gilliam gave me leave to ask your assistance with a small difficulty."

Lord Hartleigh's oversized companion cleared his throat and stepped forward. "Byrd, ma'am. Aloysius Byrd, at your service." He doffed his cap, revealing a distorted ear and a pate as bald as the eggshells from Sir Gilliam's breakfast, except for the seagull tattooed there. And then he smiled, showing two gold teeth. Bonnie shrieked and fled into the pantry. Carissa wished she could do the same. She glanced to make sure Pippa wasn't frightened, but the child was staring from one of the visitors to the other, brown eyes wide in her little face, with her porridge forgotten.

"Pippa, eat your breakfast before it gets cold," Carissa said, trying to maintain some shreds of control in this bizarre situation. Cook's mouth was hanging open, so she was going to be no help. Carissa ignored the brawny buccaneer and turned her attention back to his lordship. He looked like something her cat would be too fastidious to drag in, so she asked, "A difficulty, you say? Has there been a carriage accident? I'm not surprised, thee way you dr—" She recalled her manners and didn't even reprimand him for springing his horses on the narrow street where children were wont to play. Not her child, of course. "Ah, that is, perhaps you should call for a physician?"

"No, there has not been a carriage accident," Lesley said through clenched teeth. Damn if the starched-up crone wasn't itching to treat him to another reproach about the decadent aristocracy. He could see she was thinking it, the way her arms were crossed and her brow was lowered over dark eyes. Thunderation, all he wanted was to rest his aching head on something soft. Lud knew there was nothing soft about Mrs. Kane. Still, he had no choice but to lay his burden, and his basket, at her feet. "This arrived on my doorstep a short while ago."

Carissa was not about to touch such a noisome object. Wrinkling her nose, she waited for him to continue. Instead, he peeled back the covers. "Why, it's a baby!" she exclaimed.

"Why does everyone think I cannot recognize an infant?" Lesley muttered. "Yes, ma'am, it is a baby, and I have no idea what to do with it or for it. I was hoping you could come across the street and help."

"Lord have mercy, who'd have mistaken your love nest for the foundling hospital?" Cook had found her voice.

The viscount frowned, but addressed his answer to the housekeeper. "A, ah, friend had to travel suddenly."

"And left her baby?" Carissa was incredulous. "With you?" She was kneeling down to examine the sleeping babe when the service bell rang. "Oh, dear, Sir Gilliam is ready for his breakfast."

Cook made a rude noise. "Ain't that just like Mason, when

19

he knows you're in the middle of a hobble. The little runt could have fetched the tray hisself, for once."

Carissa stood and raised the tray, shaking her head when Byrd, filthy hands and all, would have taken it from her. "I'll just be a minute, and the child seems to be sleeping for now. Pippa, do not feed the cat the rest of your porridge." She disappeared through the door, but Lesley wasn't about to let his unlikely angel out of his sight, now that he'd found her. He hefted the basket and followed, with Byrd on his heels.

Sir Gilliam raised his brows when the threesome entered his morning room. "Thank you, my dear," he said when Carissa placed his plate before him and arranged the flowers in the center of the table. "Do you think you'll be able to assist his lordship with this, ah, small problem he seems to have?"

"Yes, sir—that is, if it is all right with you, Sir Gilliam."

He waved her off with one gnarled hand. "Go on, go on with you. Take all the time you need. The linen closets and laundry can wait. His lordship cannot, by the looks of him. Just make sure you are back by supper," he said with a smile, "to tell me all about it."

"And you'll take Cook's posset when I'm gone, and remember to wear your scarf when you go out?"

"Yes, yes, my dear. Don't fuss. I'll be fine."

Carissa looked at him uncertainly, then at the basket the ragtag viscount was dangling from one hand. She nodded, curtsied to her employer, and took the hamper away from Lord Hartleigh. "Follow me, my lord. I'll gather whatever I can think of for now, perhaps some sheets if you have nothing better."

She collected some clean bottles and soft towels into a market basket, along with the fresh bread the men were eyeing, meanwhile giving instructions to Cook and the maid. She handed Philippa's shoes to the viscount. "Someone help her with the buttons while I go fetch the sheets, then we'll be ready."

Lesley looked at the small boots in his hand, then at the small child. He looked at the cook, who was up to her elbows in dough. She winked at him. The maid was washing pots in the sink, too bashful to meet his eyes. He turned to Byrd, who grinned. "You're the one in the petticoat line, Cap'n."

Groaning, Lesley lowered himself to the floor near the stool. A small finger reached out to touch the unshaven stubble on his chin. The chit's nose wrinkled in exact imitation of her mother, then she nodded and put her thumb in her mouth, staring at the viscount. When he finished, the laces every which way, the bows in knots, Lesley wiped the sweat off his brow.

The thumb came out of the moppet's mouth only long enough for her to inform the viscount, "I could make mice feet myself."

He was saved having to answer by the reappearance of Mrs. Kane. She had her cloak, and one for the little girl. "Ah, it might be better to leave the br—uh, child here. One of the servants could watch her."

Carissa glared at the viscount, as out of place in her kitchen as she would be at Almack's. "My lord, I *am* one of the servants."

Chapter Four

No apologies, no excuses. Lords did not explain their actions to the lower orders, yet Lesley's unsettled stomach was churning as he led the silent little band across the street. The difference between Sir Gilliam's tidy property and his own dilapidated domicile was glaring by the light of day, even to his bloodshot eyes. There was, in fact, no explanation that he could have given. Instead, he warned Mrs. Kane, who clutched the baby's basket in one hand, her daughter's wrist in the other, to beware of the holes.

"I am well acquainted with these holes, my lord," she told him, picking her way across the erstwhile lawn. "We have similar ones at Sir Gilliam's, where my azalea used to be, where the rosebush once stood, where I tried to plant an herb garden, where—"

"Yes, well, here we are then." Lesley coughed and pushed open the front door. He tried to make light of the chaos within. "It's not what you're used to, I'm sure. Bachelor digs, don't you know."

He could see her looking around for a clean place to set down the baby, so he swept his arm across the hall table, sending bottles and dishes, racing forms and a painted fan, to the floor. Thank heaven, he thought, she hadn't glimpsed the risqué painting on the fan. The widow's nose was already twitching so fast she was in danger of turning into a squirrel. "There is an unused bedroom abovestairs. That should be in order."

Carissa pursed her lips. "First the kitchen, I think."

Well, they hardly used the place, Lesley reflected, so how bad could it be? Mrs. Kane's gasp told him. "The, ah, staff left

22

precipitously." So much for no excuses. "I haven't had a chance to replace them."

In two years, by the looks of things. Carissa was horrified, itching to take Pippa and the baby back across the street. But she could never bring the infant to Sir Gilliam's, she knew, even if the poor scrap didn't belong to the viscount. Mason gave her enough trouble over Pippa as it was. The martinet would stir up such a dust if she brought the baby back that Sir Gilliam would be disturbed, which she would not do, not even for an innocent tyke. Lord Hartleigh would just have to put this place in order, unless . . . "You are not below hatches, are you, my lord?" Perhaps that would explain why such a nonpareil was living in Kensington. No rumors of his pecuniary embarrassment had come Cook's way, however, or Carissa would have been bound to hear. "You know, punting on tick, I believe it is called."

The muscles in the viscount's jaw bulged from his effort not to bite her head off. "I know what it is called, Mrs. Kane. And no, I am not in Dun Territory."

She let her eyes encompass the room again before coming back to him. "Then why do you live this way, my lord?"

"Because, madam, I simply do not care."

"How sad."

The drab felt sorry for him? The gall, the effrontery! She was the one earning her keep in a menial post, or on her back, and she felt pity for him? "You are impertinent, ma'am."

Instead of putting her in her place, the viscount's words seemed to amuse the woman. She smiled, taking five years off her age, at least, and asked, "Shall I leave, then?"

It was extortion, plain and simple, and it was deuced effective. Byrd was nearly apoplectic. "It's just his way, ma'am, he don't mean nothing by coming the heavy. Do you, Cap'n?"

The viscount bowed toward the black-clad widow and bowed toward the inevitable. "My apologies, Mrs. Kane. No offense intended." No apologies, no excuses, hah! Next Miss Prunes and Prisms would have him groveling at her feet, lest she abandon them.

Carissa had cleared an area on the kitchen table for the

baby's hamper, and found a not-too-rickety chair for Philippa. She gestured for Byrd to start the fire, and was looking around for a pan big enough for a baby bath. "Very well, my lord," she called over her shoulder, "but this simply will not do. You cannot keep a child here, no matter how temporarily."

"The room upstairs will be adequate. How much space does an infant require?"

"It is not a matter of space. Pigs thrive in sties, my lord, infants do not."

"I did say I was meaning to hire servants, Mrs. Kane. I'll do so immediately."

She nodded. "I'll write a note to the employment agency Sir Gilliam patronizes. I am sure they can send the beginnings of a staff over this afternoon. Whether they stay or not is another question." Carissa was doubtful, but there were few enough positions open that some poor souls might have to accept this one. She turned to the viscount's man. "You do know how to heat water, Mr. Byrd, don't you? The child needs a bath as soon as can be." She could not help glancing toward the viscount. "Some extra hot water would not come amiss either."

Byrd grinned and set kettles on to heat, lots of kettles. Trying to appear not altogether useless, the viscount was manning the kitchen pump to fill them. With every movement, his stomach gave another lurch. He could not help the groan that escaped his lips.

"Oh, do sit down, my lord, before you fall down. Perhaps this will help." The widow placed the loaf of fresh bread in front of him on the scarred and sticky table when he did collapse onto the only other chair in the room. Her daughter was still staring at him, sucking her thumb. He sat up straighter, trying to decide which female's disdain annoyed him more.

Mrs. Kane was bending over the infant in its basket, cooing softly. She sniffed, then sniffed again, then gasped. "Why, this child smells of spirits! What have you done?"

Lesley swallowed the bit of bread, which was now lodged in his throat. "Nothing. That is, my, ah, glass spilled while I was trying to—"

Ever helpful, Byrd put in: "An' he sleeps better for it, too."

Carissa didn't want to know whether the baby slept better or the viscount. "That's why he is still napping, despite the jostling and all. The poor lamb will have a headache when he wakes, I'm sure."

Someone could have a tad of sympathy for *his* headache, the viscount was thinking, wishing they would all lower their voices, but he wisely held his tongue. No need to aggravate his savior more than his presence already did.

"My lord, you have no business having a baby."

So much for restraint, he thought. For a servant, Mrs. Kane certainly spoke her mind. And Byrd was helping her. "That's just what I told him, missus. No business a'tall."

"For the last time, my son—that is, my ward—stays here, until I can make other arrangements."

Mrs. Kane was scornful. "Do you know what kind of 'arrangements' you'll have to make for even the shortest time? You'll need a wet nurse, a nanny, a crib, clothes and blankets, an army to clean this barracks so the dust bunnies don't swallow your s—ward."

All he could do was try his infallible charm. Lesley smiled and said, "There, I knew you'd know just what was to be done. In fact, why don't you stay and oversee the overhaul of the place? I'll double whatever it is Sir Gilliam pays you."

Carissa bit her lip to keep from laughing at his hopeful appeal. "No, I could never leave Sir Gilliam. He has been much too kind to me and Philippa. But I will send that note to the employment agency. Now I think the water should be warm enough for this young man's bath. What is his name?"

Byrd and Hartleigh looked to each other, then at the baby.

"You don't know?"

"The note that arrived with him didn't say." The viscount pulled the now-tattered letter from his pocket.

"Thing is, we don't rightly know if he is a he in the first place."

Carissa could only shake her head at yet another instance of the handsome lord's lunacy, and started unbuttoning the baby's gown and infant shirt. "Whatever makes you think it's a boy, then?"

Lesley shrugged. Of course he'd have a boy. "He hasn't much hair. And . . . and he belched."

She laughed, one of the few sounds that did not seem to grate on the viscount's aching eardrums, and kept removing layers of fine cloth. "All babies expel air, my lord, and few have much hair for months. You, my lord, have a daughter."

A daughter? Lesley looked at Mrs. Kane's doll-like daughter sucking her thumb, whose big brown eyes accused him of crimes he'd never thought of committing. A daughter? No soldier or seaman or stud-farm steward, but a porcelain princess? "Bloody hell, what the devil am I going to do with a daughter?" Stunned, he didn't even try to claim he was simply guardian for a friend's child.

"The same as you would with a son. You'll find some caring family to adopt her, and give them a bit of money for her dowry. She'll never know her birth was irregular, never have the stigma of illegitimacy, and you will know she is safe and loved. Will you hand me that towel, my lord?"

The viscount was still muttering, though. "A daughter?"

While Mrs. Kane bathed the baby, the viscount tried to clean himself with the jug of hot water Byrd had brought up to his room. Fresh clothes and a hurried shave made him feel more human, and the coffee and another slice of bread made him almost confident that he'd live through the rest of the morning. Now all he needed was a nap while Byrd went to the hiring agency, Lesley decided. Unfortunately, the baby was screaming again. Now, wasn't that just like a female to be complaining when a chap was in queer stirrups? A daughter, bah! No wonder King Lear was so mad. No wonder Prinny was such a jobbernowl.

Mrs. Kane looked up when he entered the kitchen. A few honey-brown tresses had come out of her mobcap and were lying along her cheek, curling from the heat of the infant's bath. She was singing to the crying baby, rocking it in her arms. Damned if the woman wasn't looking more human too, Lord Hartleigh considered. Then she glared at him. No, he must be foxed still, to think he'd glimpsed a Madonna-like loveliness in the dried-up housekeeper.

Carissa was angry with the viscount for being turned out bang up to the mark—except for a smudge on his cheek—while his daughter was in such distress. The infant did not even have a change of clothes, and his lordship was dressed to the nines. And she did not like the way he looked at her, as if he was measuring her and finding her wanting. Well, in truth, she *was* wanting—to plant him a facer! "Your daughter is hungry, my lord," she snapped.

"Then feed her!" The noise was bringing his headache back.

"I am as ill equipped as you are, my lord, and shouting at me will not help. What you need is a wet nurse."

"By Jupiter, ma'am, you'd give a drowning man directions to the nearest lighthouse! I know I need a wet nurse; Byrd is out looking. Can't you do something until he finds one?"

Carissa hated to think where Mr. Byrd might be looking. The docks, she supposed, where some gin-soaked doxy would let her own child go hungry for a few coins. Cow's milk would have to be better than that. "I'll need a glove."

Hartleigh found one on the floor in his study. She wouldn't touch it. "No, my lord," Carissa said in a voice she might have used on her four-year-old. "It has to be clean." Cleaner than anything she'd seen in this house so far. "Do you have any new ones?"

Hartleigh was gone long enough that she feared he'd gone out to purchase a pair, leaving her with an infant who was beyond comforting. He returned eventually with a butter-soft pair of York tan leather. "I recalled these were delivered last week, but could not locate where Byrd had put them."

The gloves were more expensive than every pair Carissa had owned for the last five years, combined. They would have been custom-cut, of course, from patterns made from the viscount's hands. No store-bought, ready-made, ill-fitting gloves for his lordship. Of course not. With no compunction whatsoever, Carissa took her sewing kit out of her reticule, found her embroidery scissors, and cut off the soft thumb from the right hand.

Lesley winced, but acknowledged the justice in the sacrilege. If he'd had a glove in Vienna . . .

With her needle, Mrs. Kane poked a tiny hole in the thumb, then she wrapped thread around the whole, fixing it to a bottle filled with milk that she'd been warming in a pan of water. With great slurping sounds, the baby started suckling.

"Ah, it has to be warm! That's the secret."

Carissa just shook her head. The man's ignorance was astounding. So was his arrogance, as he tilted his beaver hat just so and turned to leave the kitchen. "Where are you going?"

"Why, I thought I would see what's keeping Byrd and the new servants. Take a ride there, clear the cobwebs from my brain, don't you know."

"You'd do better to clear the cobwebs from this place. Besides, you need to stay here to learn to feed the baby."

"Me? I?" This unprepossessing female possessed more hair than wit if she thought he was going to play nanny to the brat.

"What if Mr. Byrd cannot find a nursing mother with milk to spare until tomorrow? They are not waiting at every street corner, you know. At least I hope they are not."

He grasped at straws. "But you are so good with her. See, she's quieted right down."

Carissa smiled, at the baby, not the peer. "Yes, she is a darling, and I would love to stay with her. I wish there was a way I could keep her, even, as my own. I'd forgotten how much I enjoy holding an infant. But the little lamb is yours, my lord, and you know that I cannot remain. Sir Gilliam has been more than understanding, but I need to see he takes his medicine. Mason would let him go without, or let him have more wine than the doctor recommends. Come, sir, hold your daughter."

The viscount sat, and Carissa carefully placed the child in his arms, tilted the bottle just so, and stood back. The babe looked up at him with the same wise scrutiny Mrs. Kane's daughter had, only this chit had his own black-rimmed blue eyes. Her skin was almost as white as the milk, and her nose was just the right size. She was a beauty, his daughter, if he had to say so himself. And she was drinking happily from the bottle he held. "Look at that, she likes it."

"Not as much as mother's milk, but it will do for now, I hope." Carissa took her own daughter on her lap and combed Pippa's light brown curls with her fingers. They both watched him watch his daughter. "Don't you think she should have a name, my lord? Even if her new family changes it, she deserves more than 'Baby.' Are you sure her mother did not give her one?"

"The note merely said that she was a souvenir from Vienna. Sue. That's it, I'll call her Sue. What do you think?"

Pippa spoke up: "I think you should call her Lovey. Mama says she's your love child 'cause no lady will marry you."

While Hartleigh choked, Mrs. Kane's cheeks flooded with color. Then she smiled at the girl, and the viscount, recovered, was struck again by how her pinched features were rounded, softened by the affectionate expression. "But Lovey is only a pet name, darling, like darling. Sue is a perfect name. Sweet Sue."

"Sweet Sue," Lesley repeated. "Yes." Feeling more confident, he touched the downy fuzz on the baby's head, then her cheek to see if it was as impossibly smooth as it looked. One hand reached out and grasped his finger. Oh Lud, he wasn't drowning. He was sunk.

Chapter Five

The woman was right, again. Lesley admitted that there was, indeed, something magical about holding a sleeping infant in one's arms. What trust, what faith—and what he wouldn't give to ensure his daughter's happiness! He wanted to take her to Hyde Park to introduce her to the ton, and not simply to convince the Polite World that he was not worthy of their pampered darlings. Lord Hartleigh wanted to show off this marvel, this miracle, this—sour milk on his clean waistcoat.

"Hell and damnation, the brat spit up on me!"

Mrs. Kane was already dabbing at Sue's face. She almost wiped the viscount's chest also, but caught herself in time. Blushing, she handed him the dampened towel. Luckily his lordship was too concerned with the affront to his tailoring and his dignity to notice. "You needn't take it as a personal insult, my lord. Babies do that, you know. What with the unfamiliar milk, to say nothing of what you gave her earlier, it will be a wonder if Sue does not develop colic."

Horses died of colic. Lesley's arms tightened around his daughter until she screwed up her face in protest. "Should we send for a physician?"

"Only if you need a restorative draft for your nerves, my lord. Babies get unhappy with the colic; most survive, and their parents do, too."

He relaxed, soothed by her confidence, and Sue went back to sleep. His arm was turning to pins and needles where it rested on the chair rung, but he was afraid to move. "Did your husband help with your daughter, then, Mrs. Kane?" he wanted to know. He didn't want to be the only nodcock enchanted with a mere handful of humanity.

"No," Carissa said, turning away. She realized she must sound too abrupt, especially in light of his attempt at cordiality, so she explained, "That is, he rejoined his regiment whilst I was breeding. He was . . . gone when Philippa was born."

Lesley understood that Kane hadn't merely gone to the Peninsula, and regretted his thoughtlessness. "I am sorry, ma'am. I didn't mean to bring up a painful topic."

She brushed that aside. "It was nearly five years ago, my lord, and you could not have known." Still, her stiff back told him she would not welcome any questions as to Mr. Kane's regiment or her difficulties in providing for herself and the child. Lesley knew the army wouldn't help. His admiration for the female was growing, until she picked up a broom and started swatting at his dog.

While Lord Hartleigh sat holding the swaddled infant, Carissa had been bringing what order she could to the unkempt kitchen. Her housewifely heart wouldn't let her do otherwise. Why, she couldn't find a clean plate to serve Pippa a slice of bread. "Come, darling, help Mama tidy up a bit." Pippa carried glasses, bottles, cups, and more bottles, one by one, to the sink. Carissa was tossing spoiled foodstuffs, green cheese, a chicken carcass, other items too desiccated to be identified, into a pile by the back door. Byrd or the cleaning staff he was hiring could remove the mess later. When she went to add a sack of sprouted potatoes to the heap, however, a dog was making off with the chicken bones. Not just any dog, but a long, low, filthy hound, one she recognized well. "You!" Carissa exclaimed, reaching for the broom. "You . . . you garden wrecker! You marauding mongrel! Begone, I say."

Instead of fleeing in terror, the hound dove past her, the chicken remains firmly clenched in its slavering jaws, and raced toward sanctuary under the kitchen table by Lesley's booted feet.

"That . . . that monster is *your* dog?" the widow asked, grabbing Pippa up and onto the sink, out of harm's way. "I should have known." She held the broom to her heaving bosom in

31

case the beast decided he'd rather have bones with some meat on them.

Lesley frowned. He couldn't do much else, with the baby asleep in his arms. "You are entirely safe, Mrs. Kane. He wouldn't hurt a fly."

The dog was so fat and stubby-legged he couldn't have caught a fly. The animal's top half was a large hunting hound. The bottom half—well, there was no bottom half, just baggy-kneed, splay-footed stumps. It was as if someone had lopped off an arm's length of leg. The creature was so low, the bottoms of its drooping ears were ragged from dragging on the ground. Its eyes were sunken in folds of skin, more bloodshot than the viscount's, and the whole thing was covered in mud so thick Carissa couldn't tell what color it was. Frankly, she did not care.

"That beast is the bane of the neighborhood," she accused. "It terrorizes the butcher's boy and steals lunches from school-children. It has destroyed more greenery than a plague of locusts. Get rid of it."

"Glad? He never hurt anyone, and he's just a born digger."

"Glad? As in, Glad no one has taken a meat cleaver to him yet?"

"No, short for Gladiator. I found him digging himself out of a pen at a country fair. He was to be first course in a bear-baiting. Old Glad didn't stand a chance, being so slow, and he was smart enough to know it. I couldn't let the poor chap be tossed back in, could I?"

"He would have given the bear indigestion, I suppose." The brutal sport was supposed to be outlawed, but Carissa knew it still went on. She could just imagine the uproar at the fair-grounds when the promised entertainment made its escape. "They let you simply walk away with him?"

"Why, no, Byrd took his place. Knocked the bear out with one punch, too." Lord Hartleigh was grinning now, and she couldn't tell if he was teasing or not.

"But did you have to bring him home?" she asked.

He was still smiling. "At the time I was residing at Ham-mond House, and I couldn't think of anything that would annoy my stepmother more. Of course, I grew more creative, but when I took up residence here, I couldn't leave the poor fellow to her tender mercies. He'd have had better odds with the bear."

Carissa had to laugh at the picture in her mind. Besides, something about the viscount's smile brightened even this gloomy room. That devilish dimple he flashed must have broken many a heart. Which reminded her: "Cook will be disappointed that the gossip columns are so far off the mark. Lord Heartless indeed! Why, you are as tenderhearted as a fairy godmother. Rescuing worthless mongrels, talking sweet nonsense to an infant, keeping that unlikely, inept manservant. And I saw you trying to win a smile from Pippa by wriggling your eyebrows, my lord. You are nothing but a sham."

He winked at her. "Don't tell anyone, I pray you. My reputation is the only thing that protects me from every matchmaker in town. At least it was the only thing, before Sue."

"But don't you need to marry, to ensure the succession? I thought all noblemen were constrained to pass on their blue blood."

"In my own good time, Mrs. Kane, and when I find the right woman. I have cousins enough meanwhile."

"But you seem to like children."

"I do, don't I?" He was as surprised as she. "Perhaps it is time to start looking after all. After Sue is settled, of course."

Byrd returned with a cleaning crew and supplies, as per Carissa's instructions. Permanent staff would be sent round on the morrow for interviews and such, but there was nary a wet nurse to be found. The biddy at the agency had none on her lists, Byrd reported, and no one at the pubs knew of any mum willing to take on another ladybird's hatchling, either. He'd checked a lot of pubs, Byrd had, trying not to disappoint Mrs. Kane.

The babe seemed none the worse for a second helping of warm milk, but if Mrs. Kane thought Sue would do better on breast milk, breast milk she would have, by George. Lord

Hartleigh tossed his caped greatcoat over his shoulders, then paused. A cow he could have found easily, but this?

In the end he decided to try some other agencies, and Carissa decided to go along with him. There was no place to set the baby, with all the workers and their buckets and mops, and no place for Pippa to play. Besides, Carissa wanted to make sure his lordship hired a capable, kind woman, not just one with large bosoms. They needed to purchase some infant gowns and soft fabric for nappies, too. Byrd drove the carriage.

The viscount went into the first employment office alone. He came out alone, glowering. "The blast"—a glance toward Pippa—"blessed busybody in charge there practically accused me of immoral and unnatural conduct! She didn't believe I had a child in my keeping!"

Carissa hid a smile. "You do have a reputation, my lord."

She went into the next agency, with the baby. And came out with angry spots of color on her cheeks. Recognizing the crest on the carriage outside, the proprietor of this establishment had accused Mrs. Kane of being Lord Heartless's latest harlot, too sunk in depravity to nurse her own infant. "Why, I never!" she exclaimed, handing the infant to the viscount so she could fan her heated skin.

"What, never?" he asked, grinning at her discomfiture.

"That anyone could take me for a . . . a . . ."

"Remember the children," he teased, horrified himself that some fool thought he'd make this hitherto colorless, shapeless, moralizing female his mistress. Dash it, he had a reputation to uphold.

Byrd suggested the foundling home. Perhaps they had a surfeit of milch maids. Or perhaps his lordship would reconsider and leave the little blighter there and end all this rumgumption. In response to that bit of unsolicited advice, the viscount tossed a coin to a waiting urchin to hold the horses. Now Byrd could sit on the squabs with Mrs. Kane's daughter and the baby, since the institution held too many dangers and diseases to take them inside. Pippa was sucking her thumb and the baby was whimpering—or was that Byrd? He removed his hat to mop at his brow, and Pippa's big brown eyes widened at the seagull tattooed on his bald head. The baby started crying in earnest. Byrd took out his flask. Pippa took out her thumb. "I'll tell Mama."

Inside, conditions were worse. Children were everywhere, and so was the filth and stench and noise and misery. In answer to the viscount's request, the gray-haired, gray-complected matron explained that the infants were weaned onto cow's milk as soon as they arrived, and there was never enough of that to go around, nor willing hands to feed the poor mites. Some lived; some did not. She shrugged weary shoulders.

Carissa dabbed at her eyes when they returned to the carriage, and hugged her daughter closer to her. Lesley's pockets were lighter, but his heart was heavy. "My daughter will never, ever be sent to a place like that. I will keep her myself rather than worry that she might land in such conditions."

Carissa was rocking the infant, letting Sue suck on her knuckle. "You cannot keep her, my lord. It wouldn't be fair, for she would always be reminded of her blighted birth. A loving couple can give her a good life, away from those who would blame Sue for her parents' sins."

"You do not know my world, ma'am." Lesley did not enjoy being referred to as a sinner, no more than he liked to consider his daughter a bastard. Both were true, of course, but he did not need to hear it from a cit's chatelaine. "If I adopted her as my own, Sue would be the daughter of a viscount, with an Honorable in front of her name. That and a generous dot count far more than her mother's morals among the ton. 'Struth, with a large enough dowry, the chit could look to the highest in the land for a husband."

"She would still be your love child."

"Fustian. I can give out that she is my ward, a missing cousin or something."

"Anyone can look in *Debrett*, my lord, or into her eyes. There will always be whispers."

"Bastardy is not the end of the world, Mrs. Kane."

"Not to one born with a title, a fortune, and no blot on the family escutcheon. To those of us in the real world, it is a considerable affliction."

"You appear to feel strongly on this matter, Mrs. Kane. Is it possible you speak from personal experience?" He nodded in Philippa's direction. "Was there really a Mr. Kane?"

"How dare you, sirrah, ask such an insulting question! As if I would do what Sue's mother— Of course there was Mr. Phillip Kane!"

Lesley was enjoying seeing the colors flare across her countenance. The female might be halfway passable, with this much animation. Of course, the black gown deadened her complexion, and the bonnet, hiding her hair again, accentuated the widow's rather pointed nose. "Yet you are not baseborn, I'd give odds."

She gasped. "You are impertinent, my lord. Indelicate and impertinent to be impugning my mother's honor. I know about the prejudice against those of uncertain parentage because such intolerance exists among the working class as well as among the Quality."

"And you are no more of the lower orders than I am, my girl. I wondered what seemed peculiar about you; now I realize it is your educated speech, your polished manners, the whole aura of refinement you carry with you. No housekeeper I ever met had the airs of an heiress."

For a moment he thought he'd gone too far. The woman was going to swoon or slap him. Or both.

Carissa took a moment to gather her composure. "As you said, my lord, I am not of your world. I may have been born to a different way of life, but now I am, indeed, of the working class. I am not an heiress; I am a housekeeper. Nothing more."

"And I would give a pretty penny to find out why. Was there no family to take you in when your soldier died?"

"That is none of your business, my lord. It is your daughter's future we are concerned with at the moment, not my past."

"The child will be provided for, never fear. I might not be the best father in the world, but my girl will not end in the poorhouse."

"No amount of money will excuse your immorality."

Not even the baby dared make a peep after that.

Chapter Six

$\mathcal{I}$t was amazing how two dissimilar minds could work in concert.

Insufferable prig, he was thinking.

Insufferable boor, she was thinking.

"My lord," Carissa finally said into the awkward silence. Hartleigh's eyes were closed, but the rigid muscles in his jaw and the clenched fist told her he was not asleep. "I know of a home for wayward girls in the city. An unfortunate maid at Sir Gilliam's needed a place to birth her baby." Carissa's voice trembled still, to think of something like that happening in a household she ran. It would not happen again, by heaven. A footman had been dismissed, and most of the maids went home at night now.

"I want no doxy tending my daughter."

"We have no choice. Neither did that maid, as a matter of fact. She was forced. Besides which, Sue's mother was obviously no better than she ought to be!"

"Sue's mother, Mrs. Kane, was a princess, by Jupiter."

"Who abandoned her child into the care of a drunken rake." She hurried on, cursing her wayward tongue. "The home might have a girl there with milk enough for two babes."

Byrd had been awaiting directions, head swiveling between the two. "Lands, you're thinking to saddle us with another infant, missus? I'll be bunking in the stable, Cap'n, and you can find someone else to look after your threads."

Two infants in the house? Lesley thought he might have to move back to Grosvenor Square to get any rest. He nodded toward the housekeeper, though, signaling her to give Byrd the address.

Recognizing Mrs. Kane, the director of the girls' home was inclined to be sympathetic to Hartleigh's tale of an orphaned ward. He was wise enough to be sympathetic to any potential patron, in fact. Reverend Garapie might not have believed the taradiddle, but neither did he accuse the widow of wrongdoing, nor the peer of philandering. Unfortunately, he did not have a solution to their problem. Most of the girls left the home as soon as their infants were born, the clergyman explained without mentioning what happened to either the girls or their offspring. The only two nursing mothers now in residence were not suitable. One was sickly, which was why she remained, and the other was unbalanced since the birthing and could not be trusted with her son. The home was trying to locate her family to take her away. Reverend Garapie shook his head. "Such things happen, the good Lord knows why." He kept sorting through the stacks of papers on his desk. "We do have two young women near term, however, my lord, Mrs. Kane. A week or so should do it, then a few days for recovery."

"I don't have a few days, much less a week, damn it. Ah, dash it, Reverend."

"The good Lord cannot be hurried, Lord Hartleigh." The reverend adjusted his spectacles and read one of the papers. "Hmm. We did have a girl here last week whose infant son was born dead, God keep his innocent soul. Perhaps she is still in milk."

Lesley sat up straighter. "We'll find out. Where is she now?"

Mr. Garapie was not to be rushed either. He kept reading the paper and "hmming" to himself until the viscount almost snatched the document out of his hands. Finally the cleric looked up and removed his spectacles. While he wiped them on his handkerchief, Garapie spoke to Mrs. Kane, seeing her to be the more understanding of the pair.

"The girl's name is Maisie Banks, and it is a familiar enough story. She was gainfully employed as a parlor maid when the poor child was accosted by her employer. Her titled employer," he added, looking at Hartleigh now. "He refused to take responsibility, which I am happy to see is not the case here. Maisie had to come to us, and heaven alone knows what was to happen to her or the child after, for no one hires servants with besmirched reputations or babes. As I said, the infant died. I believe the poor girl was forced to return to Lord Cosgrove's house to seek her position back. She had no references, you see, and no family to take her in."

Carissa could well understand the girl's plight. Encumbered by an infant, she herself had had enough trouble finding a position, even in her widow's weeds. And her father had refused to lend assistance, since she'd wed against his wishes. If it weren't for a friend of her great-aunt's, who knew one of Sir Gilliam's partners, Carissa might have been forced to accept such a situation. If not for Sir Gilliam, she and Pippa might have found themselves on the street.

Mr. Garapie was shaking his head. "I am sorely afraid the poor child will be back here in a few months."

Not if Carissa Kane had anything to say about it. Lord Hartleigh was all for rescuing the chit too, if it meant his daughter would be well cared for. Besides, Lord Cosgrove was a sore loser. The dirty dish was also a frequent loser, Lesley told Carissa and Byrd as they made their plans before re-entering the carriage, with a wife he kept in the country while he spent her money as fast as he could here in Town. "I knew he was a nasty piece of goods from the start, when he wasn't paying his gambling debts on time, but to rape one of his own servants . . ."

Carissa was pleased to see that his lordship had some antipathy toward Lord Cosgrove's dastardy, right after his poor sportsmanship. "Do you know his direction?"

"Aye, but I will take you and the children home first. No need for you to speak to such a blackguard."

"I'll go, Cap'n," Byrd offered, pulling a pistol out of his coat pocket, to Carissa's horror. "I'll have the mort back in Kensington afore the cat can scratch its ear."

"Stubble it, Byrdie. We cannot kidnap the girl. He might be a rum go, but I'll convince Cosgrove to part with the maid, one way or the other."

"You are both being precipitous," Carissa put in, "besides itching for trouble. We don't know if this Maisie Banks can feed Sue, or if she wishes to, with her own infant dead. I'll go talk to her myself."

In the end, Lord Hartleigh entered Cosgrove's front door, Mrs. Kane and the two children entered the rear, and Byrd entered the nearest pub.

Since it was still before noon, Lord Cosgrove was still abed. He was not pleased when his valet announced an insistent caller, one who was known to be handy with his fives. Lord Hartleigh was not pleased to be kept waiting for half an hour. He was pacing around the shabby parlor, kicking at the unlighted logs in the fireplace. Cosgrove was practicing economies, it seemed. He ought to be happy to be relieved of paying one maidservant's salary.

Cosgrove had a drunkard's nose, all red-veined and swollen. He had pouches under his eyes big enough to store a palmed ace. He had shaking hands, bad breath, and a stomach that sagged over his waistband. Lud, the viscount wondered, could *he* look this bad in the mornings? The thought was enough to keep him from accepting a glass of the port Cosgrove was pouring for breakfast.

Cosgrove slammed the decanter down. "So how much do I owe you, Hartleigh? I tell you right off I'll need time to recoup my losses, so you've wasted the call. Don't know why you're in such a rush, dash it. Ain't like you're sailing close to the wind, blast you."

"You do not owe me anything, Cosgrove, for I won't play with your ilk."

"What's that supposed to mean, 'my ilk'?"

"I mean belligerent, bacon-brained gamblers who can't afford to pay their debts."

"What, did you come here to insult a man in his own house?" Hell, if Cosgrove didn't owe the Corinthian anything, he didn't have to take his arrogance.

"I came to ask you to release the young female in your employ who recently gave birth." Lesley had no desire to air his laundry in this midden, so he did not mention the infant. The

40

ton would find out soon enough, and this clodpole with them. "I am prepared to reimburse you for her quarterly wages."

"Maisie, eh? She gets pennies." And none of his servants had received their last wages anyway. But Maisie? "Now, what would a swell like you want with such a dab of a maid? You've always had nothing but the highest flyers. What, did you hear she was a tasty morsel?"

"An adolescent parlor maid? Hardly. I need the milk, man, that's all."

A crafty look came over Cosgrove's shifty eyes. "I never thought of that. And I never knew you had such unconventional appetites. I'm not surprised the houses of accommodation cannot accommodate you."

"It's for an infant, you clunch."

Cosgrove ignored him, lost in a fantasy of his own. "I have half a mind to taste it for myself."

"No, you have half a mind, period. And I've a mind to put my fist through your nose. I want that girl, by Zeus!"

"It'll cost you a monkey then, Hartleigh. Right fond of the girl, I am."

"I'll see you in hell first." He got up to leave, nauseated all over again, this time by Cosgrove, not last night's carousal. Byrd could come back later and kidnap the girl after all.

Meanwhile, Carissa was enjoying a nice coze in Cosgrove's kitchen. Pippa was playing with some string, and the baby was watching. Cosgrove's housekeeper was impressed at how well behaved the widow's daughter was, and even more impressed that her neighbor, the one they called Lord Heartless, was taking responsibility for his pretty little by-blow.

"It's not every man what will, you know," the housekeeper declaimed over the second cup of tea. "And hardly any of the nobs. Think they can have their way with the girls, then ignore the consequences, they do. I warn my girls, over and over. Not that it helps in this household. Not at all, not at all. "

She paused only long enough for Carissa to mention her own trials with young servants and older scoundrels. "I have the maids go home at night now, or sleep with Cook."

The older woman nodded and handed Pippa a biscuit. "I

tried to hire old women, but they couldn't do the work. And the master don't care. Young or old, pretty or ugly, willing or not. I'd move on, I would, for such conduct is not what a body is used to, but jobs are worse than hen's teeth to come by. I don't have to tell you how it is, dearie."

Carissa agreed that life was hard for a woman earning her own living. "But perhaps I can make things easier for Maisie."

The other housekeeper shook her head. "I don't know. I'd feel better if she went, yet I don't want to see the poor child go from the frying pan to the fire. That Lord Hartleigh has a wicked reputation, he does."

Leaning closer, Mrs. Kane confided, "It's all a hum, but he doesn't want anyone to know. Why, the man positively dotes on little Sue. And he is taking the responsibility for her very seriously indeed. In fact, on the way here he bought every infant dress the store had in stock."

"And if Maisie comes, you're sure he won't . . . ?"

"He wouldn't." Carissa was certain of that. She couldn't explain how, but she knew without a doubt that Lord Hartleigh would never take advantage of a weaker opponent. "He treats me with respect, like a true gentleman. Naturally we would have to warn Maisie not to fall in love with him."

The housekeeper laughed. "That much of a charmer, is he?"

"Some women might find him so." Never her, of course. She would never toss her bonnet after a silver-tongued devil, no matter how many dimples he had. Not again. Carissa folded her hands in her lap and waited for the housekeeper to send for Maisie.

The maid was barely seventeen, with red hair and freckles. She would have been comely except for the gap between her front teeth, that and the pale listlessness that draped her like a shawl. Until she saw the baby. "Hello, lovey," she cooed to Sue after making her curtsy to the two housekeepers.

Carissa started to ask if Maisie thought she'd like to care for Sue, but Pippa exclaimed, "She already knows Baby's name, Mama!"

Maisie did not know much about babies. She never had the chance to learn, but she thought she'd like it just fine. And the milk was hurting something fierce. "I think I would be happier anywhere than here, Mrs. Kane, if it's safe."

"It will be, I swear. And when his lordship finds a new home for Sue, either you'll go along or he'll find a place in his household for you."

Maisie's satchel was already packed. They were all waiting in the carriage when the viscount stormed out of Cosgrove's house. "And good riddance."

Back on Gibsonia Street, Maisie and Sue were quickly settled in the spare bedroom, which had been cleaned first. The infant was suckling happily when Carissa returned to find Lord Hartleigh anxiously awaiting her report.

"Is it working? Sue is going to be all right?"

"Yes, and Maisie will be also, I think. I must warn you that I have given my pledge that she will be unharmed in this household."

He was outraged. "You felt you had to give your word that I would not rape that poor girl? What kind of monster do you think me, that I might even be tempted? I am not Cosgrove, madam, that you have to warn me to be on my best behavior around innocent children."

"Maisie is no longer innocent, thanks to Cosgrove."

"She is still innocent. He is the cad. The girl is now in my employ, which means she is under my protection, not to be trifled with by anyone."

"Well, I am sure I am happy to hear all that, my lord, but what I pledged to Maisie was that she didn't have to worry about the dog. Gladiator has to go."

Chapter Seven

"Unsafe. Unsanitary. Unkempt and uncouth."

Was she talking about him or the dog? Lesley checked his neckcloth for spots. He hadn't had time to tie anything intricate this morning. Hell, he'd felt like tying a noose this morning. Now Mrs. Kane had everything under control, bless her starched-up soul. Every time he was coming to like the prickly female, though, she got on her high horse. He was in no mood for a grump-gallop. If he did not get some sleep soon, he was like to collapse in one of Glad's holes. Mrs. Kane, he was certain, would kick dirt over him and plant posies on top. "You go too far, madam."

She wasn't listening. "He brings in fleas and filth, and cannot be trusted around an infant."

"Dash it, ma'am, Glad isn't about to gnaw on the baby's toes or anything."

"How do you know? You've never had an infant here before, have you? Besides, Maisie is afraid of dogs."

Only Maisie? he wondered. Aloud he asked, "What do you expect me to do, toss him out with the trash?"

"He'd never go hungry there."

"Come now, Mrs. Kane, be reasonable. Think of the weather, the traffic, the hungry beggars. Surely you have more compassion than to believe I should evict poor Glad?" The dog wouldn't go; he'd tried.

"I believe that if you can find a home for Sue in the country, you can find one for that beast also."

"Ah, I can see the advertisement now: Wanted, kind, loving family for girl child and male hound, both of uncertain pedigree."

She sniffed at his attempt at humor. "Meantime I think the cur should be in the stables."

"Oh, no, you don't. You have never heard Glad howl when he cannot dig his way out of a prison. Werewolves baying at the moon cannot hold a candle to him. And he keeps it up for hours. I did try, you know, to keep him from bothering my neighbors' yards. It was either their roses or their rest, however, so I chose to let him roam."

"You could have avoided the problem altogether, my lord. You should never have brought the impossible creature home with you in the first place."

"There are many things I should not have done, but it is too late for regrets, ma'am." Lesley was thinking that he shouldn't have had that fourth bottle last night—or was it the fifth?

Carissa was thinking of the motherless baby. "We will return to the issue of the dog presently. For now I have compiled a list of what you will be needing if you are to keep Sue here for more than a day or two."

The house already smelled of beeswax and lemon juice. The carpets were not really gray, it seemed, and his study windows actually looked out on a pleasant vista, now that they were clean enough to be seen through. What more could the woman want? Since his plans involved parading the child before the Polite World, for however long it took to give the doyennes and duennas a disgust of himself, Lesley took the proffered paper. He'd been right about Mrs. Kane not belonging to the servants' class, he noted. She wrote an elegant hand, the kind that came from expensive governesses or exclusive finishing schools.

"A cook?" he read. "I take my meals at the clubs or social engagements."

"Yes, but Maisie cannot. Nor can the rest of the staff you will be hiring to keep the house presentable."

He raised one eyebrow. "I will?"

Carissa went on. That topic was not open for debate. "And Maisie cannot be expected to cook. She has been in service all her life and was never taught how, for one thing. And she will be too busy with the baby, for another."

"I bow to your superior knowledge of running a household, Mrs. Kane, but surely women have been doing the cooking, cleaning, marketing, and mending for centuries—with babies on their hips."

No woman he knew, she'd be willing to wager. Aloud she said, "Yes, and those women help their husbands plow the fields, too. And then they die young. Maisie needs nourishing meals if she is to nourish the baby. From what I have seen of Mr. Byrd's cooking, tea and hardtack are about his limits."

"That's not hardtack, ma'am," Byrd put in as he brought a fresh pot of tea into the viscount's study. "They are scones."

"And I am sure they will be excellent teething biscuits for Sue in a few months, Mr. Byrd."

Lesley tried to bite into one of the lumps. He'd always assumed Byrd had lost his front teeth in a prizefight. Now he wasn't so sure. "Very well, a cook. One who can also act as housekeeper, I see."

"Yes, you'll need someone to oversee the female servants, especially since you said you wished to retain day help only."

What he'd said was that Byrd would leave his employ if he filled the house with gossipy, giggly housemaids. He kept reading. "Bootboy, tiger, undernursemaid, scullery maid— Gads, ma'am, this household consists of one person and a child, and I am gone most of the time. You are staffing a palace."

Carissa bit her lip. "I know my estimates are a trifle extravagant, my lord, but the matron at the foundling home happened to mention that she had a quantity of youngsters ready for employment."

Byrd took the pot of cold tea away. "Half-pints and females," he muttered. "Females and half-pints. It's enough to make a body go back to sea."

"At least he hasn't served notice again." Lesley sipped at his tea, wondering how he could sneak the scones out to Glad while Mrs. Kane was busy adding lines to her list with a pencil from her pocket. She handed it back to him. "An exercise boy?

46

Why the deuce do I need an exercise boy? I only stable my chestnuts and a gelding here. My other horses are kept at Grosvenor Square or Hart's Rest, my country seat. Both of which, you'll be delighted to know, employ a veritable army of servants."

"The dog, my lord. It occurs to me that if the creature were kept on a lead, taken on long walks—outside this neighborhood—he would not be such a threat to Lovey, ah, Sue. Or the shrubbery. At night the boy could sleep in the stables, guarding the horses." And keeping the wretched mongrel company.

"I will consider all of this if you will consider coming to-morrow to help with the interviews. You have already been a lifesaver, accomplishing far more than I ever hoped or expected, but I confess I would not know how to begin hiring a cook-housekeeper, to say nothing of an exercise boy."

"I was going to come to see how Maisie and the baby are getting along, but I would be happy to select candidates, for your approval, of course, if Sir Gilliam does not require my presence tomorrow. And I can talk to Matron also, if you wish."

There was a teasing sparkle in the widow's brown eyes that Lesley found enchanting enough that he nodded his agree-ment. The female was a conniver, like all her sisters, but she was not underhanded about it. He admired that in Mrs. Kane, if not her efficiency. The blasted woman was handing him yet an-other list.

"They need you at the War Office, madam, to keep the troops better supplied. What is this list about?"

"The other list was what the household needs. This list is what the baby needs, if she is to be here any length of time."

The list was two pages long, in neat double columns. "Good grief, ma'am, Wellington travels with less."

"Wellington is not an infant, my lord. Sue cannot be ex-pected to sleep in a food hamper, you know."

Lesley didn't see why not. The little darling looked adorable in her basket.

"As soon as she learns to turn over, she'll tumble out onto

the floor. If you place her on a bed, she might creep to the edge."

Lesley borrowed Carissa's pencil to circle *crib*. "But all this other paraphernalia? Surely babies do not need so many . . . things."

Surely they did, Carissa proceeded to convince him. A pram so the child could get outside for healthful fresh air, a rocking chair to help her get to sleep. More blankets and bonnets and booties. Talcum and special soap, a rattle and a teething ring. A cradle so Maisie could lay her down when she came to the kitchen for meals.

"Did you have all of this for your daughter?"

"Yes," she answered curtly, volunteering no further information.

Hartleigh looked around. "Deuce take it, where the devil is she? The chit is so quiet, I forget she's around half the time."

"Pippa is upstairs with Maisie and the baby, having a nap. And yes, she is a quiet child. Living at Sir Gilliam's, she had to learn to be unobtrusive and well behaved."

Granted the viscount did not know much about youngsters, but he knew the brats on the street were always running and shouting. He could not believe that Philippa Kane's reserve was quite natural. Lesley wondered if the sobersided little chit ever laughed or cried or played with other children, and why not. His curiosity about Mrs. Kane and her daughter was growing.

As was Mrs. Kane's list as she thought of new items an infant needed. "Bibs, of course. How could I have forgotten?" She'd embroidered scores of them for her baby, and smocked so many infant dresses that Pippa hardly wore the same one twice before outgrowing it. Then there were tiny undergarments, for warmth. And wool for sweaters. Carissa could teach Maisie to knit if she did not already know how.

"Where the devil am I going to get all this stuff?" the viscount demanded. He'd be chasing from dry goods stores to furniture warehouses to carriage makers—if the manufacturers of his curricles were the same ones who made baby carriages. And Lesley could just imagine himself going into Mme. Fou-

quette's millinery shop, where he was used to shopping with
his latest barques of frailty, and asking for baby bonnets.
"Byrd!"

"I ain't picking out no dainties," the man replied when
shown the list. "You want a cravat, that I can buy. Handkerchiefs are at the haberdashers, no argle-bargle there, Cap'n.
But nappies and nightgowns for the nit? No way."

Carissa took pity on the helpless males. "Most likely you
have nearly everything you need right in the attics of your
family home. Most households do."

Hartleigh saw sweet salvation. "Do you have all of your
daughter's infant things over at Sir Gilliam's then?"

"No, I had to leave it all behind when I came to London."
Carissa had had to sell everything, the tiny lace-edged caps and
the cradle she'd commissioned, everything Pippa had outgrown or could spare, to pay her coach fare. "I didn't need any
of it since I was unlikely to have any more children, and there
were too many years to wait for grandchildren. I would have
been happy to see it used for Sue."

Lesley wondered at the sad look in Mrs. Kane's eyes. Did
she miss her husband so much, still, or was she regretting the
change in her circumstances? He could not keep from specu-
lating whether she really was what she seemed, a respectable
widow fallen on hard times, or a rich man's mistress. She
spoke so fondly of the old gent, it was possible. And hidden behind the dreary demeanor was a spirited woman who might appeal to certain men. Not himself, of course, but Sir Gilliam
might not desire a dasher. Mrs. Kane was kind and gentle;
anyone could see that from watching her with her daughter.
Hell, he owed her his life for finding Maisie, for showing the
maid how to change the infant's diapers. He'd have traded his
gelding, his diamond stickpin, and Byrd for that alone. But
there was some secret Mrs. Kane was holding, some hesitation
about her past, as if she were weighing each word. He'd never
trusted a woman yet, and saw no reason to take at face value all
this one said, or didn't say. But he owed her. He was fairly certain she would not take money for her efforts, but Mrs. Kane

had a small, doe-eyed weak spot. She'd never deny her daughter some toys and books, and Lesley knew right where there were cartloads.

"Now that I think on it, the attics at Hammond House must be full of baby things, for my mother never threw anything out. I know all my old toys are still in the nursery. Agatha, my father's second wife, would never exert herself to climb to the upper stories, so I am sure everything is exactly where my mother left it."

"Excellent. Then all you have to do is go over there with a wagon."

Byrd slapped his knee. "Aye, and listen to a lecture on your wicked ways. Lud, I can't wait to hear you tell Lady Hartleigh you're outfitting an infant."

"I was hoping she'd hear of it through the gossip vine and wash her hands of me entirely." For Carissa's benefit he explained, "The woman is a carping shrew who uses her health as an excuse for her bad behavior. As much as she deplores my style of living, Agatha still has hopes of haranguing me into holy matrimony with one of her rabbit-faced relations. I would not put it past her to try to catch me in parson's mousetrap, either, so I cannot say I relish bearding the lioness in her den. Unfortunately she is my father's widow, so I cannot give her the cut direct, or her marching orders."

He did not speak for a minute, contemplating the dire fate of being buckled to one of the Spillhammer sisters. Then he looked up. "But wait. Tomorrow is Wednesday, is it not? They will be attending Almack's, without a doubt. Agatha's agues never seem to occur on evenings of social importance, and there is none more crucial to her sisters' success than the weekly assembly. She'll never snabble them husbands if she can't pass them off as Quality there."

"Surely the, ah, Spillhammer sisters are Quality or they would never be granted vouchers to attend in the first place," Carissa chided, revealing a telling familiarity with the ways of the Polite World.

Lesley waved a manicured hand. "Jumped-up gentry. That's why Agatha wanted my father's title so badly, so she'd have the cachet of Hammond House behind her when she tossed the dismal duo on the ton. No, they'll be hunting at Almack's tomorrow night, I guarantee it. Hammond House will be vacant, therefore, so we can steal in, get what we need with no one the wiser, and be gone in less time than it will take Sally Jersey to dragoon some poor sods into dancing with the chits. Madam Housekeeper, how would you like to be a housebreaker?"

Chapter Eight

"*Y*ou mean to say Lord Hartleigh is going to sneak into his own home to purloin his own baby clothes?" Sir Gilliam laughed himself into a coughing fit. Carissa jumped up from her seat next to him to pat his back and hand him a glass of water before Mason could. The butler scowled, making him look more like a weasel than ever.

Sir Gilliam had requested that Carissa join him for dinner that evening, as he did on occasion, to Mason's disapproval. She'd put Philippa to bed in the room they shared, hoping she wouldn't awaken, and donned her one evening frock. It was hopelessly out of fashion and she had sewn it herself, of course, but the dark amber crepe made her feel almost pretty. It wasn't black, at least. Carissa coiled her hair into a crown atop her head, not her usual severe bun, and even let a few wisps of soft brown hair curl around her cheeks.

Sir Gilliam had smiled appreciatively, indicating that she should move her plate closer to his, at the top of the linen-draped table. Mason muttered about females knowing their station, female ewes parading as lambs, and females playing off their tricks, too softly for his employer to hear. Mason, of course, had set Carissa's place at the foot, as far away from the aged knight as possible. Sir Gilliam, however, did not wish to miss a word of her report on the neighborhood's most renowned resident.

With tears of laughter in his eyes, the old banker asked her to begin again. "You mean he nearly required smelling salts? Hartleigh?"

"He turned every shade of green as soon as I asked him to

dispose of the baby's soiled linens. In all honesty, his lordship wasn't in prime twig to begin with, but that sent him for the nearest basin—and not to put the diapers in, either."

"And then?"

"And then Sue smiled at him. 'Twas gas, most likely, but our supposedly hard-hearted lord turned to mush in front of my eyes. Why, if Sue could have asked for the moon, I am sure he'd be thinking of ways to get it for her. The little sweetheart will have him firmly wrapped around her tiny fingers as soon as she figures out how."

"And you are going along with him to Hammond House?"

"With your permission, of course, Sir Gilliam."

He brushed aside her concern for his approval. "I have no objection, my dear. You have this place organized so efficiently, it runs itself without you. But is it necessary for you to accompany his lordship?"

"Heaven knows what he will fetch back, else. Between him and his odd manservant, they wouldn't know a cradle from a coal scuttle. And I will put Philippa to sleep at his house, where Maisie can look out for her. Pippa seems fascinated by the baby, and Maisie seems both conscientious and caring." That suggestion had been Lord Hartleigh's, when Carissa had objected that she could not leave her daughter alone at Sir Gilliam's, for there would be no one to comfort the child if she awoke in the night. In truth, it was Carissa who was anxious, since she had never been parted from Philippa for more than an hour or so, in the four years since her birth.

Sir Gilliam was not convinced of the wisdom of pillaging Hammond House. "Does the child really need so many things?"

"His lordship is going tomorrow to speak to his solicitor about finding a good home for her. He thinks it might take some time, however, since he has no proof that the child is his to give away. Those distinctive blue eyes do not count in a court of law, I suppose. The fact that Sue was left on Lord Hartleigh's doorstep should be proof enough, but he fears his man of affairs will have to track down Sue's mother or a baptismal record or some such."

"I am sure his lordship's man will know which fist to grease, to see him named legal guardian."

"Yes, but that could take considerable time, time in which Sue deserves a proper place to sleep. She might have been born on the wrong side of the blanket, but she is entitled to as many blankets as she needs."

Sir Gilliam placed his gnarled hand over hers at the table. "Be careful, my dear."

Carissa knew he wasn't thinking about the raid on Hammond House but the rake.

Lord Hartleigh decided to stay in that evening. Byrd asked if he was ill, and the dog sniffed at him, as if he were a stranger in the house at night. He was exhausted, for one thing, not that he expected to get much sleep with a crying infant around, and worried about Maisie and the baby, for another. Would the young maid know what to do if Sue took sick? What if, heaven forfend, the babe did indeed fall out of the basket? Lesley knew precisely what to do: run across the street to fetch Mrs. Kane.

The widow had to be the most competent woman in his extensive experience. As he lay between clean, fresh-smelling sheets, Lesley mused how he had never considered competency to be a requirement in a wife. A fellow certainly didn't look for brisk efficiency in a mistress. He could see how life could be more pleasant in the hands of a capable female, however, easier on one's constitution. He was looking forward to the occasional meal at his own board, finding his books all in one place, having his apparel in order. Why, if the new cook and servants turned out to be halfway acceptable, Lesley thought he might even invite some of his cronies over for dinner and cards one evening. Repay their hospitality, as it were. No, he amended, imagining the widow's pursed lips and pointed chin, dinner only. His acquaintances tended to become too raucous as the hours passed, much too loud for a sleeping baby.

Lesley had his best night's sleep in ages, dreaming about Mrs. Kane. He only checked on the baby three times, when he heard a noise, or pretended he did. The first time Maisie was sitting up in bed, nursing Sue. She was mortified, not because of the baby at her carefully draped breast, the way Mrs. Kane had shown her, but because she'd let the baby's cries disturb his lordship's rest. She'd get faster about the diapering, she promised. The second time, when no one answered his soft scratch on the door, he tiptoed in. By the light of the oil lamp left burning on a dresser, he could see Maisie fast asleep on the wide bed, with the baby's basket next to her, and pillows mounded on the basket's other side. Sue was in no danger of falling. He leaned over the pillows and touched her angel-soft cheek. "I will find you a good family, little one, never fear." The baby reached out and grabbed his finger and raised it to her mouth. She sucked a few times, then went back to sleep. "A very good family."

After the child's supper Wednesday night, Carissa prepared to take Philippa across the street, along with her nightclothes, her doll, her favorite blanket, two books, and some gingerbread to share with Maisie. Carissa would also have brought Pippa's pillow, the miniature of her father that Pippa was used to saying her prayers to, and a jug of warmed milk. It was Pippa who dissuaded her, declaring, "Mama, I am not a baby, you know."

"You are *my* baby." And what business did she have, Carissa asked herself as she put down extra food for her cat, going off with a notorious womanizer? Why, she'd feel like an intruder, if not a burglar, visiting a house whose front door was firmly closed to her by reason of her position. Lord Hartleigh should have sent her with a note to his housekeeper. Better, he should have had the staff at Hammond House pack up whatever baby things they found and send it all on to him in Kensington, to sort through there. Best of all, the blond-haired rogue should have kept his britches buttoned. But then they wouldn't have Sue, of course.

And Mrs. Kane wouldn't be abandoning her duties at Sir Gilliam's, for which she was guilt-ridden. Neither would she be abandoning her own precious daughter in a strange house with an inexperienced nursery maid, for which Carissa was petrified. Pippa could get eaten by a dog that should have been abandoned to his fate ages ago.

"Gladiator is harmless, I tell you," Lord Hartleigh said, trying to reassure his nervous coconspirator, "and Philippa seems to like him."

Carissa looked around the tidied study until she found her daughter. Pippa was sitting quietly alongside the hearth. The fingers of her left hand were in her mouth; Pippa's right hand was in the dog's mouth, feeding that filthy, hulking cur her gingerbread! If that wasn't enough to strike terror in a mother's heart, Pippa switched hands. Carissa shrieked, causing Byrd to drop the plate he was carrying of the new cook's excellent pastries. Glad was there before the first macaroon touched the floor. Of course, he'd had to knock Pippa over to get to the fallen delicacies and step right across her, too. Mrs. Kane screamed again. The viscount dove to right the child, tripped over the dog, and bumped his head on the mantel. And Pippa laughed.

Lesley glared at the child, Mrs. Kane glared at him, Byrd glared at the widow, and Pippa laughed some more. The dog, of course, ate the rest of the macaroons.

Carissa was wiping Pippa's hands with her handkerchief. "That's enough. I cannot go to Hammond House with you, my lord. You might choose to leave your daughter with a ravening beast, but I do not."

"Mama, you are fussing again."

Now Lesley looked at the child approvingly. "Yes, Mrs. Kane, you are worrying over naught. I for one enjoyed hearing the child laugh, even if it was at my expense. But if it will make you feel better, we can take Glad with us."

Ride in the carriage with the creature? Carissa would rather go to the tooth drawer. "No, this is simply not a good idea. Surely you can locate a cradle without my assistance. I can draw you a picture."

"The dog can ride up with Byrd, ma'am. Unless you are getting cold feet? I thought you were made of sterner stuff, Mrs. Kane."

Somehow she did not wish to appear one of those niminy-piminy females, afraid of their shadows. And she wanted this handsome lord to look on her approvingly, also. Without stopping to inspect her motives, Carissa agreed. If she was lucky, perhaps the animal would fall off, or run off. If she was luckier yet, perhaps their route would take them past the Tower menagerie. Gladiator could be tossed to the lions.

The butler at Hammond House should have been guarding the palace gates, he was so stony-faced and toplofty. He looked past the viscount's shoulder to welcome Lord Hartleigh to his own house, ignoring the unaccompanied, unfashionable female with him. "I regret, milord, that Lady Hartleigh and the Misses Spillhammer are not at home. Almack's, milord." His tone said he regretted having to open the door to anyone not granted vouchers for that pillar of propriety. "Would you care to leave a message?"

"Agatha insisted I hire Wimberly," Lesley whispered to Carissa. "She thought Hammond House needed a more dignified majordomo than a retired prizefighter."

"I thought Mr. Byrd was a sailor." Carissa would have laughed at the idea of Lady Hartleigh's morning callers being welcomed by a tattooed butler, but Wimberly was staring down his nose at her cloak. The viscount had removed her worn woolen mantle from Carissa's shoulders and held it out. The butler snapped his fingers for a footman to come remove the plebeian garment from the marble entry.

"No, Wimberly, I did not come to visit with the ladies. Mrs. Kane and I have come to select some things from the attics and the nursery. We'll need a couple of strong footmen to bring the things down, and a carriage to transport it all to Kensington."

"The nursery, milord?"

"Yes, you know, where one places small persons to keep them from staining the upholstery."

"But, milord, you cannot. That is, Lady Hartleigh would wish to—"

"Wimberly, whose house is this?"

"Yours, milord, but—"

"And who owns everything in it?"

57

"You do, milord, but Lady Hartleigh will have my—"

"And who pays your overinflated salary, Wimberly?"

"How many footmen did you say you required, milord?"

So they started in the attics, with lanterns. Lord Hartleigh had been right: His mother never discarded anything, nor did the three viscountesses previous to her. Luckily most of the trunks and boxes were labeled. While Carissa went through bundles of blankets and linens, all laid out with lavender, Lesley searched for the larger things they needed. He went past sleds and small beds and cricket bats and half-size top hats, until he reached a low-ceilinged section. He found an elevated chair, but that wasn't on Mrs. Kane's list, likely because Sue couldn't sit up yet. He directed the footmen to carry it down, just in case. He couldn't decide between his choice of three cradles, so he took two. He preferred the wicker pram to the heavy wooden one, but thought he'd have a new one made for Sue anyway.

Carissa had unrolled a frayed carpet onto the floor, noting that the attic was cleaner than the viscount's other house had been before the cleaners came. She started opening trunks and placing her selections on the rug, which could be folded over and carried down the stairs. "Some of the bonnets will need to be bleached, and I fear moths have gotten into one or two of the sweaters, but I should be able to mend them. The rattle needs polishing, of course, but I think that is everything, my lord."

The mound was as high as his waist. "Lud, I should hope so. There will be no room for Sue in that little bedroom."

On their way out of the attics, they passed a stack of paintings. The first one was of a beautiful woman in court dress of the previous century. "My mother," Lord Hartleigh told Carissa. "Right after her marriage. This portrait used to hang in the library, before Agatha got here."

Carissa couldn't blame the viscountess for banishing the painting. What woman wanted to be compared to her husband's exquisite first wife? "Why don't you take it with us? The Kensington house could use something pretty."

Lesley nodded to the footmen. He also pointed to a vase he recalled from his mother's sitting room, an embroidered fire screen, and a footed sewing basket. "Perhaps Maisie could mend the baby's clothes if needed."

"We are going to require another wagon soon if you don't stop."

"But we haven't even inspected the nursery."

"I cannot imagine what's left that an infant could use, especially in the short time Sue will be in London. You did see your solicitor today, didn't you?"

Lesley said something about the man making inquiries but was already on his way to the lower level. Carissa had to trail behind him, hoping the viscount did not intend to give the baby his toy soldiers or some such. He was looking around the schoolroom, directing the footmen to lift this small chair, that pile of picture books. The rocking horse, with its flowing mane and glass eyes, he carried himself.

"It will be years before Sue can ride that thing," Carissa protested. "And you said yourself how crowded her room will be."

"It's not for Sue. I thought Pippa would like it."

Chapter Nine

A rocking horse? Carissa thought of all the things she had never been able to give her daughter, would never be able to provide: other children to play with, a proper governess, riding lessons, and more. Toys were the least of it. She'd saved her pennies just to provide ribbons for Philippa's hair and a scrap of lace for her petticoats. Carissa had never so much as considered a rocking horse, it was that far beyond her finances. Pippa would adore it, but . . .

They were on facing seats of his carriage, the rocking horse on the floor between them. Carissa almost reached out to touch the wooden steed's silky black mane, but she caught herself in time. "I am sorry, my lord, I cannot accept."

"The toy is not for you, Mrs. Kane. It is for your daughter."

She rubbed her hands together, cold from the chill of the attics. "You must know that it would not be proper for me to accept so lavish a gift."

He leaned closer, as if he would take her hands in his and warm them. Speak of improper! Carissa sat back against the squabs.

"Mrs. Kane," he was saying, "if I wished to make you an improper present, I would offer jewels or furs. Or a real horse. Do you ride?"

"Of course," she answered without thinking, though there was no "of course" to a housekeeper's equine experience. "And now you are talking fustian. You must know I could never let you provide me a horse, even if I had the time to ride, which I do not. You forget that I am in service."

"No, I don't. I only wish you worked for me. I don't suppose you'd reconsider?"

"Leaving Sir Gilliam? Never. But you are merely trying to change the subject," she accused, and his boyish grin in the glow from the carriage lamp proved her right. "I cannot accept such an expensive gift, not even on Pippa's behalf."

Lesley sighed. He'd known this was going to be difficult. "Mrs. Kane, do you have any idea how helpful you have been to me?"

"Gammon. Anyone would have done the same."

"Hardly. So-called ladies wouldn't know where to start, if they deigned to acknowledge Sue's existence in the first place. They let nannies and governesses rear their own infants, then send them off to school. No, Mrs. Kane, you have been invaluable. And you will not let me reward you financially, will you?"

"Pay me? Of course not! Why, that would be infamous, taking money to help an innocent child. Especially when Sir Gilliam already pays me a very fair wage. Besides, I quite enjoyed myself. Why, the look on Wimberly's face when you walked out with the rocking horse was worth every minute of my time."

"And Pippa shouldn't enjoy herself?"

"Whatever can you mean?" Carissa asked, ready to take affront that he'd think she would deny Pippa anything in her power to provide. "She likes the baby very well and was quite looking forward to the adventure of sleeping away from home tonight."

"I mean, Mrs. Kane, that it seems to me your daughter does not laugh nearly enough. Winning a smile from Miss Philippa is a rare and golden treasure that I would hope to repeat. If I cannot repay you for your goodness, at least let me show my gratitude in this simple manner. I am not being extravagant, either; Old Blackie here has been gathering dust for decades. And I am not asking you to compromise your principles. This is just a repayment of debts, between friends. "

"Friends." Carissa repeated the unfamiliar word. It had been so long since she'd had a real friend. And it had been forever

61

since anyone had given Pippa a gift, she realized, other than herself. Certainly not the father who couldn't wait for his daughter's birth to leave them for the army, and not the grandfather who refused to acknowledge the child of a match he had not arranged. Sir Gilliam was generous, handing Carissa a shilling or two to purchase something for the child at Christmas or her birthday, but that money was carefully hoarded against the future. Carissa had vowed never again to be at the mercy of callous fates. Now this. Blackie was the most beautiful gift anyone had ever received, right after Lord Hartleigh's friendship.

"You must be the kindest man I have ever known," the widow said through a curtain of tears.

Kind? What a night for firsts. This was the first time that a woman had refused a gift from him, and the first time in his life that anyone had called Lesley Hammond kind. Mrs. Kane must have known some bounders in her time, he thought. If a shabby wooden horse could bring moisture to her eyes, that Phillip Kane had a lot to answer for, leaving her so unprotected and vulnerable. "Then you will let Pippa have the toy?"

She nodded, sniffling into her handkerchief.

"Good," he said, trying to tease her out of the weepiness, "for who knows what I might require of you next. Hammond House tonight, perhaps the Egyptian Collection tomorrow, to steal Sue a mummy of her own."

Lord Hartleigh insisted on carrying Pippa across the street. The rocking horse and a few other items, books and trifles, he claimed, would be delivered in the morning. Carissa could not argue and chance waking any of the neighbors to see her coming in so late, in such company. The service door was locked, of course. She had expected nothing else from Mason.

"They might have left a candle burning," Lesley complained as she fumbled in her reticule for her key.

"What, for a mere servant?"

"Your Mason makes Wimberly appear positively amiable. It must be something in the breed of butlers."

"It's not the blood, my lord, it's the power. Men like Mason and Wimberly thrive on feeling superior to those weaker souls beneath them. I have seen enough of their kind to know. Besides, Mason is terrified that I might usurp some of his influence with Sir Gilliam. He is horridly jealous of our relationship."

Whatever that was. Hell, Lesley realized he was jealous too, but he merely shifted the child's slight weight to his other arm, so he might reach for his flint.

Carissa's fingers were suddenly stiff and clumsy as she tried to fit the key to the lock. The carriage ride, the cavernous attics, none seemed as intimate as her own doorstep. She was alone, for all practical purposes, with a practiced rake. All too aware of the viscount's masculinity, his size and easy strength, Carissa knew she did not want such a virile presence in her little sitting room, much less the bedroom she shared with Pippa. He was too large, too handsome, too used to women throwing themselves at him.

Once the kitchen candles were lit, Carissa reined in her own racing emotions. No, her imagination, she told herself. She was being a gudgeon, thinking that Lord Hartleigh might be interested in her. He was charming to everyone, that was all. They were not equals, and he would never trifle with such a dull, decorous female as herself. They were friends. Still, she reached out. "I'll take Pippa from here."

When the child was safely transferred to the widow's arms, never having fluttered an eyelash, the viscount did not step back as Carissa expected. Her pulse thundered as he took a step nearer and lowered his head. Surely he would not try to kiss her, not with Pippa in her arms? Surely she would never stand still and let him? But her feet were not listening to the orders from her brain, which were drowned out by the pounding of her heart.

No, the viscount did not kiss the housekeeper. He merely reached out and tugged the mobcap from her head. That was much, much worse. Brown curls tumbled to her shoulders and down her back, coming out of the bun in a flurry of fallen hairpins. Gold highlights flashed in the candle's glow.

"Ah," was all he said as he bowed, then left.

Hartleigh came to deliver the rocking horse, as promised, in the morning. And he came via the front door, to aggravate the niffy-naffy butler. Mason tried to bar the entrance. "Deliveries go to the rear," he insisted. "And so do Mrs. Kane's callers. On Saturdays. Her half day off."

Lesley carefully lowered the wooden horse, polished and brushed to a fare-thee-well, to the floor of Sir Gilliam's hallway and took out his quizzing glass. With enlarged eye and exaggerated sneer, Lord Hartleigh drawled, "You grow wearisome, my good man. I have half a notion to report your insolence to Sir Gilliam." He stared down at the smaller, thinner, older, and entirely less prepossessing butler, who seemed to shrink, and not merely because he was seen through the wrong end of a magnifying lens.

It was not the viscount's threat that had Mason holding the door wider, nor his arrogance. It was the sight of Byrd's grin, gold teeth, cauliflower ear, and tattooed skull that blighted the bully's bluster. Byrd was looming over the viscount's shoulder, his arms full of the "few trifles" from the shelves of the Hammond House nursery.

"No need to show us the way, Mason. We can locate the lady from here."

"Lady?" Mason sniffed, turning his back to them.

"Want I should pop his cork, Cap'n? Mrs. Kane is more a lady than half the gentry morts in London."

"Three quarters, I make no doubt. But this entry is much too charming to ruin with spilled claret. Flowers, fruit, ferns . . . Mrs. Kane's handiwork, I suppose. Next time, Byrdie." With that promise, the viscount and his man went down the hall toward the kitchen.

Pippa's eyes grew even larger and her thumb fell out of her open mouth when she saw Lord Hartleigh and his gift. "For me?"

The viscount winked at the buxom woman at the stove. "No, it's for Cook, so she'll come make gingerbread for me."

The child looked from Lesley to her mother, then grinned and hurled herself into the viscount's embrace, wrapping her thin arms around his neck and kissing him soundly on the cheek. "Now can I ride the horse?"

Carissa feared she was turning into a watering pot. Pippa was so happy, and her pride had almost denied the child this treat. She watched the viscount lift her daughter to the leather saddle and show her how to hold on. And she listened to Pippa jabbering away about how the horse was black, like her cat, and how it was almost as good as a real pony, and how Sue could ride it too, when she was bigger. Carissa never knew Pippa wanted a pony, never knew she could chatter like a magpie to a virtual stranger.

"How can I ever thank you enough, my lord?" she managed to ask past the lump in her throat.

"That's easy. You can come help us find places for everything we brought back last night."

Byrd had put down his load of packages. "More stuff'n a hundred babies need," he grumbled. "And that red-haired widgeon had me moving it all morning. Upstairs, downstairs, to the laundry, to the clothesline. What do poor babies do, is what I want to know, without a different blanket for every day of the week?"

"They get the croup, inflammation of the lungs, or pneumonia." Cook had filled a plate with slices of poppy-seed cake and set it in front of Byrd at the kitchen table, recognizing that so large a man was never filled. Carissa nodded for the viscount to help himself while she fetched the tea things. Tea in the kitchen, with earthenware mugs, was not what he was used to, she was sure, although Lord Hartleigh was smiling, thanking Cook, laughing at Pippa's excitement. What a complicated man, she thought again, as if the puzzle that was the prodigal peer would look any different by the light of day. He lived in a house that was smaller than the stables of his family home. His morals were abysmal, yet his manners were everything pleasing. He was arrogant and overbearing, but melted at a child's smile. He could outstare pompous despots like Wimberly and Mason, yet befriend those far beneath him in status. Truly, Lord Heartless was an enigma.

"Then you'll come?"

She'd been woolgathering. "Come where?"

"Across the street to help Maisie sort through the baby things, Mrs. Kane. And perhaps have a word with the new servants."

"No, I cannot interfere any more than I have done. You have a competent staff now." She ignored Byrd's blatant snort of disbelief. "Besides, I have to go to the apothecary this afternoon. Sir Gilliam's cough was worse this morning, and I promised Pippa a visit to the duck pond on the walk back."

"Excellent. We'll go with you, Sue and I, if we may. Test out the perambulator, don't you know, and give Maisie a rest. Maybe she can make sense of the piles if Sue is not around. And we'll take Glad. You said he needed the exercise. And that babies need fresh air. I've decided to take your advice, you see, so I do not consider anything you might tell me to be interference."

Carissa didn't like the sound of this at all: Byrd fetching and carrying, Maisie struggling with the laundry, the two men devouring every last slice of cake as if they hadn't breakfasted. And pouring the butter boat over her. Eyes narrowed, she asked, "What happened to the boy Matron sent over to walk the mongrel?"

"A squirrel. Glad went east, the lad went west and refused to come back."

"Then your housekeeper can interview another boy for the position."

Lesley cleared his throat. "The, ah, cook-housekeeper decamped earlier."

"Glad?"

"No, she was a damn—deuced good cook."

"I mean was it the dog that sent her to the right-about?"

"No, but he did eat the new footman's hat. You cannot blame Glad, though. The fool was storing a meat pasty in it."

"So the footman is gone, too?"

"And the new underbutler," the viscount confessed. "He, ah, had an accident on the way to the necessary last night. 'Twas dark, he was unfamiliar with the grounds. . . ."

"He fell in one of the dog's holes, didn't he?"

"Yes, and the scullery maid heard Glad baying and thought it was a banshee, and the bootboy turned spotty around dog hair. So, you see, we desperately need your services again."

Byrd nodded his agreement. "The place was running fine, for about a day and a half."

Carissa had to smile. "But what happened to that nice Mrs. Bennett? The housekeeper assured me she didn't mind children or dogs. What did Glad do to her?"

Hartleigh frowned at his manservant. "That was Byrd. He decided to show the staff how he could make his tattooed seagull flap its wings."

Byrd wiggled his eyebrows, causing the spread-winged bird on his bare scalp to move slightly, in imitation of flight.

Carissa shook her head. "And that disturbed Mrs. Bennett?"

"Not that tattoo, Mrs. Kane. The one on his cheek."

"But Mr. Byrd doesn't have a tattoo on his— Oh."

Chapter Ten

*H*e feathered his corners, he steadied his wheeler. His Belcher neckcloth flapped in the breeze. So did Glad's ears. Ah, if the Four-in-Hand Club could see Viscount Hartleigh now! But Sue squealed, and then her eyes drifted shut as he pushed the pram across the street. No race victory was sweeter.

He called at the front door of Sir Gilliam's town house, out of sheer perversity this time. He did offer to wait on the stoop with his carriage and his faithful hound while Mason went to fetch Mrs. Kane. He would have had a long wait but for Pippa being on the watch for him. She skipped along the side of the house toward the viscount and the pram, her mother following with a market basket in her hands.

"I do wish you wouldn't tweak Mason's nose that way, my lord," Carissa chided after greeting him and tucking the blankets more firmly around the baby.

"But that officious, pointed beak is just begging to be pinched."

"Yes, but it does make him more difficult to live with."

He smiled. "Then you'll come live with us."

"Ah, I see what it is now. You hope to give Sir Gilliam cause to dismiss me so you'll have a reliable housekeeper." She spoke severely, but he could see a spark of humor in her eyes, now that he knew what to look for, under the abysmal mobcap. "I must inform you that I do not cook."

Lesley wondered what else she did, or didn't do. He was wise enough to keep the question to himself, although he'd thought of little else last night after seeing that glorious hair tumbled around her shoulders. Sobriety and abstinence did that to a fellow, he decided, after one day of both. Giving Mrs. Kane a disgust of him did not suit his current plans, however. Not at all. As he pushed the pram with Mrs. Kane strolling beside him, therefore, he tried to make polite conversation. He was sorely out of practice, it seemed. "How did your husband die?"

To give herself time to recover from the unexpected question, Carissa looked back to check on her daughter. Pippa was marching along, one hand on the horrible hound's collar, one in her mouth. Carissa bit her lip and looked straight ahead again. "I am, ah, not entirely sure. The War Office was not forthcoming with details." That was an understatement. The War Office had never heard of Phillip Kane.

"Yes, those chaps can be closemouthed. Would you like me to look into it for you? What regiment was he in?"

"I am sorry, my lord, I do not like to discuss my husband. Please understand, it is simply too painful."

After four years? Or was the man such a rotter she did not wish to be reminded of him?

Then it was her turn to try to fill an awkward silence. "Have you made any progress toward finding Sue a foster family?"

That was another sore subject. "Oh, look, we've reached the apothecary already."

Hartleigh greeted the chemist in a friendly manner and purchased some peppermint drops. Then he returned outside while Carissa waited for her order to be filled, offering one of the sticky treats to Pippa, one to Glad. As Carissa watched through the window, shaking her head, the viscount tipped his hat to a fur-clad matron who stopped to admire the infant and nodded to a bewigged barrister hurrying past. He chatted with a young woman with two children in tow and smiled at an aproned abigail come to fetch her mistress's Denmark lotion. His lordship was not high in the instep at all, she marveled, when it suited him. Or else the infant was having a mellowing influence. He positively beamed when anyone complimented him on the pretty baby. What kind of heartless rake was this?

When they left the apothecary, they passed a butcher shop. The viscount groaned, recognizing the place where Glad preferred to do his own shopping. Lesley could have bought the store thrice over, for the damage reparations he'd paid. He let go the carriage to grab for the dog. The pram continued rolling. Mrs. Kane cried out. So did the driver of a wagon careening around the corner.

"Bloody hell!" Lesley dove for the carriage and snatched Sue out of it just as the first dray horse crushed the fragile wicker beneath its platter-size hooves. "There, Lovey," he soothed the startled child. Guilt tore through him, even before he saw the condemnation in Mrs. Kane's fine brown eyes. Damn, but he wasn't fit to own a canary, much less a baby. And damn, he needed a drink.

Mrs. Kane took the baby from him, as if he couldn't be trusted to hold the sprout now, Lesley lamented. So much for his plans to impress the widow. At least Glad hadn't caused any trouble at the butcher's. The dog was sitting at the corner, with Pippa holding one flopping flap up so she could whisper in his ear. Whatever she was promising him as reward for good behavior seemed to be working.

"Gingerbread," she confided at his lordship's questioning look.

"Then gingerbread it shall be! There must be a bakeshop somewhere nearby."

Carissa was afraid her daughter would grow spoiled, but she kept still. The poor man was so remorseful over his lapse—and he'd been so magnificent in his rescue—that she couldn't disappoint him. As they left the bakery, however, they passed their neighbors, the retired schoolmistresses. The Misses Applegate pulled their skirts aside, as if afraid of soiling the hems, when the viscount's little party went by. And Glad hadn't even marked the spot so he could come back for more gingerbread.

"I am afraid our neighbors do not approve," Lord Hartleigh said.

Carissa was enjoying her pastry too much to be upset. "Oh, those ladies do not approve of anything. They are barely civil to me on the best of days."

"Still, they used to dip a shallow curtsy in my direction now and again. Honoring the title if not the man, I suppose. The baby seems to have sunk me beneath contempt, though. I do hope you won't be tarred with the same brush, accompanying me and the child."

"Think nothing of it, my lord. If you are concerned that anyone might suppose the infant to be mine, rest easy. I wasn't enceinte or on holiday in recent times, so there is no suspicion of that. Everyone in this neighborhood knows the tale of Sue's landing on your doorstep, anyway. It was too good a story for the servants' grapevine, I am sure."

"Still, you cannot like being part and parcel of the gossip. We should turn back."

"But Pippa hasn't fed the ducks yet, and I did promise. Besides, my lord, I had no reputation to lose in the first place. People are always ready to think the worst of one, do you not agree?"

"Most definitely!"

"Why, do you know that there are persons who believe Sir Gilliam is my . . . that is, that he has, ah, designs on my person?"

"You don't say?" his lordship exclaimed. "Tsk, tsk."

"As if the dear man would even think such licentious thoughts."

"Absurd," he agreed.

She nodded at his understanding. "Sir Gilliam's is not merely an empty title handed to him in exchange for large donations to the Crown, I'll have you know. He is a true gentleman in every sense of the word."

"Here, here."

"No one who knows him, or you, for that matter, could ever suspect such a thing."

The viscount choked on his gingerbread.

They found the ducks, but Glad found them first and happily splashed through the stagnant waters to chase them off. So Pippa fed him the bread crumbs from her pocket.

"I told you he wasn't stupid," the viscount said.

Then it was time to return home. Carissa had chores and Pippa needed her nap. The baby was growing fussy, too, and needed Maisie.

"Dash it," the viscount muttered. He'd been enjoying himself, teaching Pippa to skip stones, jiggling the baby, listening to the widow's cork-brained comments. He was thoroughly unused to curtailing his pleasure for anyone else's convenience, especially a hungry infant's. "I suppose a father is de trop most of the time."

Hers was, Carissa concurred, and Pippa's. But she thought a doting papa just might have a place in a little girl's heart. If he didn't break it.

As he left, the viscount invited Mrs. Kane and her daughter to accompany him to Hyde Park on the next nice day. The ducks in the Serpentine wouldn't be afraid of any old dog, he told the girl, and if they were, the swans would send Glad to the roundabout. And there were horses too, not as fine as Blackie, he assured her, but very handsome. If she was very good—and he could not imagine the sprite being anything but—he might take her up in front of his horse.

How could Carissa say no? Especially when he made the engagement for her half day off? She fussed over Pippa's frock and her braids for an hour, after spending two hours on her own appearance. She wore her least shabby day gown, brightening it with the paisley shawl Sir Gilliam had given her last Boxing Day. And she wore her Sunday straw bonnet with fresh flowers tucked in the brim. For a housekeeper, she thought, she would not shame his lordship, not until the flowers wilted or the sunshine grew too warm to wear the shawl, at any rate.

Looking more handsome than ever in his buckskins and boots, blond hair gleaming in the sun, the viscount rode his gelding alongside an open carriage that held Maisie and Sue. Byrd drove, with Glad beside him on the bench, lop ears like windmill vanes in the breeze. Maisie was almost as excited as Pippa, and even Carissa had to admit that it had been ages since she'd been in an elegant rig, behind prime goers. When they reached the park, Lord Hartleigh lifted Pippa out of the coach and onto his horse. Carissa couldn't doubt his power or his prowess, but she couldn't look, either. After a gentle canter, they all got down to feed the ducks and walk on the pedestrian

72

paths toward some benches, where Byrd produced a jug of lemonade and some tarts.

The refreshments were from Gunter's, since Lord Hartleigh's most recent cook, a French chef, actually, had left his employ the evening before. It seemed Glad did not understand *allez, allez*. He did understand fricassee. Every last bite of it. The previous cook had been overheard to speak of Sue as a foreign bastard. She hadn't lasted for breakfast. One of the new footmen had ogled Maisie while she was feeding the babe, and the maid-of-all-work had decided she'd rather work on her back, in the viscount's bed. Never had a man been so bedeviled by his employees, Lesley complained as they sat on the bench, eating and watching Glad chase squirrels. His lordship was thinking of trying another employment office.

"Perhaps you should try another city," Carissa replied dryly. "The owner of the agency you've been using complained to me that his hirees would rather starve than serve in such a havey-cavey household. 'Queer as Dick's hatband' was the expression he used, I believe. And no, I will not leave Sir Gilliam."

"Well, Maisie offered to learn to cook, so I bought her a book of recipes. Now all I have to do is find someone to teach her to read. I don't suppose those Applegate women would, do you?"

Carissa had to laugh. And she had to offer the lessons, for she was starting to teach Pippa her numbers and letters. What was one more pupil, if Sir Gilliam was not discomposed by it? She would ask him.

When the last tart was gone, they returned to the carriage, walking away from the benches that were filled with shouting nannies and their rambunctious charges, shy young lovers and irate old ladies who'd come to feed the squirrels. The viscount tied his gelding behind and sat across from Maisie and Carissa, with Pippa on his lap. He pointed out to his fellow passengers all the trees and shrubs he could identify and made up names for the ones he could not. He asked for Pippa's opinions on the horseflesh they passed, and Carissa's on the fashions of the riders. He waved to friends, nodded to acquaintances, bowed to the long-nosed dowagers with lorgnettes, and ignored the garish women who tried to catch his eye. He did not stop for introductions, but neither did he hurry his companions away from society's gaze until they passed Lord Cosgrove. He was riding a showy hack, and both of them were already winded after one turn around the tanbark. Maisie hid her face in the baby's blanket.

"Let's leave, Byrdie," his lordship directed, loudly enough for those nearby to hear. "The park is growing too crowded with the raff and chaff of the city." Lesley reached across and patted Maisie's hand. "No one can ever hurt you again, my dear. Remember that."

What a nice man, Carissa thought yet again, and what a delightful day. Pippa had fallen asleep without her supper, after a surfeit of treats, but Mrs. Kane knew she'd have a harder time of it. Why couldn't he be old and ugly, mean and miserly? Why couldn't Lord Heartless live down to her expectations? And why, oh, why, did she have to be growing so fond of the man when there was no future in it? Not with his reputation, not with her past. The other thing keeping Carissa awake was the niggling feeling of being watched in the park. She did not mind the passersby who barely concealed their curiosity at the odd caravan, but she'd felt something furtive, half seen. It had been enough to bring shivery goose bumps to the back of her neck. Her past, again?

The viscount was entirely pleased with the day. His plan was working perfectly. The news would be served up at any number of fashionable dinner parties that evening, that Lord Heartless had a family. Not a sanctioned marriage, but a ménage. The baby was his—he'd never made an effort to deny it—and if anyone chose to wonder if Mrs. Kane's moppet belonged to him too, well, that was a bonus. Today's performance should put paid to his stepmother's matchmaking once and for all, if it didn't give her an apoplexy. Not even the most desperate female would align herself, or her relations, with a gentleman so lost to propriety that he paraded his by-blows in the park. No marriage-minded mother would push her daughter into a match that was already adulterous, with no

74

signs that the groom meant to cut the connection. No right-minded father would betroth his daughter to such a loose screw. Lesley knew he wouldn't. Why, let a rake like himself look twice at his little girl, or Pippa, for that matter, when they were of marriageable age, and Lesley would call the scoundrel out, by George!

Chapter Eleven

*F*atherhood was fine, but the straight and narrow was beginning to suffocate Lord Hartleigh. He did not wish to make his daughter feel unwanted, but a fellow couldn't spend every evening by his own fireside, talking with an infant. Sue didn't have much conversation and she tended to fall asleep at the best part of his stories.

He did not want to give Mrs. Kane cause to curtail their growing friendship. To Lesley's surprise, the idea of not calling on her, not going for walks with her, bothered him, and not only because his plan would work better with her cooperation. If he brought a Cyprian home, he knew, he could say good-bye to their easy familiarity.

Most of all, the viscount did not want little Pippa to see him disguised and disheveled again. He liked seeing the light of hero worship in the child's eyes, Lesley realized, and it was so easy to put there. A toy, a treat, a horseback ride—would that her mother fell into his lap as easily. But no, he would not think along those lines. Nothing would send Mrs. Kane fleeing faster than an improper proposal. The thought, the one that he wasn't supposed to be thinking, sent him into the night, seeking companionship.

Lesley took himself to White's, where he had no intention of losing a lot, drinking a lot, or finding a harlot. He did not intend to get into a duel, either.

After an hour or two, he was sorry he'd come. The air was fetid, the cognac was cloying, and he began to realize that he'd rather hold Sue's featherweight than a deck of cards. Winning a smile from her was more of a challenge than winning another fortune from the gamesters at his table. As he stood to leave, however, he heard his name mentioned at an adjoining table. He had no doubt that Lord Cosgrove meant him to hear every word. He sat back down and nodded for Harry Falcroft to deal him back into their game.

"I say," the raddled peer was slurring, "did you hear Heartless has taken to keeping a harem?" Cosgrove was in his cups, and so far in Dun Territory that nothing could save him. He was going to have to rusticate in the country with his wife, by thunder. He hadn't won a hand since Hartleigh and his handmaiden had invaded Cosgrove House, carrying off the little red-haired maid. Silence greeted his words, so Cosgrove continued: "Seems that expensive bit of fluff from the opera house ain't enough to satisfy the sod, nor that countess from Kent who's been throwing herself at his neck. Stealing other men's wives must've grown tame sport, 'cause now he's stealing other men's mistresses."

"I say," one of the other men at Cosgrove's table put in, knowing full well that Lord Hartleigh could hear Cosgrove's rant. "That's a heavy charge." He laughed, trying to dispel the growing tension. "Everyone knows Heartless don't have to steal any females. They just flock to him, like bees to honey. You're just hipped 'cause your pockets aren't deep enough to afford the dashers he keeps."

"They ain't dashers, I tell you. First he stole my convenient, right out of my house, and then he made off with Parkhurst's, y'know, the banker. Saw them with my own eyes, I did. Riding in the park as bold as brass. That female masquerades as Parkhurst's cook or something. Hah! The only baking she does is to keep buns in the oven!"

Hartleigh had heard enough. So had every other man in the room, in his opinion, if the oaf meant to make free with Mrs. Kane's reputation. He stood and turned to face the sot. "Did you have something you wished to discuss with me, Cosgrove? Perhaps we can meet tomorrow, say at Gentleman Jackson's?"

What, and get beaten to a pulp by this student of the Fancy?

Cosgrove was angry; he wasn't insane. "What I wish to say, I can say right here, Hartleigh. I want my maid back."

"Why, so you can abuse her again?" He sneered. "Crawl back under your rock, Cosgrove, for only a slug would take his pleasure on a servant too helpless to refuse. And only a sack of slime would toss a wench onto the streets when she was increasing."

Now Cosgrove was on his feet, too. "What, is it noblesse oblige you're practicing, Hartleigh, keeping your bastards around, parading them in the park? I swear, decent people have to be offended!"

Anyone who knew Lesley would have been warned by his narrowed eyes and the muscle twitching in his jaw. "Cosgrove, you would not recognize decent if it came up and bit you on your sottish snout."

"What, are you impugning my honor?"

"I couldn't, sirrah, for you have none. And I would not waste my breath on you; I'll simply take my whip to your worthless hide if you offend me further." With that warning, Lesley nodded to the gentlemen at his table, most of whose glances did not meet his eyes, and turned to leave.

Cosgrove reached out and latched on to the viscount's sleeve. "Hold, varlet. I am of a mind to call you out. You cannot insult a gentleman and then walk away."

"I didn't," Lesley said briefly, staring at the other's hand until it fell away. Then he flicked his fingers at his coat sleeve. "Insult a gentleman, that is."

Cosgrove was turning purple in his fury. "Why, why, I will have to issue a challenge for that slur."

"An invitation to the field of honor? I told you, such honors are not open to scum like you. Your abuse of women, your card playing—"

"What, are you calling me a cheat now?" Cosgrove was screaming. Waiters and footmen were scurrying around, gentlemen were pouring out of the reading room and the dining parlor.

"Zounds, do you do that, too?" Lesley held up one hand. "Not that I am accusing you, Cosgrove. I'd never play with you to find out, but I'm sure all these other members appreciate the warning."

Since Cosgrove seemed to be reduced to sputters, Lesley went on: "If you are still thinking of slapping my cheek or tossing your wine at my face, think again. As challenged, I would get to choose weapons. Do you know, I believe I would have a hard time trying to decide whether to blow your ballocks off with my pistol or slice them off with my sword. Be assured, Cosgrove, that you'd never get to rape another half-grown girl."

Cosgrove sank onto his seat; the color fled from his face as sobriety—and self-preservation—settled in. Hartleigh was a master swordsman and a crack shot. Cosgrove's country estate was looking more and more welcoming, even if he'd have to tell his shrewish wife that he'd lost everything else. Of course, if he left now, he might as well admit he'd been marking the cards. And that he was lily-livered to boot.

Hartleigh wasn't finished. "If you still wish satisfaction, or still think you can bandy my name around in public, or that of my companions, my offer to meet you at Gentleman Jackson's still stands. Shall we say Monday morning? Harry, will you make the arrangements?" At Falcroft's nod, Lord Hartleigh bowed to the room and made his exit.

Carissa had not seen Lord Hartleigh in a few days, on purpose. She was not precisely avoiding him so much as staying close to the house, for she kept feeling that prickling sense of being watched. And she had a perfectly good excuse for not being available when he called, at the front door or the back: Sir Gilliam's cough had worsened, and Carissa convinced him not to go to the bank for a few days, to recover his strength. She was helping him with correspondence, as a result, or keeping him entertained with backgammon and piquet. She and Pippa did look in on Maisie and the baby a few minutes here and there, slipping into the viscount's house via the back door and leaving as quickly and quietly. A few times she accepted Maisie's offer to watch Pippa for an hour or so, since the child was not getting out as much as usual, or getting as much attention. The two of them could practice their letters together, thank goodness. Other times Mrs. Kane silently thanked the viscount for Blackie and the books and the games from Hammond House, which kept Pippa happy for hours in their tiny sitting room.

Byrd and Maisie seemed to be coping with the kitchen, Carissa discovered, between cooks. The last one drank too much, the one before that stole the silverware. His lordship would not permit one of the new footmen in the house with Sue because the man caught a congestion. Another caught Gladiator in his bed and almost killed the mutt. But none of that was her problem, Carissa told herself. The house was still reasonably clean, so she did not have to worry over Pippa or the baby playing in dirt—in the kitchen. And they all seemed to be eating well enough. According to Maisie, anything was better than the swill Lord Cosgrove saw fit to feed his servants.

No, Lord Hartleigh's domestic worries were none of Carissa's concern. Why, if she took a hand in his household, people might think she was tossing her ugly mobcap at the viscount. Worse, *he* might think she was just another flibbertigibbet female ready to fall at his feet. Carissa would not throw herself at him, nor give the appearance that she wished to. There was too good a chance that he would catch her, and that was entirely too dangerous for her peace of mind. She'd noted his gleam of appreciation when she dressed for the park; she'd noticed that he held her hand longer than necessary when helping her into and out of the carriage. And she'd known that she was falling under the spell of Lord Hartleigh's fatal charm. Much too dangerous indeed. There were precisely two offers a viscount made to a housekeeper, and Lord Hartleigh had already offered her one of them, repeatedly. Carissa wouldn't be his chatelaine, and she wouldn't be his *chère amie*. If the world were a different place . . . there still would have been Phillip Kane.

Carissa knew what people were saying, of course. Mason made sure of it. Sir Gilliam's good opinion of her was the only one that mattered, however, and he merely patted her hand when she put another blanket across his knees.

"You've a good head on your shoulders, my dear," he said. "I won't worry about you."

Mason also made sure that Carissa knew that the viscount had made a public spectacle of himself, defending her name. He announced it at the servants' luncheon in the kitchen, savoring the news as much as Cook's steak and kidney pie. In disbelief, Carissa looked to Cook.

" 'Twere in all the columns this morning, dearie, as how he and that snake Cosgrove had words. Your name weren't mentioned." She waved her paring knife in Mason's direction.

Mason was not intimidated. "But Sir Gilliam's was," he gloated. "Leastways 'Sir G P, eminent financier,' was. Set the master back, it did. Told me to call for his solicitor, he was feeling so poorly."

They were all silent at that. Then Cook said, "Go on with you, no one thinks any the less of the master because two swells butt heads."

"Like stags in rut," Mason slyly added, "over a doe in season."

Cook slammed a mug of ale down in front of Mason, letting a few drops spatter on his pristine uniform. "You watch your tongue in my kitchen, Mr. Mason, else I'll cut it off and serve it to Mrs. Kane's cat."

"Cleo's too fussy an eater." Carissa was touched by Cook's defense, but she could not help feeling guilty for any distress Sir Gilliam might have suffered. Whilst she was enjoying Lord Hartleigh's company, she'd thought her peace of mind would be the only casualty. She should have realized that anything the viscount did was bound to become grist for the gossip mills. If a rake smiled at a milkmaid, her morals would be suspect. But to be throwing down gauntlets in White's? How dare that reprobate involve her—involve a totally innocent gentleman like Sir Gilliam—in an adolescent, asinine act of arrogance? She did not think much of Lord Cosgrove either. Luckily for him, he was already packing for the country.

Unluckily for Lord Hartleigh, he was at home, already packing ice around his bruised knuckles when Mrs. Kane marched across the street. "How dare you?" she said by way of greeting, ignoring the basin of ice and the bloodied towels. "How dare you let Sir Gilliam's name be bandied about that way? You knew Cosgrove was a serpent. Bullies like him love an audience, and you had to provide it, didn't you? You could have left at the first word out of his forked tongue. With no one to aggravate, he would have subsided."

This was not what Lesley had in mind for his next meeting with the widow. No thank-you for defending her name, no congratulations for routing the rum touch. He shouldn't have been surprised, because nothing about the woman was what he expected. He also shouldn't have tried to excuse his actions. "I did try to muzzle him."

"The way you muzzle the mongrel?" she shot back. "You practically challenged Cosgrove to a duel, by all reports! A duel! Let's ignore the fact that dueling is illegal, for now. What about Sue?"

"Sue? Did Cosgrove call her out, too?"

"You know very well what I mean. What happens to Sue if you get slain in a nonsensical set-to with that swine, or have to flee the country for killing him? You haven't made the least push to see your daughter placed in a real home with a real mother and reliable father. Will the cousin who inherits your title also inherit Sue? Will he look after her the way you would, or will he turn his back on your by-blow? If she is lucky, the new viscount will take her in to become an unpaid servant, a poor relation not fit to take out into company. Lucky? She'll never marry, never have a family, never be treated with respect. How dare you take chances with your life before hers is settled? And what about Pippa? She thinks you the nearest thing to heaven in her life, and you could disappear at dawn. A child does not understand about manly honor or gentlemen's pride. She understands that you promised her another ride on your horse! The gabble-grinders are right: You are a care-for-naught, my lord Heartless, and I never want to see you again!"

She likes me, Lesley thought as the door slammed behind Carissa. She likes me a lot.

Chapter Twelve

Sir Gilliam was dying. When his physician said so, Carissa made Mason call in another. That doctor shook his head and handed her some more laudanum, for her nerves, he said. The solicitor came, not Mr. Alistair Gordon, who had conducted Sir Gilliam's legal affairs for the last forty years, but his son, Mr. Nigel Gordon. The senior Gordon having passed away last winter, the younger was taking over the business.

"It's a dying generation," Cook lamented, wiping her eyes on her apron.

Carissa could not help recalling the evenings when she and Sir Gilliam and his solicitor had played three-handed whist for hours, or when she had sat to table, at Sir Gilliam's insistence, with Mr. Gordon and his wife. Mr. Nigel did not so much as acknowledge her presence when she brought him tea in the sickroom. No "Thank you," no "How do you do?" The world was going to be a sadder place without all the courtly old gentlemen, Carissa thought, dabbing at her own damp cheeks.

Nigel did find time for a coze with Mason, most likely going over details concerning pensions for the staff and addresses of those to notify, Cook guessed. "Sure and Sir Gilliam will do what's right, iffen Mason and the young vulture don't talk him out of it whilst he's so poorly."

Having instantly taken control of the household, Mason was doing his best to keep Carissa away from Sir Gilliam. "It would not be proper for you to sit up with the master at night, in his bedroom," he took pleasure in telling her. "You do remember the rules of propriety, don't you, Mrs. Kane? Or are you too busy chasing after your nob to recall the demands of proper conduct in a *gentleman's* house? Go off where you'd rather be, across the street, and leave Sir Gilliam to those as care for his welfare."

She hardly left the house, waiting for Mason to eat or sleep or go off on business of his own, though heaven knew what or where. Most of those times, when she tiptoed into the sickroom past a drowsing footman, Sir Gilliam was in a drugged stupor, oblivious to her visit. She sat by his side anyway, saying prayers and listening to his labored breathing.

A few days later Mason summoned her to the master's bedroom. "He's calling for you, won't take his medicine till he's had his say. It'll be on your head if he takes a turn for the worse."

How much worse could the poor man get? Carissa wondered as she stood next to the bed, fighting back tears at the sight of the shrunken, shaking body, struggling for every breath, it seemed.

"Don't be sad, my dear," the old man said with a gasp, reaching out one wizened hand for hers. "I have led a long life, made my fortune, made the knighthood, made my peace with God. It's time to make my farewells."

"No, dear sir, don't talk like that. You cannot leave us! Save your breath, I beg you, so you may recover."

He tried to smile, but the effort was too much. "Very well, I shall lie here quietly and listen to you for a spell. How is Lord Hartleigh going on?"

So she told him about the duel that wasn't, and the harsh things she'd said, and the servants who would not stay.

Sir Gilliam coughed, as laughter was beyond him. After Carissa held the glass of tonic to his lips and he'd taken a sip or two, the aged knight managed to say, "You are just what that young man needs."

"What, a competent housekeeper?"

"Aye, you're that and more, my dear. A pearl beyond price."

She shook her head. "I wouldn't put up with that dog, either!"

"And you won't have to, Carissa. I have made other provisions."

84

"Sir?" His voice was so soft Carissa had trouble understanding.

"You won't have to keep house for anyone but yourself and your daughter. Tell Philippa good-bye for me, my dear. I shouldn't want her to see me this way."

"She sends her prayers," Carissa said, no longer able to contain her tears.

"And thank you for sharing her with me, for the little while. I never wanted children of my own, you know."

"Please, Sir Gilliam, please don't strain yourself to speak."

"Have to, my dear. There won't be another chance. Did you ever want more children, Carissa?"

"Once, sir, but I stopped thinking about it until I held Lord Hartleigh's infant. I am content with my daughter."

"It's still not too late for you. Handsome woman, I always thought so. In your prime. I often wondered if that was why you would not accept my proposal. You should have, my dear. I could not offer you mad, passionate romance—my spirit might have been willing, but this old body would not have cooperated. But your future would have been secure now, yours and Philippa's both." A tear rolled down his sunken cheek.

Carissa wiped it away and tried to smile for him. "You mustn't worry about us, Sir Gilliam. You've been so generous I've been able to put some money by. And you said yourself, I am an excellent housekeeper."

"No. You weren't meant to keep another woman's house. I've seen to it. Rather take care of you than that nodcock nevvy of mine. You and the lass are more like family than the coxcomb could ever be."

"That's the nicest thing you could say, dear sir." She leaned over and kissed his pale cheek and brushed the silvered hair off his forehead. "I am going to miss you more than I can ever express."

He squeezed her hand feebly, but a squeeze nevertheless. "You'll be fine, my dear. I've seen to it."

Mason sent for the rector of the nearby church, and for the nephew. While the clergyman was praying for Sir Gilliam's soul, Mason was closeted with Mr. Broderick Parkhurst, a would-be dandy, a ne'er-do-well who'd gone through his five-and-twenty years at his uncle's expense, and was going to the devil on his own. He'd refused Sir Gilliam's offers of a university education, a position at the bank, an army commission, or an introduction at the East India Company. He'd refused everything but an allowance, which he spent on clothes that did not flatter his spindly frame and horses that he could not stay aboard. Broderick's sole ambition in life, Sir Gilliam had often despaired, was to become a gentleman of leisure. No matter that his birth was only respectable and his fortune negligible, Broderick Parkhurst was not going to work for a living.

Especially not while his wealthy uncle lay dying.

Broderick moved into the house, demanding constant service, keeping irregular hours, creating havoc in the kitchens. If he visited Sir Gilliam's bedside once, it was more than the exhausted Carissa noticed.

"Good," Cook announced. "Let the poor man die in peace."

Carissa prayed he had.

She had no time for grieving, for Broderick filled the house with his rowdy friends for the funeral observances. She was run off her feet changing linens, changing menus every time another young man arrived. More foodstuffs had to be ordered, and more wine. A lot more wine. She hired more maids, which were her domain, and insisted Mason hire more footmen, to haul bathwater and coal and the occasional castaway guest off to a bedchamber. They suddenly needed grooms to manage the horses and a boy to polish the riders' boots, after they'd tracked mud throughout the house. The new servants needed quarters and uniforms and meals. They were not all what Carissa considered fit company for Pippa, especially the footmen Mason hired. The guests, with their foul mouths and reckless ways, certainly were not. Pippa spent more time with Maisie than with her mother.

Lord Hartleigh came to call, to pay his respects to those who truly cared about Sir Gilliam. That time he came in the back door.

"I will have Byrd here in two shakes," he offered, "to carry your things across the street. There is no reason for you to stay on here when a perfectly suitable position is going begging. Can you believe the last woman that agency sent over was cloth-headed enough to feed Glad beans?" He shook his head. "Parkhurst and his peep-o'-day boys will turn the place into a gaming hell before they are done. Come away before I am forced to do something they will regret."

Carissa smiled but had to refuse. "I owe Sir Gilliam more loyalty than that. At least until the will is read, when things shall be more settled. Then I will decide what's best for me and Pippa." She had no idea what Sir Gilliam intended for them, so she could not make plans. She did know how dangerous re-siding under the same roof with this handsome rake could be. She'd take her chances with the louts upstairs.

"So long as you don't mind that Pippa is underfoot at your place?" she asked.

"Of course not. She is no trouble at all, I assure you." And she was keeping the tongues wagging when he took the little moppet to the park, perched in front of him on the saddle. "Besides, she is the only one Gladiator listens to."

"She is the only one with gingerbread in her pocket, most likely."

"You are sure you can manage these young sots? Some of them fancy themselves hellrakers."

She'd managed *him* so far, hadn't she? But now that she thought of it, Carissa hadn't seen his lordship disguised since Sue arrived, hadn't seen him come home at daybreak, and hadn't seen any birds of paradise fluttering about. She'd think about that later, after she made sure there was ample hot water for those of the houseguests who deigned to bathe before dinner, or ever.

Lesley left, reluctantly.

Carissa let him, reluctantly.

The day the will was read, Sir Gilliam's nephew wore a black stock, a gray coat with black armbands, and a smug ex-pression. Broderick was already seated in the library when Carissa and the rest of the servants filed in to stand toward the rear, there being no chairs set out for them. They all shared the same sorrow to find the new solicitor sitting at Sir Gilliam's desk instead of their beloved employer. Nigel Gordon had a glass of wine at one elbow and Mason hovering at the other with the decanter. Nothing was offered to the staff, of course. Bonnie, the maid, started sniffling, until Cook pinched her.

Carissa barely listened to the legal terms and the long explanations Mr. Gordon seemed determined to make, ensuring the validity of the will. Then he got to bequests for the servants. Mason was to get a pension, Cook was to have a year's salary. The others were to have a quarter's wages. Carissa's name was not mentioned.

Next came donations to charities. Sir Gilliam was generous, but Carissa's name was not mentioned.

The remainder of Sir Gilliam's estate, the lawyer was reading, including this house and the balance of his financial assets, was herewith bequeathed to his nephew, Broderick Parkhurst. Carissa's name was not mentioned.

Stunned, she leaned against the wall as the other servants left the library, looking at her and shaking their heads. She did not understand, could not understand. How could that kind man, that gentleman who'd offered to marry her so she and her daughter would be provided for, how could he not have remembered her in his will? Worse, how could he have lied to her? Carissa could not believe it of him. On trembling legs she approached the desk where Broderick and the solicitor were shaking hands while Mason poured them each another glass of Sir Gilliam's finest sherry.

"Excuse me, sirs, but I think there must have been some mistake."

Nigel Gordon looked up—he did not stand up—and then looked through his papers and notes. "Ah, yes, the housekeeper. Mrs. Kane. We wondered why there was no mention of you, until Mr. Mason pointed out that you had not been in Sir Gilliam's employ when this testament was created."

"Not in his employ? I have been here nearly four years."

"And this will is five years old. You would have heard the

date, had you been listening." He turned back to Broderick and his glass.

"Pardon me," Carissa persisted, "but Sir Gilliam made a new will when he took ill. You yourself came to call."

Nigel swallowed his wine before bothering to answer: "I was called to his bedside, indeed, but the man was nearly comatose."

"That was due to the laudanum. He was not so stuporous all the time!"

"The twice I called he was not lucid, I am sorry to say."

"He was clear enough in his head to assure me that provision had been made for me and my daughter."

"Ma'am, his mind was wandering at the end. Surely you saw that he was delirious." He looked toward Mason, who confirmed his assessment with a nod. Broderick was cleaning his fingernails with the penknife on the desk.

"No, he knew me. He mentioned my daughter by name. We talked about the neighbors! He was *not* rambling or vague, and he did say that he'd left me a bequest."

"I am sure he meant to, Mrs. Kane. Sir Gilliam was generous. However, even if he had managed to express his desires, the will could have been overturned. No court of law would have believed Sir Gilliam was in sound mind at the time."

Not with Mason and that worm Broderick to say otherwise, she saw now. They'd kept him drugged, kept poor Sir Gilliam nearly unconscious, so that he could not change his will in her favor. Broderick's motives were obvious, and Mason had always hated her. Perhaps he was even getting a bonus for his part in the scheme to rob a dying man of his last wishes, and her of dying hopes. Carissa had to steady herself, but she would not swoon, not in front of these . . . these criminals.

"I say, it's a rum go, Mrs. Kane." Broderick was swinging his fob watch—no, it was Sir Gilliam's fob watch, Carissa saw now; the carrion-eater had not even waited for the will to be read. "But I mean to do the right thing. Respect for m'uncle, don't you know. The other servants got a quarter's wages, eh? Well, you shall have a half year's, ma'am." He beamed at the solicitor. "And the opportunity to stay on, of course. La, couldn't put m'uncle's loyal helpers out in the cold, now could I?"

"You are too generous," she said, and Broderick was too stupid to hear the irony in her voice.

He polished the watch on one of Sir Gilliam's handkerchiefs, one that Carissa had embroidered an ornate *P* on, for Christmas. "Think nothing of it, m'dear."

She didn't.

Chapter Thirteen

*W*hat was she going to do? By all that was holy, what was she going to do? How long could she live on the crumbs Broderick had tossed her? London rents were high, but there were more positions here than in the country. Carissa had some savings put aside, but they would not go far, either. They were supposed to be for Pippa's dowry, not her daily bread. Carissa did not know if she could bear to stay on in Sir Gilliam's house and watch Sir Gilliam's nephew destroy the peace and quiet the old gentleman had cherished. She knew she could not remain here if Mason did. The man had been difficult under Sir Gilliam; he'd be impossible under a weakling like Broderick. Carissa would not be under his thumb. Mason had been left a pension, though, a pension she thought she'd been promised, along with the house. Perhaps he'd leave.

Cook was already packing, instead of making dinner. "They can go out to supper, for all I care, onct they're done celebrating, and the master not even in the ground two days." She folded her aprons and stuffed them into a small trunk, slamming the lid. "I won't stay here with that young bugger, I won't. It ain't what a body is used to, that's for sure. Taking food out of my larder in the middle of the night so a body doesn't know what's left to cook come morning. Not telling a soul how many are coming to dinner. Strutting into my kitchen like a gamecock, 'n' leaving it a shambles. No, I'd rather go to my sister's house and cook for her brood than feed the likes of him."

Pippa's cat was twining itself around her legs, so Mrs. Kane picked it up and collapsed onto a kitchen chair with Cleo on her lap, stroking the soft fur and getting some small comfort from the purring. "But you don't like your sister's husband. You said he curses at her."

Slamming a knife into a drawer, Cook said, "Not with me there, he won't. You can count on that."

Carissa nodded. Cook was a formidable woman. Her brother-in-law's days of intimidating his wife and children were over, unless Carissa missed her guess.

" 'Sides," Cook was saying as she reached for a bottle of Sir Gilliam's finest wine, "that man-milliner Broderick will go through Sir Gilliam's blunt in a month, you mark my words. Let loose on London with all that brass in his pockets, the ninnyhammer will be plucked by every Captain Sharp in town. Look at the way he already lets those bosom bows of his barracks themselves here. No, it won't be long afore he goes through what should have been yours, dearie, and has none left for my salary, much less my pension."

"Can he do that?" Carissa wanted to know, accepting a glass for herself. She deserved that, at least. "I thought the monies Sir Gilliam bequeathed had to be set aside, held in trust or some such."

Cook clucked her tongue at the housekeeper's naïveté. "And who's to make sure he does, then? That no-account solicitor? Why, if he isn't getting a share of Sir Gilliam's groats, then I'll eat my Sunday bonnet. And you know how much I like my new hat."

It had fruit on it, and a little stuffed bird. Carissa hated the thing, but she'd miss seeing it every Sunday. "Now you can have two new bonnets," she said in a quavering voice.

Cook blew her nose into a spotted kerchief. "I'll miss you too, dearie. What are you going to do?"

Carissa shook her head. "I haven't decided. Mr. Broderick says I can stay on as housekeeper."

"Faugh. Why work for that popinjay when you can work for his lordship acrost the street? You know he's always asking, and you practically run the place for him now. Did you know that dog of his bit that scurvy solicitor this morning? The flat tried to pat your little one on the head, he did, when she were out walking with Maisie and the babe. Trying to turn Maisie up sweet, I'd wager."

"I could almost grow to like the mutt." The cat turned big green eyes up at Carissa in reproach, whether for the compliment to the dog or for the tear that fell on her fur. Carissa scratched under her chin. "But not enough to take the position. It would be too . . . difficult."

"You mean it would be too easy to fall for the nonesuch, like every other female alive. Why, was I twenty years younger and a few stones lighter, I'd be batting my eyelashes at him too."

"I never did!"

"No, I didn't mean you, dearie. You're too much the lady for a quick tumble, and don't I know it." She downed her glass, poured another, and shook her head again. "Still and all, it ain't right what they done to you. It ain't right at all. Could you go home to your da? A gentle-born lady like you hadn't ought to be working no ways, and Sir Gilliam was the first to recognize that fact."

The cat rolled to her back, to get her stomach rubbed. "No, my father washed his hands of me when I wed. I tried to seek his help when Phillip left us, but he was as adamant as ever. I would work for the worm who stole Sir Gilliam's money, rather than go begging of my father."

"And that husband of your'n didn't leave you his army pension or nothing?"

"Phillip Kane left me, period, as soon as he realized my father wouldn't release my dowry since I'd married without his permission. He rejoined the army before Pippa was born." Or so he'd said at the time. "Oh, he did manage to go through the small inheritance I had from my mother first. I was able to sell my gowns and jewelry to live on, hoping he'd come back. He never did." He never so much as sent a letter, never inquired about the child or her welfare. "I know now that he never loved me, that he was just after my father's money, but I was too gullible to see it at the time. It galls me that Papa was right. But I was young and would not listen to anything but my schoolgirl romantic notions."

"And then that Kane bastard up and died. Good riddance to him, I say. The Frogs did you a favor, dearie."

Phillip had died, at least in Carissa's heart.

Cook poured out another glass. "It ain't right."

Carissa knew it wasn't right, she just didn't know what she could do about the damnable situation. First she went to fetch Pippa, avoiding the viscount, his manservant, and his mongrel. She hugged the child so hard that Pippa protested. Then she bathed and fed the girl, brushed Pippa's light brown hair until it crackled, and listened to her prayers.

"Say a special one for Sir Gilliam in heaven, sweetheart," she advised, hoping the dear man wasn't spinning in his grave after this day's work. Then she put Pippa into bed early, telling her they had to get up sooner than usual to say good-bye to Cook in the morning. After one story from the viscount's nursery books, Carissa waited for her precious baby to fall asleep, the cat tucked under her chin.

Then, and only when she was absolutely positive that Pippa would not stir, Mrs. Kane returned to her tiny sitting room, threw herself onto the sofa there, and cried her eyes out. She cried for the man who was almost like a father to her, for hadn't she run her father's household too? And she cried for Pippa, who would never know a front-parlor life, unless she had the dusting of one. And she cried for herself. An inheritance that would make her independent, that's what Sir Gilliam had said. She wouldn't have to keep house for anyone else, he'd told her. With a house and a bit of money in the bank, and letting her father's name be known, and the devil take him, she could be almost anyone's equal. The highest sticklers would never forgive her for going into service, of course, even if it had been the only way she could eat. No matter, she did not care to reenter Society, anyway, for she could never marry again, as the old knight had thought she would, and that was the only reason for taking her rightful place in the ton. But she would have people's respect. She would have the viscount's respect. He would not look at her as if she were a plum ripe for the picking, not if she were Lady Carissa, the Earl of Macclesfield's daughter, with a tidy competence.

Instead she had nothing. Worse, she'd had her hopes dashed. What was she going to do?

Carissa must have fallen asleep eventually, there on the sofa, for she woke up cold and stiff, with her black gown twisted around her. The fire had gone out, and only the tiny glow of the oil lamp she left burning for Pippa in the bedroom they shared let her read the mantel clock. Two o'clock. Broderick must have come home, she thought, with his boisterous friends, disturbing her exhausted slumber. She just hoped they wouldn't decide to make a foray on the nearby kitchen.

While she was washing her face, still in the same wrinkled gown she'd worn all day and half the night now, she heard a scratching on her door. Carissa was *not* going to wake a footman to carry wash water for the cawker. Hers was frigid; let Broderick make do with cold water, too. And if the gudgeon wanted tea at two of the clock, he could jolly well go to China to find it.

The scratching continued. Standing perfectly still, Carissa pretended she hadn't heard it, even though Cleo wouldn't have made as much of a racket. Then came a hoarse whisper: "Mrs. Kane, I need to talk to you. I heard noises, don't you know, so you must be awake. I'll wait."

"I am sorry, Mr. Parkhurst, but you will have a very long wait. My duties begin at six of the A.M., not until. I shall be pleased to speak to you first thing in the morning."

"But I need you now. I really do," he whined.

Oh, Lord, had the clunch come a cropper already? What if he was bleeding or ill? What if his conscience was bothering him so much he wished to offer her the deed to this house? Pigs would fly first, but she opened the door a crack. She didn't see any blood or bruises, though the coxcomb did seem the worse for wear. His neckcloth, which had been tied so high he had to look past his chin to see, was now limp and hanging to one side. His Cossack trousers, the latest thing, he had assured her that morning, had also come unstarched and unpressed, making him look like a failed balloon ascension. The hot air must have gone to his face, for it was flushed and damp with perspiration. Either he had the influenza or he'd imbibed too much. Carissa bet on the bottle.

When she tried to shut the door, he put his foot inside. "Dash it, just want to talk, don't you know."

She knew there'd be no getting rid of the rattlepate till she heard him out. "Very well, Mr. Parkhurst. What is it?"

"Didn't want to say it in front of Gordon, but you're welcome to stay on in the same city—no, the same capacity, is what I mean—as with m'uncle."

Carissa nodded, tapping her foot impatiently. "Yes, sir, you did say that this afternoon. And I am considering your kind offer. I shall inform you of my decision on the morrow."

"But there's more. Didn't want to say it in front of the fellows, either. Or the bra—your daughter. Or Cook." He shuddered. "Reminds me of the knacker, back home."

"Yes? What more did you wish to tell me in confidence?" Carissa thought it had to be something about the will. Perhaps he was feeling so guilty, he couldn't sleep until he'd made amends.

"Mean to say, I won't share you with Heartless."

"Lord Hartleigh? Of course not. He'll be getting a permanent housekeeper of his own any day now."

"Tol-lol, ma'am, we're alone now. You know I'm not referring to keeping the accounts and counting the sheets. It's sheet-play, though, and I don't mean to share. Uncle mightn't have minded his dolly-mop spending time with the viscount— hell, the old man couldn't have kept a prime article like yourself satisfied." Broderick puffed out his pigeon-breasted chest. "Daresay you won't have anything to complain about on that score, m'dear."

Carissa was dumbfounded. "You dare come here, in Sir Gilliam's own house, and slander him this way? You dare come to my own private rooms, where my daughter lies sleeping, to spew your filth?"

"And that's another thing. The chit's always staring, never says much. Puts me off m'feed, it does. There must be a school for the little nipper, eh? Teach her some manners and conversation. Be better for the chit in the long run, don't you know.

And you'd have more time for your, ah, duties, ha ha." He reached out to pinch her cheek.

At least now Carissa knew what she was going to do. Right after she shoved the dastard's writhing body out of her sitting room and locked the door behind him. 'Twould be a long time before Broderick would be performing any of those particular duties. Ha ha.

Chapter Fourteen

*I*f she was going to work for a rake, Carissa decided, let her master be a master of the art, not a pretentious, pawing puppy.

Pippa would love it, moving into Lord Hartleigh's house.

And oh, how the Applegate sisters would love it, too. Even though Mrs. Kane had no reputation to speak of, there would be tongues wagging aplenty. She was young for a housekeeper, shielded from scandal, if not speculation, only by Sir Gilliam's great age and dignity. To move into Lord Hartleigh's house? She might as well paint her face and dampen her petticoats.

The gossipmongers would all be wrong, of course. Viscount Hartleigh was not interested in getting up a dalliance with Phillip Kane's relict. He wished his household run properly, was all, and his daughter's welfare seen to. Carissa would be his employee, and the viscount was too much the gentleman to importune one of his dependants. She was safer than ever, despite the loss of her good name. Lord Hartleigh had principles. Even if he did make improper advances—which he wouldn't, of course, since she was not one of his high fliers—Carissa was too much of a lady to accept, despite Phillip Kane, the Earl of Macclesfield, and Sir Gilliam's botched bequest.

No matter that the viscount had seen her with her hair down, and spoiled her daughter, and cradled Sue like a butterfly in his hands, Carissa had principles, too. Didn't she?

She was all packed by dawn, staying up the rest of the night to wrestle with her belongings and her emotions. Her trunks could be fetched later; her wits, she needed with her. At quarter past eight, Pippa in hand, the cat in a basket, Carissa knocked on the door of opportunity. No one answered.

The back door was unlocked, so she went in. The stove was unlighted, the sink was full of dishes, the pantry shelves were empty. He needed her. Carissa looked around for the useless dog that hadn't barked, but Gladiator was most likely out marauding in the neighborhood, so she let Cleopatra out of the basket. While Pippa skipped up the back stairs to see if Maisie and the baby were up, Carissa hung up her cloak and took a deep breath. Then she got to work.

When Byrd stumbled into the kitchen an hour later, scratching his armpit, his jaw dropped open. Coffee was on the stove, muffins were in the oven, hot water was raising steam, and a bouquet of flowers sat in the middle of a tray on the scarred kitchen table. The flowers were in a pitcher with a chipped lip and glued-on handle, and the tray was dented and scratched, but Carissa was determined that the viscount would see she could make him comfortable, by George.

Byrd was jolted back to his senses when he saw Carissa adding wood to the stove. "Here now, missus, let me do that. And you hadn't ought to be lifting that heavy kettle, no, nor pumping the water. Why, the Cap'n will be so tickled to see you here, he's like to burst his britches."

Just what she feared. But what she told Byrd was: "Such enthusiasm is unwarranted but appreciated, I am sure. Would you be so kind, when you take his lordship his breakfast tray and hot water, to inform him that I would like a few moments of his time?"

Byrd scratched some more. "I don't know how soon that'll be, Mrs. Kane. He were up late and—"

He wasn't up as late as Carissa was, she'd warrant, and she wanted everything settled before she lost her nerve. Carissa slapped a cup and saucer down on the tray, the only matching pair she'd found. "Now, Mr. Byrd."

"Aye, I mean right away, Mrs. Kane. I'll just be fetching the Cap'n then. He can have his coffee later." For a big man, Byrd flew.

Not too many minutes later, although every agonizing one of them seemed like ten to Carissa, Viscount Hartleigh stumbled into the kitchen. His flowing white shirt was open, with no cravat and no coat, only chest. At least his trousers were buttoned, thank goodness. Carissa hurriedly raised her eyes. He needed a shave, and his blond hair was mussed. He looked like a Greek god waking on Mount Olympus. After an orgy.

Carissa tried to recall her prepared speech. Heavens, she'd be lucky if she recalled her own, *no*, ah, name. "If I come, the dog goes," she finally blurted out.

Lesley combed his fingers through his hair, not affecting his tousled appearance one whit. "I take it you are applying for the post of housekeeper?"

She nodded. "If you still need one."

Lesley waved his hands around the room. "More than ever. The place needs a woman's touch." He bent his head to sniff at the flowers, smiling. "Maisie is too young and inexperienced. Besides, I don't wish her taking time from Sue to look after the linens and things. Do you know, the last housekeeper—"

Carissa did not want to know, else she might turn craven altogether. Rudely interrupting the viscount, she said, "I have three conditions. One, the dog goes."

He looked around. "He's gone. What are the other two?"

Carissa realized he hadn't agreed to anything at all. She also realized that she was staring at his golden-haired chest. She licked her dry lips. "Number two, you help me break into a solicitor's office."

Lesley choked.

"I went with you to Hammond House," she reminded him.

"Of all the featherheaded notions . . ." He crossed his arms over his chest and leaned against the table. "Strolling into my own home cannot be compared to breaking into a man's locked office, Mrs. Kane. That is a criminal offense. You—and I— could go to jail."

"Very well then, I shall have to go myself. I am sorry I took you away from your rest so early, my lord." If he was not going to help her, then she was wasting her time, and her reputation. Her hopes thoroughly dashed, Carissa vowed not to show the viscount her distress. She took her apron off and started to look under the table for Cleo.

"Hold, Mrs. Kane. Don't go yet. I take it this has something to do with Sir Gilliam's will?"

"A missing will, not the one Nigel Gordon read. The one Mr. Gordon had was dated five years ago, and I was not mentioned, naturally, as I was not even in London yet. But I just know there is another, later one. Sir Gilliam practically told me he'd changed it in my favor."

"But you have no proof?"

"Without the will? Of course not. But I have thought about it all night, and I do not believe that Sir Gilliam waited until his deathbed to dictate the new terms. He was so sure he'd done the right thing for me, and so pleased with his actions. Besides, he was too downy a businessman not to know whether he'd signed something or not. No matter what they said, he was not in his dotage; his mind was as clear as when he handled all the details of the bank. The will must be at the new solicitor's. Perhaps it got mislaid when old Mr. Gordon passed on and his son took over. That's why I have to go look."

"Are you certain that Sir Gilliam did not mislead you? I know you thought highly of the gentleman, but is it possible he was telling you what you wished to hear, for his own satisfaction? Such things happen, you know."

"Not Sir Gilliam. The man would have married me anytime these past three years. Why should he lie about his bequests?"

"And you turned him down?" Lesley couldn't help the note of disbelief that entered his voice.

"Of course I did," she bristled. "I would not take advantage of a lonely old man, merely to feather my own nest." Regrettably, she might have reconsidered it, if it were possible.

Lesley didn't know that, of course, and his estimation of her character was rising. Not many other females of his acquaintance would have turned down a respectable offer, especially when it came with a handsome fortune. "Let me think about this," he told her, starting to pace. "You say Mason seems to be involved too?"

"They have all been quite chummy: Mason, Broderick, and

the solicitor. I cannot imagine what else they might have in common, other than Sir Gilliam's will."

"Well, I am not surprised that mawworm Mason is up to no good, but as for the solicitor, I am not sure. Besides, the fellow would have destroyed any evidence. Wouldn't you if you'd cheated your client and broken the law a hundred different ways? He'd be unfrocked or whatever they do to crooked solicitors, if he were caught with the evidence in his possession. And wills do not simply get lost at legal offices, so it's not a matter of searching through old folders and such. If there had been another document, it was removed, I make no doubt."

Carissa was disappointed that he made so much sense. She checked on the muffins so he could not see her distress.

The viscount was still thinking. "On the other hand, no one makes a will without getting a copy to keep. Your man Mason would have known where it was kept."

"Of course. We both had the combination to Sir Gilliam's safe. Oh, how I wish I had thought to look there before I left."

He kept pacing, thinking aloud. "Don't blame yourself. Mason would have removed it long ago. But he, as opposed to the lawyer, has no reason to destroy the new will, and every reason to keep it hidden away somewhere safe."

"He does? I am sure Sir Gilliam provided generously for him in both versions."

"Ah, but what about young Broderick? He was cut out in the second, I'd wager, or the nearest thing to it, and Mason knew it. That's his hold on the heir. And Mason wouldn't destroy the new will, because it's his meal ticket. He'll bleed the cawker dry."

"Cook thought he was acting like the cat in the cream after the reading. It's possible. Then Nigel Gordon is innocent?"

"Not by half. The scoundrel was likely paid to lose his copy."

Carissa had to agree. "Very well, then all I have to do is find the duplicate that Mason kept. I ought to be able to find some excuse to return to Sir Gilliam's when he is out, to search."

"No! That is, it's too dangerous, and besides, he'd be a fool to leave the thing lying around. Broderick is not so stupid that he wouldn't think to look. No, we'll have to consider this further, watch where Mason goes. I could set Byrd to watching his movements."

Carissa listened to the big man hauling more coals from the bin belowstairs. "Mr. Byrd is not exactly unobtrusive, you know."

Lesley stopped pacing and smiled. "You're right. A Bow Street Runner is what we need."

"I cannot afford such an expense." She'd looked into the cost of such an investigation once already.

The viscount was not deterred. "If you are in my employ, your expenses are mine. Agreed?"

She was more relieved than convinced. "Very well, but you will please keep track of such expenditures, for Sir Gilliam was a wealthy man. As soon as the will is found, I shall insist on repaying you."

"Naturally. You'll be tending the household books here anyway, so you can keep the tally. And do not worry, I can stand the cost. Of course, I might tell the Runner not to rush about finding the evidence, though, until you get my house in order and properly staffed."

She ignored his attempt at humor. "There is one other thing."

"Ah yes, the third condition. More pay? You've got it, double, triple what you've been earning. Sole authority over all the servants? I'll pull Byrd's tongue out myself if he interferes with how you run the house."

He was smiling, and Carissa had to smile back, but she also had to make one thing perfectly clear. She swallowed, audibly, she was sure, and said, "I am your housekeeper. Nothing but."

"I know, no cooking."

"Cook might be willing to come, since she hates her brother-in-law, but that is not what I meant." Dash it, she was blushing like a schoolgirl.

Her blushes must have led him to the right conclusion, for

Lord Hartleigh drawled, "I do not recall making you any other offers, Mrs. Kane."

She could breathe again. "Fine."

And "Fine," he said, holding out his hand to seal their agreement. "Now, about the dog . . . ."

Chapter Fifteen

"*Y*ou have a what?" If Viscount Hartleigh had yelled any louder, the Applegate sisters next door wouldn't have had to keep their ears pressed against their windows.

"A cat, my lord, a perfectly behaved, perfectly groomed cat." Carissa kept looking in the corners of the kitchen for her pet. What she found in the corners was better left unmentioned, but she did not spot Cleo.

"Fine, your perfect cat can go live in the stables. I'm certain there are some perfect mice just waiting for it."

Mice? Carissa instantly vowed never to visit the stables. "My cat does not eat vermin, my lord, no more than she eats trash." Hah! Let him say as much for the hound from hell! "She is an indoor cat."

"Glad will never accept a cat in the house."

"Good, then he can go live in the stables. That's where he belongs anyway."

"And your pet doesn't? What did you do, overfeed the pampered puss so it's too fat to hunt? A cat will eat anything it can catch, Mrs. Kane. Of course, your sadistic little tabby will torture its victim first. At least leftovers don't suffer like birds and baby rabbits and squirrels and—"

"Stop it! I know very well that some cats have to hunt for their livelihood. Cleo is not one of them. She has never been out of the house since the day I found her at the doorstep as a tiny kitten, and she isn't going out now."

"What, never? Not even to . . . ?"

"I have a box of soil for her that I clean every day. That way she brings no mud or dirt inside."

"No, only clumps of cat hair."

"Not if I brush her. And dogs shed, too, my lord. Or were those hairs Byrd is always trying to brush off your clothes from an incipient bald spot?"

He immediately raised his hands to the back of his head to make sure the damnable thinning area was still covered. "Deuce take it, I am *not* going bald. And I am not having a sneaky, slinky feline in my house."

"Cleo is neither of those things, and how dare you condemn her without a fair trial? I'll have you know that because she does not go outside, she never gets fleas or worms. Can you say that for the disaster you call a dog? Cleo does not get into fights with other creatures, and she does not bring home unwanted kittens."

Lesley was enjoying himself hugely. He loved when the widow came alive with feeling, how her eyes flashed and her cheeks flushed and her bosom rose and fell with each angry re-tort. Her whole life was in tumult, yet the silly, loyal chit could think only of defending a fur-ball. He decided to enjoy himself a while longer: "Glad's never brought home a kitten in his life, wanted or not. I daresay he most likely swallows them whole before he gets here."

Her foot tapping angrily, Carissa told him, "You know what I mean. You ride a gelding."

This wasn't quite as humorous. The viscount unconsciously crossed his legs. "What, are you suggesting I geld poor old Gladiator?"

"He'd be happier."

"Now who is judging without having all the evidence? Trust me, Mrs. Kane, no male creature will be happier without his, ah, freedom."

This was a highly improper conversation, and to be having it with one's employer, and in the first hours of a new position besides, was unheard-of, outrageous, and foolish beyond per-mission. And Carissa was not backing down. It might cost her this post, but she could not put poor Cleo out with the rats. "Your dirt-ball of a dog is not happy, my lord. He is a hazard.

A hazard and a glutton. And the laziest, meanest, most cantankerous animal I have ever seen."

"But he is my dog, and I own the house, lest you forget."

"And Cleo is my cat, and I will not move in without her."

"Well, I won't have any witch's familiar near my daughter. They steal babies' breaths, in case you didn't know."

"Fie, my lord. That is an old wives' tale."

"And how do you think they got to be old wives? They listened to such lore because it is founded in truth. The ones who didn't listen likely died young, suffocated by some feline felon."

"Fustian. That bit of nonsense came because cats like to sniff at new scents, is all. Cleo knows to stay away from grasping little fingers, and she never bothered Pippa in all the days of her infancy. They grew up together, for heaven's sake. If it makes you feel better, the nursery door can be kept closed when Maisie is not there watching Sue. Cleo comes, my lord. Glad goes. That is final."

Now, Lesley was prepared to let Mrs. Kane move a menagerie into his home, but he was not going to let her think he'd live under the cat's paw. Literally or figuratively. He did have some backbone, although it seemed to turn to bread dough in this female's presence. "Glad gets to come into my bedroom, my study, and the front parlor," he insisted. "That's only fair."

It was more than fair, and Carissa knew it. She nodded, but had the last word: "Only if he has a bath first."

Just then Byrd called from the cellar steps, where he'd gone to fetch the coal. "Cap'n, you better come see this. You know that old French cognac you was keeping for special occasions? The bottles what were put down before the embargo?"

"Not the cognac, Byrd. Please tell me nothing has happened to the cognac." He was on his way to the stairs.

"Something happened. I reckon the mutt chased a cat up on the wine rack. I guess I didn't hear the bottles fall 'cause of moving the coal around."

"A cat?" Carissa screamed, dashing past the viscount and tearing down the stairs. "Cleo!"

With sinking heart, for both the cat and the cognac, Lesley

followed. Three bottles remained in their niches. Four bottles were down. Two were broken. A black cat with white socks was lapping daintily at one, Glad was like a pig at a trough at the other. The cat sneezed. Glad burped. Then they changed places.

"I don't believe it," Carissa murmured. "And what do you think will happen when the wine is gone?"

"I'd wager they'll both have god-awful headaches," Byrd offered.

"No, for I believe I'll kill each of them," Lesley announced, retrieving the unbroken bottles. "But our problem seems to have resolved itself. For now, at any rate. I make you no guarantees that Glad won't change his mind."

If he did, he was liable to have a pawful of claw marks on his nose. Carissa didn't think even Gladiator was that stupid. "If that dog chews my cat, his head will be on your breakfast platter, my lord. And make sure he has a bath or he is not coming near my child, my kitchen, or my clean house."

Her clean house, eh? Lesley thought he liked the sound of that. Byrd didn't. After his coffee and muffins, he asked the viscount just who was working for whom. "For it's hard to figure anymore, what with the gentry mort giving all the orders. Now she's sending for that cook from the sir's house," he complained. "And that's another blasted female here, besides them two and the nipper and the nursemaid. I ain't never served on a ship what had a single one of them, and now the place is crawling with women. It's enough to make a grown man cry, Cap'n. And a cat, b'God. A black cat besides, even if Mrs. Kane pointed out its white mustache and feet. So it ain't a hundred percent bad luck. It's the closest thing to it. And we didn't need no more bad luck, Cap'n, not with babies landing on the doorstep and all. Maybe if I stop down by the docks tonight, I'll meet up with the press gangs. Now, that'd be lucky, by comparison."

"Stubble it, Byrdie," his lordship ordered. "And pass the soap."

* * *

Cook was delighted to be fetched back from her sister's house. The brother-in-law, it seemed, had discovered religion. Now he was a Reformer, with no cursing, and no tippling either, allowed in his home. Not even a sip here and there, Cook complained. Instead of being a mean fool, now he was a mean, preachy fool, who meant to see that everyone was as miserable as he was.

Besides, Cook told Carissa as she unpacked her aprons, it would be a treat to cook for gentlemen who appreciated fine foods. Sir Gilliam had barely picked at his dinners, after Cook worked all day at them, and the harebrained heir was usually too deep in his cups to notice what was in front of him. Cook could feed him the cat's dinner and he'd be none the wiser.

Warned about the dog, Cook did not turn a hair. She was bigger and smarter and tougher than any mismatched mongrel. "He couldn't be worse than that Mason, always snooping around, filching a jar of jam or a tablespoon of tea, for his private stock. 'Sides, once the mutt gets the idea of who feeds him, he'll be trying to turn me up sweet, just you watch, dearie. Like every other male what knows which side his bread is buttered on."

Cook also reasoned that if he was fed well enough, the dog wouldn't go scavenging, bothering the neighbors. His thieving wouldn't bother her, for she wasn't one for leaving foodstuffs out where creatures and casual visitors to her kitchen could just help themselves. She'd put locks on the pantry, if that's what was needed. No, the dog was no problem.

That heathen Byrd, however, was another kettle of fish.

"You show me any more of your tattoos and I'll show you my fry pan, alongside that ugly head of yours."

"Ugly? Why, you wouldn't know ugly lessen you looked in the mirror." Byrd raised huge, beefy fists. "And I ain't one of your sissified swells, you old bat. You hit me with the frying pan and I hit back."

"You raise one hand to me, birdbrain, and I'll get me the meat-ax."

It was love at first fight.

As Carissa knew it would, Cook's expertise in the kitchen

soon won Byrd over, especially when they discovered they each liked a wee bit of spirits now and again. And a good game of backgammon. Besides, Byrd was under orders to make sure this set of servants stayed on. All of them. In a few days two footmen from Sir Gilliam's house arrived, seeking positions, so Byrd didn't feel as outnumbered. The men related how Mason was even more tyrannical than ever, while doing less of the work.

"You'd think he was the master, the way the old sod gives orders and throws tantrums," the younger servant said, sporting a bruised jaw.

Arranging quarters for all the newcomers was a challenge. The menservants were bedded in the room above the stable, in the mews. Byrd refused to give up his room off the kitchen, which should have been Cook's or the housekeeper's. He needed to keep an eye on the comings and goings, the old sailor declared. And he needed to be able to blow a cloud without bringing the house—and Cook's wrath—down around his ears. So Cook had the attic room, sharing with Bonnie, who refused to stay with Broderick and Mason without Cook or Carissa to protect her. Mrs. Kane was to have the other guest bedroom, next to what was now the nursery suite. Unfortunately, it was also across the hall from his lordship's apartment.

"Very well," she agreed, tight-lipped, "and we can bring in a pallet for Pippa."

"I thought she'd be happier in the nursery." Lord Hartleigh was leaning against the door of the pink chamber. The room was most likely intended for the mistress of the house, he supposed, and that suited him just fine. Now that it had been cleaned and aired, the soft tones suited Mrs. Kane's coloring, too. Cats, yes, but he would not back down on this.

"But she has never been apart from me," Carissa insisted.

"And it's more than time. The child is not a baby anymore, Mrs. Kane. You have to let her grow up a bit. Besides, we can do over the dressing room next to the nursery so Pippa will have a room of her own. She'll have lots of area for play, and Maisie can watch her more easily."

Carissa had unhappily followed him down the hall to the adjoining suite. Pippa was already riding Blackie in the center of the large, airy sitting room, which was filled with books and toys and games, even a dollhouse his lordship had unearthed somewhere. In the next room, the bedchamber, Sue's crib was to one side, so filled with more dolls and toys that the child had to sleep in the cradle next to Maisie's bed. Sue's basket had been claimed by Cleo.

"This room is large enough for me to have a cot also." It really wasn't, not with the rocking chair, the dressers filled with baby clothes, and the little desk brought in for Maisie's schoolwork.

"Yes, but that is unnecessary. Besides, your later hours might disturb the children or Maisie."

"Later hours?" Scorpions and spiders?

Lesley smiled. "Why, yes. I understand that you used to take dinner with Sir Gilliam on occasion. Surely you cannot deny me that same courtesy? We will need to speak about the children, the household, that type of thing."

"Of course." Dinner with him? Was she to be the dessert? She might as well give up now, Carissa thought. She was doomed. Lord Hartleigh was impossibly handsome, incredibly charming, and inflammatory to her senses. "I would be honored, my lord."

"That's another thing. I am deuced tired of all this my-lording. I would much prefer you call me Lesley, or if that is too familiar, Hartleigh. Hart will do. And I shall call you— What the deuce is your name, anyway?"

"No."

"No? I knew your family was a slew of shabsters, leaving you to fend for yourself, but to give their daughter such a name . . . ?"

"Do not be foolish, my lord. I mean no, such familiarity is not pleasing."

"Well, all the bowing and scraping isn't pleasing to me, madam." He stood up to his commanding height and glared down at her, a stance calculated to intimidate. "Recall, if you will, who pays the piper here."

Carissa put her hands on her hips. "Recall, if you will, *my*

lord, who decides how much starch goes in your unmention-
ables and how often asparagus appears on your table."

He hated asparagus.

"You do not play fair, Mrs. Kane," he conceded. "At least
tell me what the blasted name is."

"It is Carissa," she told him, hurriedly adding, "it's Greek
for 'loving.' "

"It sounds like a caress. No wonder you aren't free with it to
strangers." It suited her, though, he thought.

"Yes, well, my family called me Carrie." And so did Phillip.
She hated it.

"No, no, Carissa is perfect—when we are better acquainted,
of course."

"When hell freezes over, my lord."

Chapter Sixteen

Carissa was upstairs, checking the bedrooms with Bonnie to see what in the viscount's house should be replaced, what should be repaired. Lord Hartleigh had given her a generous budget, a free rein, and a commission to fulfill. He wanted the house appearing presentable enough, he said, to hold interviews there for prospective foster families. He'd go visit their homes, of course, to make sure the premises were suitable for Sue, but he also wanted to see the strangers with his daughter, in her own surroundings. His solicitor had declared him dicked in the nob, making such a to-do over a simple adoption procedure, but the viscount was adamant. He was also immovable about providing for Pippa's needs as well as Sue's. Carissa was to purchase a child-size desk, a globe, and a chalkboard. The viscount had already purchased a pony.

The pony, a shaggy cream and white Shetland mare, was just the perfect size for a little girl, and of such pleasant temperament that Carissa had no qualms about letting Pippa near it, so long as she herself did not have to visit it in the stables. She had a great many qualms, however, about accepting more of the viscount's generosity.

"She's not for Pippa, Mrs. Kane, so you needn't get on your high horse. The mare I brought over from Hammond House for you to ride is quite the right height."

"If it is not for Pippa and not for me, my lord, who is to ride the pony? Byrd?"

"Oh, Pippa shall have the riding of the pony, and the naming of her, too, I suppose. But you see, I purchased her for Sue. Now, I know you are going to tell me Sue has no use for a pony, but she will in a few years, and Pippa will have the little mare perfectly trained by then, won't you, poppet?"

Pippa had nodded. She would have agreed to anything Lord Hartleigh said. If he wanted her to teach the pony to count, well, she knew up to ten.

"And when Sue is ready for her pony, Pippa should be ready for a real horse, which she will deserve, having done me the favor of exercising the pony while we wait for Sue to grow. There is only one problem, poppet."

A tear had already been forming in Pippa's big brown eyes. Problems usually meant no.

"Yes, a pony needs two hands on the reins to guide it."

The thumb had come out of the little girl's mouth like an arrow shot from a bow. And hadn't gone back in yet, except at night. Carissa was more grateful to the viscount for that than she was for the pony.

He'd insisted on buying Carissa a riding habit, also, so she could accompany them for Pippa's riding lessons. Gentle pony or not, Carissa was not about to let her baby on any horse but Blackie unless she herself rode at Pippa's side. But her old habit, old before Pippa was born, had been hopelessly out-moded, worn at the seat and cuffs, and too tight. She'd cut it up to make Pippa a riding outfit, complete with feathered hat. For herself, Carissa had carefully tallied the cost of her new habit in the accounts ledger, for when she could afford to repay his lordship. Even if she sewed the brown velvet herself, her debt was mounting.

The least she could do for now, Carissa had decided, was make his home fit for a king. Or a viscount, at any rate. The narrow stone building could never compete with the grandeur of what he was used to at Hammond House, of course, but the Kensington place could be a gem. It would be, if she had to drag Byrd and the footmen to every furniture showroom and upholstery warehouse in London.

So far, the list of furnishings and such that needed replacing far outnumbered the repairs. As for the list of those items that were good enough for now, it consisted of Blackie—except where Cleo had been using the rocking horse as a scratching post. Carissa made a note to place some fabric around the pony's legs, quickly, before his lordship noticed. She also made a note to ask Lord Hartleigh what colors he preferred for his chamber's new drapes. She would *not* select his bedhangings.

The only reason she'd proceeded with her inspection in the first place was that she knew the set of rooms was empty. Lord Hartleigh had gone to his club, and Byrd had taken the gelding round to the farrier. The sitting room was tidier than she'd expected, since Byrd was haphazard about anything except the horses and his food, but the footmen were conscientious, and so was Bonnie. Carissa did not see much that was personal, no portraits, no miniatures, no trinkets or knickknacks from his travels. Of course, he had Sue as a memento. . . .

She was not comfortable in Lord Hartleigh's bedroom. His lemony cologne lingered, even amid the musty furnishings. But she was too conscious of all the other women who must have come here to share that enormous bed with him, mingling their scents with his. Joining their bodies. She hoped they'd all gotten stuffed noses and watery eyes from the mildew.

Carissa crossed to the window to inspect the curtains, and to avoid the bed. From the viscount's chamber she could look out at Gibsonia Street, and across to Sir Gilliam's house. Mason was just leaving, headed east up the street. He did not look back—why should he?—and so missed seeing a nondescript sort of fellow leave the alley between two houses and follow him. So far he'd gone to the local pub, but the Runner thought he acted furtive, exactly like a ferret-faced malefactor. The pub was west, down the street.

Why not? Why shouldn't she go look for the will? Most likely Lord Hartleigh was right and Mason had stashed it elsewhere, but what if he wasn't that clever, only cruel? What if the rodent was so confident that he'd tucked it under his mattress, or in a book? No one would dare enter Mason's room without permission, to find it by accident. No one but Carissa.

She wouldn't ask either of the footmen to go with her . . . or Bonnie. There was no way to explain their presence at Sir Gilliam's, and she would only be exposing them to danger for nothing. Carissa could say she was looking for something of hers that she'd forgotten in the attics, a sewing basket or some outgrown clothes of Pippa's. Mason's room was just down the hall. If he came home, however, and found her there, not in the attics—she wouldn't think about that.

She was not going to worry about Broderick Parkhurst either. The popinjay was undoubtedly on the strut in Hyde Park at this hour. What he had to peacock about was beyond her comprehension, since by all accounts his last showy hack had shown him the Serpentine. Young Broderick was making a splash in Society, all right.

She did not think he'd dare approach her anyway, not after the last contretemps. Just in case, though, Carissa threaded another long, sharp hatpin through her mobcap.

The decision was obviously made; the rationalizations had come after. Carissa was going after what was promised her, what Sir Gilliam had wanted her to have: a place of her own, an end to uncertainty, not having to be beholden to any man for any thing.

More than the rest, Carissa wanted a home for her daughter, where she could laugh and play and slide down the banisters. One that wouldn't be taken away when their current employer died or married, as Lord Hartleigh was bound to do sooner or later. He adored children, and the novelty of having them around did not seem to be wearing off on him. He'd discover, shortly, Carissa thought, that having a wife would make the begetting of them—and the keeping of them—much simpler. Carissa well knew that no wife of Viscount Hartleigh's was going to live in a paltry pied-à-terre outside of Mayfair. That wife wouldn't want Sue around either, nor a young housekeeper with a child of her own. This was a temporary haven only, then Pippa would be uprooted again. Unless Carissa could find that will.

She left the house before she had time to lose her nerve. And she went out the front door so she did not have to explain her mission to Cook or the others. Head down against the chill wind, she did not see the second shadow that had been hiding in the alley between houses.

The footman at the door of the Parkhurst place was known to her, although not well. He grunted at her story of a missing sewing basket and went back to his solo dice game. He did not offer to assist, but he did not demand she wait for Mason to come home, either, thank goodness.

Mason's room looked as if he'd moved in yesterday, but Carissa knew he'd been there for decades. In contrast to Lord Hartleigh's, which had nothing terribly personal, this stark chamber had nothing. It might have been a room in a hotel, waiting for the next paying customer. Not even a comb rested on the dresser.

In the first drawer she opened, shaving items were laid out as if on display. Everything faced in the same direction, and nothing touched. In the second drawer, every stack was aligned precisely: hose, handkerchiefs, neckcloths. The third contained a white nightshirt and black fabric slippers, nothing else.

Carissa was afraid to disturb the narrow bed, for she'd never get the coverings so tightly tucked. Instead, she opened the clothespress. Two coats, two pairs of trousers and two waist-coats, all black, hung in regimental order. One pair of shoes was on the bottom. One formal wig on a stand stood on the top. She felt the clothes for hidden pockets, and beneath the wig. She checked the drawers for false bottoms, and lifted the braided rug in case a floorboard was loose. Nothing seemed wedged between the clothespress and the wall, not so much as a hair. The single chair had one cushion, which did not crinkle when she shook it. The Bible on the table next to it had no loose papers, no writing on the flyleaf. And that was it. There was no place else to look. The man lived like a monk.

But Carissa knew Mason was no ascetic, no pious church-goer. He drank, he swore, he did not attend church with the other servants on Sundays. And nowhere in that nearly new Bible did it say *Do unto others as much as you can get away with*. Lord Hartleigh was right: Mason had another life some-where else. No one could live so long in one place without ac-cumulating something, even a letter. Although Mason never seemed to have mail, Carissa had always assumed he'd re-moved his personal correspondence before she saw the day's delivery. He never took a vacation, either, now that she thought of it, only his days and half days off.

Where was he going then, on his frequent trips away from the house, and what was he doing with his money? Most of all, Carissa wished she knew why he needed so much more—hers.

The footman didn't look up when Carissa walked past him, her hands empty. She told him she couldn't find the sewing box. Perhaps one of the maids had borrowed it and forgotten to restore it to the attics. The footman cared more that his right hand owed his left hand a month's wages.

Broderick was limping up the walkway when she was leaving. His face brightened considerably. "What, did you reconsider m'offer, then, m'dear?"

"If I had reconsidered your offer, you clunch, I'd have had Lord Hartleigh run you through."

Broderick lost what color he had in his sallow complexion, and almost lost his lunch. A duel with the paragon? He'd heard what Lord Heartless had done to rearrange Lord Cosgrove's features. He liked his nose right where it was. He hurried to tell her: "Meant no offense, don't you know. Not hunting on the gentleman's preserves. Isn't done, of course, by Jove. You were visiting with the servants, of course. Foolish me, ha ha."

He was a fool, but that story would not fadge. "I was looking for something I left behind. My mother's sewing box. I thought it was in the attic, but could not find it. If it ever turns up, you might send it over."

"Of course, of course." Broderick bowed and dashed into the house, lest the jade's new protector take umbrage at the conversation. He had enough trouble without annoying a nonesuch like Hartleigh.

Carissa's plate was full, too. Now she had no hopes of finding the will, no hopes of repaying his lordship, no hopes of avoiding his wicked, winsome ways. Staring at the ground in front of her, Carissa slowly trudged the short distance back to her new place of employment, where her respectability was receding as fast as her dreams. So lost was she in dismal thoughts that matched the dismal day, she again never noticed the figure that observed her from between houses.

The shadow detached itself from the gloom the better to watch her cross the street. When Carissa was one door away from her own, a hand reached out and grabbed her, dragging her into the alley. Positive it was Broderick, letting his wants override his wisdom after all, Carissa pulled the hatpin from her cap and stabbed it through her attacker's hand.

"Bloody hell, darling, is that any way to welcome your long-lost husband?"

Chapter Seventeen

She wasn't surprised, not really. Oh, Carissa was startled by the assault, but she was not shocked to see her long-lost, unlamented husband again after four and a half years. She'd had that feeling, that uncomfortable sensation of being watched. And she'd always feared he'd show up again to plague her, because that's what the man did best. He was still sucking on his thumb, where she'd stabbed him. Tarnation, Pippa *had* inherited something from the toad.

"You ain't going to swoon, are you, *cara mia*?"

She might have hoped he was, indeed, dead, but no, she was not astonished to see him alive. She was a bit confounded that Phillip Kane wasn't nearly so handsome as she remembered. Why couldn't she have seen beyond the uniform—most likely stolen—and the sweet talk, to see how coarse his features were? How his thin hair was mousy brown and greasy, how he had black spots in the pores near his nose? Why, he had hair growing out of his ears and was barely two inches taller than she was. How could she have thought him so attractive?

"No, Phillip. I am not going to get missish. What are you doing here and what do you want?"

"Sharp-tongued as ever, I see." He sneered at her mobcap, the shapeless black dress she was wearing. "And you still don't know much about pleasing a man."

"I know that my father's blunt was all that you found pleasing. I was everything admirable, until you realized the money was not forthcoming. You abandoned me, you dastard, while I was about to have your baby. Not once since then have you provided for us, so why have you come now?"

"Now, Carrie, don't be so harsh. I've been out of the country, don't you know. And with the war on, correspondence was difficult. I meant to get in touch with you—"

"You were never with the army, Phillip. I had them search and search their records. I don't know where you got the uniform, and neither did the War Office, so cut line and tell me what you want."

Kane must have realized that his adoring little wife had grown into a woman of backbone, for he traded his Spanish coin for bluntness that matched her own. "I had a spot of trouble with the military, so I left. Then I saw no reason to meddle when you were snug as a bug in the banker's bed. I've been hanging around, waiting for the old man to stick his spoon in the wall. Been an expensive wait, I'll have you know. And now it turns out he never left you a groat. What did you do to queer that deal, show him your hatpin?"

"That deal, as you call it, was never legalized. Sir Gilliam did mean to mention me in his will, but it seems I have been swindled by yet another scoundrel."

"Damn, I had plans for that house." Kane stared across the street at the tidy brownstone. "An exclusive club, gentlemen only, don't you know. High stakes, high fliers, all the best."

"You were going to turn my house, Sir Gilliam's house, into a gaming hell? I suppose I should be thankful you weren't thinking of a bordello instead. There is no way on earth or in heaven that I would permit you to do such a thing, if I had, in fact, inherited the property."

"Now, Carrie, my love, you just ain't behaving like a proper wife. A wife whose property belongs to her lawful husband."

He could do it, she thought. Phillip Kane could claim everything she owned, trifling as it was. He could claim his marital rights. He could claim Pippa. An icy chill clutched at her insides. Carissa feared she might swoon, after all. "Oh, why couldn't you have stayed gone?" she cried. "I could have had you declared legally dead in a few years, and been rid of you once and for all."

Phillip examined his frayed cuffs. "Because I didn't have the brass to stay gone, that's why. I tried to get the rhino from your father, you know."

"My father?" Now she was surprised. "Why did you think he'd give you my dowry now, when he wouldn't while we were living together?"

"I told him you were in Hartleigh's keeping. I thought he might care to finance your trip abroad, with your loving husband, of course, to avoid the scandal of anyone knowing Macclesfield's daughter was a demimondaine."

"I'm not in—"

"Trying to get soup out of a stone, it was. The earl said he didn't care if you were living with Old Harry, you were no kin to him. I'll admit I miscalculated there, darling. Never thought the old stick would cut you off without a shilling, and me with you. Then I figured he'd take you back in, and the babe."

"Oh, so you weren't altogether coldhearted when you deserted me?"

"Never had anything against you, Carrie, until you started getting all touchy about the money."

"It was my mother's money, which she'd left to me! You went through it in a month. Then you left!"

He sighed. "Water under the bridge, *cara mia,* water under the bridge. You must have put some money away since then. For sure you ain't spent it on your wardrobe. You won't need the blunt now that you've landed in clover. Hartleigh's said to be rich as Golden Ball, though you'd never know it, looking at you."

"I am his housekeeper, Phillip, his employee, that's all."

"And that's why the shabby clothes? Well, let me tell you, darling, the masquerade hasn't fooled anyone yet, according to the chitchat in the local pubs. You might as well give it up and start asking for silk and fur."

"The only thing I would ask his lordship for is better locks on his door, to keep out riffraff like you, Phillip Kane."

"Hoity-toity, my lady. And how long do you think he'll keep you if I charge him in a criminal conversation case?"

"You wouldn't! He hasn't shown me anything but kindness! How could you think of doing such a thing?"

Phillip shrugged. "How can I live, else?"

Carissa untied the strings of her reticule and pulled out what money she had there. Some of it was from the household account. She'd have to make a new entry in the ledger, she thought, her mind in a muddle.

Phillip pocketed the coins and bills, but it wasn't enough. "I know you've got more squirreled away, Carrie. Frugal little thing like you most likely has a fortune tucked under her mattress."

"My savings are for Pippa, so she'll have some kind of future."

"Ah yes, the child. I have to say I was touched when I heard you'd named her for me. Very affecting, my dear."

"I wanted her to have *something* from her father. A name and a miniature painting are little enough for a child."

Kane reached for her arm. "You know, perhaps you're right and I should go make her acquaintance right now."

"No! You stay away from her. I'll . . . I'll get you some more money, by tomorrow. But don't think to bleed me, Phillip, for the well will run dry very quickly. I was hoping as much as you were that Sir Gilliam would leave me a bequest." Then she had a brilliant idea. "In fact, he might have. . . . "

Carissa managed to convince her dead husband that it was very much in his interest to break into Mr. Nigel Gordon's law office to look for an updated will. They could split the inheritance, whatever it was, and he could go off again, hopefully forever this time. She knew there was small chance of the will being at the solicitor's, about as small a chance as Phillip Kane giving her a fair share. Still, he couldn't collect anything without her, so Carissa stood to gain something, even if it was seeing the last of the muckworm. With any luck, he'd get arrested.

No, with her luck he'd name Carissa as an accessory to the crime and she'd be transported with him. It made no difference, for she would never be free of the villain she'd married. She'd never feel safe again, even if he went away, not knowing when he'd run out of money and return to plague her, like a seven-year locust.

He'd declared his intention of coming back at the end of the week for her savings. Carissa decided she simply would not leave the house. Cook could do the marketing, the footmen could do the errands. She was much too busy anyway, what with the renovations, the lessons for Pippa and whatever servants were interested, the menus, and sewing her new habit. No, she wouldn't step outside the house. Or else, if she needed to match her thread, she'd take Byrd with her to carry the bobbin.

She'd be safe in Lord Hartleigh's house. Pippa would be safe there too. The viscount wouldn't let anything happen to her, to them. Carissa knew it, as well as she knew Phillip Kane would seek her out again and again. She couldn't help thinking the only truly safe place for her was in Lord Hartleigh's arms. He'd know what to do, how to protect her and Pippa. But she was just an employee, as she'd told Phillip, with no claims to his protection. She was just the housekeeper.

Damn if faro's daughters weren't half as entertaining as Mrs. Kane's daughter. Lesley was having a grand time, sitting on the floor of the nursery, playing at jackstraws. If his friends at White's knew he'd come hurrying home to play with the poppets before their bedtime, he'd be the laughingstock of London. They all thought he was rushing away to embrace his new inamorata. The rumor mill was working quite up to his expectations. Already he was receiving fewer invitations to debutante balls and various hopeful mamas were looking at him askance. Askance was better than as a catch.

His new ladybird was a soldier's widow, the gossip went. An upper servant. A rich man's mistress. She was the mother of his child. She was the mother of his children. If Prinny could have a common-law wife, the *on dits* went, so could Lord Heartless. He wasn't growing tamely domestic, just tripping down the primrose path with a new demirep, who happened to have a child or two.

Lesley couldn't wait until he took Mrs. Kane to the park in her new habit, with the fashionable bonnet he'd purchased this morning. She would be a stunning woman, he thought, and so no one would doubt the dalliance. Pippa on her pony between them should put paid to his stepmother's scheming, even if Maisie and Sue stayed home. A few days more and then he really had to do something about finding Sue a good home. Lesley couldn't imagine a better one than this, however, where the infant was the center of attention, both servants' and master's.

Another reason the viscount left White's earlier than usual was that he really did wish to take dinner at his own table. His new cook could outdo the finest French chef, and the menus were designed around his own preferences for once.

Who was he fooling? Not himself, obviously, judging from the time he was spending at his bath and toilette. He'd come home with hopes of convincing Mrs. Kane to have dinner with him. There, Lesley could admit it to himself, as peculiar as the notion was. She wasn't a comet; she wasn't even accommodating. She was softhearted and sincere, though, and could show real affection, unlike the brittle beauties of the ton. He would rather watch ideas and emotions flicker across her face than watch the half-dressed dancers scamper across the stage at Drury Lane.

She'd wear the gold gown to dinner, he envisioned, with her gleaming hair up and the neckline down. By George, he should forbid her usual attire in his house, say that wretched mobcap and those dreary black gowns made him bilious or some such. Of course, his efficient Mrs. Kane would likely fix him a posset, because that was her job.

Because she was the housekeeper.

The housekeeper, by Jupiter! What the deuce was he doing, lusting after his prim and proper housekeeper, destroying her reputation, using her for his own purposes? Blast, he was no better than that churl Cosgrove.

And what the deuce was Carissa doing coming from Sir Gilliam's? Looking out the same window that Carissa had earlier, Lesley could clearly see Parkhurst's house, even in the dusk. He saw Mrs. Kane crossing the street, then saw a man step out of the shadows and accost her. Lesley reached for the pistol he kept in his nightstand, but the dirty dish had already released her and was stepping back, bowing. She inclined her head only slightly and held herself rigid, he could see, yet she made no effort to leave the alley.

He was waiting when she came through the rear door.

Chapter Eighteen

*L*ord Hartleigh was furious. If Carissa had noticed, she would have been afraid. Right now all she knew was that he was detaining her from rushing up the stairs to make sure her daughter was safe and sound, asleep under the watchful eyes of Maisie and the despicable dog who wouldn't bark. So she brushed past him. "Excuse me, my lord."

"Like hell I will," Lesley said, reaching for her arm.

So she stabbed him with her hatpin, too.

"Blast!" He grabbed the weapon from her and tossed it to the ground while Cook and her helpers watched, amazed. Lesley was not about to put on a raree show for their edification, so he spoke softly, for Mrs. Kane's ears only: "If you do not accompany me to the study, I shall throw your mobcap into the oven, then I shall go looking for the blasted cat."

"Fustian." But she followed him to his private room, where he shut the door, then dabbed at the drop of blood on his finger.

"I thought better of you," he said when she sank onto a chair. In truth, her legs could not have held her up much longer.

She barely had the stamina to raise her head. "What, for sitting in your presence, or for striking you with the pin? I apologize, but I thought you another— That is, I was not thinking, my lord. I beg your pardon. Now may I be excused? Pippa will be waiting for me to hear her prayers." Carissa really had no time or energy to waste on his lordship's megrims. What, had Cook served him asparagus again? Or had Cleo used his Hessians for a scratching post?

"No, Mrs. Kane, you may not leave, and you know deuced

well that I am referring to the man you met in the alley not five minutes past."

Obviously there was no use denying it. "What about him?"

"What about a man who does not call for you at your door but lurks down alleys? I actually thought you were a virtuous woman."

Carissa sat up straighter. "He was a stranger, asking directions."

"To where, the Canadian provinces? Those were complicated instructions you gave, fifteen minutes' worth, by my watch." So what if he revealed that he'd been keeping time, ready to fly down the stairs and skin the man alive?

Carissa didn't notice. "I did not think I had to account for every minute of my day, my lord. If my work does not meet your expectations . . . " She started to get up.

"And do you pay strangers' fares, too?" he demanded. "I saw you hand him your purse."

"Where I spend my salary is even less your concern than to whom I speak on my own time." Then his words sank in, and her anger almost matched his own. "But you were spying on me, keeping track of my comings and goings, how many seconds I was away from the job? That is despicable."

"I was not spying. I happened to be looking out of my own window, checking the weather, when I noticed a man come out of the alley. How was I supposed to know he was a friend of yours? I thought you might be in trouble, so I continued to keep an eye on him." And her.

"Trouble, my lord? I have been in trouble since I was born a female and not the son my father wanted. He could not have disowned a male, for the boy would have been his legal heir. My feckless husband could not have stolen my meager inheritance, for a man does not lose all rights to his own property as soon as the marriage vows are spoken. And I might, I just might, had I been a man, have been taught to use a sword instead of a sewing needle. *Then* I might not be in trouble."

"Then I would be bleeding all over the kitchen floor, I suppose." Relieved by her diatribe, for she wasn't defending the man in the alley, only bemoaning her sex, Lesley poured her a glass of wine from the decanter on his desk. "Here, drink this and tell me what is wrong. What did the fellow say to upset you so?"

Carissa wanted to tell him. More than anything, she wanted to lay her burden at his feet and beg him to help. But. But he might be so disgusted at her lies that he'd throw her out. Or he might insist she return to her legal husband. Or he might treat her as a wayward wife, ready for an affair. Most of all, if one more person knew that Phillip Kane was alive, she would never be able to have him declared dead in a few years. She would have a hard enough time as it was, swearing under oath that she'd seen neither hide nor hair of her husband since his disappearance. Wishing would not make it so.

"I cannot tell you," she said in a whisper, not denying that the man in the street was known to her after all. "It is a personal, private matter."

"You mean you will not." He nodded curtly, hurt that she did not trust him, but knowing he did not have the right to demand more from her. "Very well. If you wish to unburden yourself in the future, feel free to do so."

Carissa was starting to her feet again when he added, "Oh, by the way, if you do not feel I am overstepping the bounds of an employer's authority, what the deuce were you doing at Parkhurst's place?"

Recognizing his barely controlled fury despite his milder tone, Carissa took a step backward. "I believe that the missing will exists. I went across the street to search Mason's room for it."

Lesley took the glass from her hand and drained down its contents. "Excuse me, I thought you said you'd gone to Mason's room."

"I did. I'd seen him leave the house, so took the opportunity. The will wasn't there as far as I could tell. Nothing was. You were right that he must have another room somewhere."

"And you could not wait for the Bow Street Runner to find it? You could not trust me to do what I said I would? Are you that desperate to leave my employ? Dash it, I've done everything I could think of to make you happy here. I've even got blasted cat hairs on my pillow."

Now was not the time to tell him those were his own blond hairs on his pillow, not Cleo's black ones. "You have been more than kind, my lord."

"And you have been a peagoose, Mrs. Kane. Good grief, that Mason character is a bully at best, a thief, a blackmailer, and who knows what else besides. And you decide to search his bedchamber, as if he were a parlor maid accused of filching milord's snuffbox. By all that's holy, madam, do you know what Mason would have done if he'd found you there?"

Carissa could well imagine. She could also imagine that Lord Hartleigh was wishing Mason had strangled her, or whatever, to save himself the effort. She took another step closer to the door.

Lesley was in a rage. She hadn't trusted him, yet she'd confided in that slyboots who met her in alleys. Now he had a focus for his anger. "You dared to lecture me about fighting duels, Mrs. Kane, if you'll recall. My responsibility toward Sue dictated I keep myself whole and hearty, you said. Is your daughter less vulnerable than mine? Less worthy of her only parent's regard?"

"Of . . . of course not."

"Dash it, you could have been murdered! Or arrested for attempted burglary. What would have happened to Pippa in that case, other than the agony she would suffer? You've seen the blasted foundling hospital! Would she have ended there or would your father have taken her in?"

In a small voice, she answered, "No. He'd see her in the poorhouse first."

"Some other relative, then?"

"There is no one but my mother's aunt Mattie. She lives in straitened circumstances herself, barely sustaining a livelihood on the tiny annuity she receives. And her landlord does not permit children. We tried when I first came to Town, before I started working for Sir Gilliam."

"And yet you dared to endanger your life. That was foolish beyond permission, Carissa."

Carissa did not have the energy to condemn his familiarity. What was one more insult on this day, after all? Besides, he was correct. Being found by Mason was nothing compared to being found by Phillip Kane, of course, but she should not have gone. She bowed her head in acknowledgment.

Lesley wasn't finished. "And what if Parkhurst had discovered you in his house? He'd probably be in his cups at this time of day and—"

"He was."

"He was, by Zeus? You met up with the whopstraw? What did you do, fend him off with your hatpin?"

"No, I invoked your name. It might have been Beelzebub's, he was that loath to call down your wrath."

"So the clunch has a dram of intelligence after all. Unlike others I could name." His hands were still shaking with the urge to wrap themselves around someone's throat, anyone who dared to threaten his . . . his friend. So he placed them on her shoulders and shook her, not hard enough to rattle her brains, only enough to knock some sense into her. And that monstrous mobcap off her head.

Seeing Lord Hartleigh's lowered brow and narrowed lips, Carissa had meant to apologize for upsetting him. When he touched her, she meant to shout back at him that none of this was any of his affair, and he had no right to mock or manhandle her for things he did not understand. What she did, however, was cry. She simply could not be strong any longer. Carissa put her hands to her face and cried.

Then his arms were around her and she was crying into his neckcloth, the one Lesley had taken an age to tie. "Good gods, ma'am, don't cry. Whatever the problem is, we'll fix it, I swear!"

"There's no way to fix it," she sobbed onto his shirtfront.

He stroked her hair, then her back, feeling the dampness soak through to his skin. "Of course there is. Enough money and influence can fix almost anything, my dear. You ought to know that by now."

"I"—sniff—"have neither."

He handed over his handkerchief so she could blow her

nose. "But I have both. They are at your disposal, whether you wish it or not."

Which kindness called forth another bout of tears. Devil take it, his waistcoat was beginning to wade. Lesley kept stroking Carissa, the way he would an agitated horse, only now his hands, without thought, were pulling out hairpins, loosening the tight knot of hair and spreading it across her shoulders.

She blew her nose again. It was not an elegant gesture. Nor did she look very appealing with her eyes all puffy, her lashes stuck together, and her nose a bright pink. A half-drowned rat was possibly more attractive. And Lesley found her irresistible. So he kissed her.

He'd been wanting to do it almost since he'd met the woman, so prim and proper he was challenged to see if he could melt her icy disdain. Then, when he'd seen her hair down, he'd wanted to taste her lips, to prove to himself that he was right, that a real woman lived inside the shell of sanctity she wore like a chastity belt. Recently, however, having come to know her sweetness and humor and intelligence, he'd simply wanted her.

Carissa did not struggle, did not kick him or slap him or stab him with her hatpin, wherever the thing had gone. She did not even take a step away, full knowing that he would release her at the first sign of resistance. No, she kissed him back. She'd been wanting to do that almost since she'd met the viscount, to see if a rake's kisses really were more proficient, more pleasing, more profound. They were. She'd been wanting to feel his arms around her since seeing him cradle his baby daughter so tenderly, since seeing his dimple, since forever, it seemed. She'd been lonely, starved for a man's attentions, aching for someone to love, even if it was only a pleasure-seeker's passing interest.

Who knew where the simple kiss of discovery, a gesture of comfort really, would lead? Lesley had hopes of his bedroom, the sofa, the rug in front of the fireplace. Right here, against the wall, before he embarrassed himself. Carissa was beyond thought, reveling merely in the almost forgotten wonder of his embrace: his hard chest beneath hers, his powerful thighs against hers, his sighs of desire pressing on her lips. Or were those her sighs?

Carissa was lost. Lesley was foundering.

Then the voice of reason spoke up: "Mama, don't you want to hear my prayers?"

Chapter Nineteen

*A*unt Mattie arrived the next day. The old lady was almost dancing a jig, so pleased was she that all her cronies at the boardinghouse had seen a magnificent crested coach pull up and a handsome swell hand her in. Would she be so kind as to move into Lord Hartleigh's town house to safeguard her grandniece's reputation?

"Laddie, I'd be your mistress m'self," she cackled, "if it gets me out of that rooming house for rheumatic relics. Why, they're all just waiting around to die there. Here you've got children. You've got life!" And he had food in abundance, servants in attendance, fires in every hearth. Aunt Mattie was in alt. She was also in a muddle. What did a housekeeper need with a chaperon? She wouldn't have blamed dear Carrie for becoming the handsome peer's mistress, and could understand why everyone would think the worst, but they were going to do so no matter how many old ladies he invited to stay. As far as the good opinion of the members of the ton, her grandniece was sunk beneath reproach already, merely by going into service. What good was an old lady, one who never went about in Society anymore, going to accomplish?

It was a good question, one Lesley kept asking himself. He did not like the answer. Aunt Mattie, as she told him to call her, wasn't so much guarding Carissa's reputation as guarding Carissa's virtue. She was there as a buffer, pure and simple. The viscount knew he was not going to be able to keep his hands off the housekeeper, otherwise. Thunderation, he'd had a hard enough time getting to sleep, knowing she was in the other room. He'd find sleep twice as long in coming now that he knew how warm and responsive the demure widow could be. He'd be in her bed in a minute, and to hell with sleep. Lesley didn't think she'd refuse him, either, not after that kiss. Hence Aunt Mattie.

Her job was to take dinner with them when he dined at home, to sit with Mrs. Kane when he took them for carriage rides, to sleep in the widow's bedroom so he could not.

Lesley had expected Carissa's aunt to be a pensioned servant, from her description of the old woman's situation. He did not expect Aunt Mattie to be Lady Mathilda Wakeford, the well-connected, genteel widow of an impoverished baronet. He also did not expect her to hate cats, loathe dogs, and possess a canary that chirped its little yellow heart out from dawn to dusk.

"Another woman and another beastie nattering at me all day? Iffen she stays, I'm leaving, Cap'n, and this time I mean it."

"Nonsense, Byrd. Aunt Mattie is a delight. And with any luck the cat will relieve us of Dickie Bird. If we are really lucky, Cleo will choke on the feathers." The cat was sitting in his lordship's lap at that very moment, purring and kneading his leg, digging the stiletto points of its claws into Lesley's thigh. He did not stop petting the silky black fur, but cursed, "Blasted cat. Aunt Mattie stays."

Aunt Mattie was full of surprises. The fact that she was an astute whist player appeased Byrd somewhat, and her avid appetite pleased Cook. She declared the infant precious, winning Lesley's instant, unbiased approval. Some of her other surprises were about as welcome as the canary. For one, her widespread correspondents kept her au courant with the gossip. For another, she passed on her vast store of information to anyone in the vicinity. So Carissa learned what the rumor mills were saying about herself, and Lord Hartleigh was hearing about his housekeeper's past.

He'd been having licentious thoughts about a lady, by thunder. Lesley was furious that he was right, that Carissa had not been born into service. But into an earldom? He'd tossed a gently bred female to the clattering crows, and all for his own purposes, if not his pleasure. Lud. And thank the Lord for Aunt Mattie.

Carissa thanked Lord Hartleigh in person and in her prayers for rescuing her aunt from impoverishment when she'd been unable to do more than send a few shillings now and again. She would have had none to send soon, after handing her coins to Phillip. And she thanked the viscount for thinking of her reputation, although he was wasting his time, which he couldn't know, of course. Thanks to Aunt Mattie, Carissa now realized that he'd purposely set out to give the appearance of an affair between them, a long-standing, fruitful affair. The rides in the park, the walks in the neighborhood, were all to show his involvement with this cupboard family. In a way she did not blame him, for Carissa knew what it meant to be pursued for one's assets only.

She did blame him for the string of sleepless nights she was suffering. Oh, she would have found it hard enough getting to sleep, wondering about him across the hall. Knowing from the laundry that he did not wear a nightshirt to bed, Carissa's imagination alone would have kept her tossing and turning. And her anxious worries over Phillip would have kept her from slumber anyway.

But Aunt Mattie did a good job of keeping her awake on her own. The bed was wide enough for two, and for Pippa when she crawled between them in the mornings. But no amount of pillows over Carissa's ears could deaden the sound of her great-aunt's snoring. Like the new steam engine she'd taken Pippa to see, Aunt Mattie gurgled and hissed and wheezed and rumbled. And then, when daylight was only dreaming of making its appearance, the canary took over.

Carissa was exhausted, in addition to being as apprehensive as Dickie Bird when Cleo was in the room. How much longer could she avoid her onetime husband? Aunt Mattie would recognize him, and then the fat would really be in the fire. Further, Aunt Mattie was no kind of chaperon. She was a welcome presence at the dinners they now shared, for Carissa did not know how she'd make simple conversation with his lordship, not after that kiss, but the old lady was so grateful to the viscount that she would have served her own grandniece to him on a platter. Further, Lady Mathilda went to bed shortly after dinner, slept late in the mornings, and nodded off in the afternoons. Carissa depended on the children and her work to keep her away from the viscount. She surely could not depend on her own inclinations.

To make certain she was surrounded by servants when Aunt Mattie was napping, Carissa hired more servants. With Aunt Mattie's help she could train young girls from the foundling home to be proper parlor maids or ladies' dressers, so the girls could later get decent jobs for decent wages. Since Aunt Mattie's wardrobe was as limited as Carissa's, the girls were taught to be nursemaids as well. Mrs. Kane also hired a strong lad to be gardener. His job mainly consisted of filling in Gladiator's holes in the backyard, so that Maisie could sit outside with the baby on nice days, Pippa could play out of sight of the street—and her father—and Aunt Mattie would not fall and break her brittle bones. Carissa found a small measure of peace directing the boy as he planted flowers and shrubs. The dog would likely dig everything up, so at least the lad did not have to worry about *his* future.

The viscount also added to his payroll. In addition to the man following Mason, he took on two additional Bow Street Runners, one to keep a watch out for the brown-haired scum who'd upset Mrs. Kane, the other to discover what he could about Phillip Kane. Lesley was sure the answer to Carissa's problems involved her deceased husband. Perhaps the alley-lurker was a gambling crony of Kane's, come to dun her for past debts. Or a bloodsucker, here to offer details of the dead soldier's demise in exchange for a fee.

Lesley was determined to make things right for Carissa Kane. It was the least he could do after the grievous wrongs he had done to her standing, even among the neighbors in Kensington. The shopkeepers were less respectful to her, he could see, and the wives made their husbands serve her. Soon Cook was doing more of the marketing, and the hordes of other servants were doing her errands. Carissa seldom left the house, for fear of being humiliated, he supposed. She would not accept his invitation to the opera, although Aunt Mattie drooled at the opportunity worse than Glad drooled at an opened bottle of wine. They did not have proper evening wear, Mrs. Kane informed him, her clenched fists almost daring him to make the admittedly scandalous offer of purchasing her a gown. Mrs. Kane did not have enough gumption to face down the stares, Lesley decided, and he could not really blame her. What a damnable coil, on top of which she looked like . . . like an overworked housekeeper.

Where was Hartleigh's high flier? Mrs. Kane's nonappearance caused almost as much talk as her rides with him in the park had done. Had he sent the woman and her children off to the country? Had he tired of her as he had every other woman? Speculation was rampant, but no one dared ask the viscount himself. The last two gentlemen who'd made mention of his mistress had been issued an inescapable invitation to Gentleman Jackson's Boxing Parlor. The last lady who'd simpered at his supposed unspeakable liaison had been treated to Lesley's quizzing-glass stare, then his back.

One female was not deterred. One woman was so offended by the reprehensible relationship that she vowed to get to the truth—and then get rid of the trollop—even if Hartleigh murdered her. Of course, she wasn't foolish enough to actually confront the viscount; she waited until she knew he was busy with his steward, in the estate office at Hammond House.

Agatha, Lady Hartleigh, knew her husband's son was at Grosvenor Square, not because he called on her to pay his respects, but because that wretched dog of his was *in* Grosvenor Square, destroying the shrubbery. Agatha would have to listen to the complaints from the neighbors again if she stayed home. She didn't. She went to call on her stepson's Kensington convenient.

The crested carriage pulled up at the front door and a bewigged, liveried footman let down the steps for Agatha to descend. She turned up her less-than-straight nose at the size of the house, the scruffy boy digging in the dirt, and the gold-toothed, baldheaded butler who answered the door. Without a greeting for the man who'd served the viscount for longer than she'd known him, Lady Hartleigh demanded, "I wish to see Lesley's . . ."

A proper female did not use such words. A true lady did not admit to knowing the words.

"Daughter?" Byrd was being helpful.

Agatha almost had a conniption. So that much of the story was true. She was so mad that Hartleigh had flaunted his by-blow in front of her friends that she forgot her fine manners. "His whore, you hairless cretin. I wish to see the mother of his bastard."

Byrd took his time answering. "I wish I could send you to her, ma'am, 'deed I do. The babe is out in the back with her nursemaid, taking the fresh air, but fact is, I don't rightly know where the nipper's mum is right now."

"And you'd be too insolent to tell me. I have never understood why my stepson keeps you on, except to aggravate me. The same reason he does every provoking, pestilential prank, I presume. Very well, I'll find her myself."

Agatha hiked up her skirts lest they touch the floor, even though she could see that the house was well kept, with the furniture polished and flowers on the hall table. She went up the stairs and began opening doors. It was her right, she told herself, nay, her duty to her dead husband, to look after Lesley's interests. Especially as he seemed too smitten to show any sense. The man needed a wellborn wife, preferably one of her own father's second wife's children from her first marriage. The Spillhammer sisters had been foisted on Agatha when she married Hartleigh, and she saw no way to get rid of them except by marrying one of them to the current Lord Hartleigh. Then they'd be his concern. Meantime, the family name was her concern. Why, she could barely hold her sausage-curled head up in company, what with all the gossip Lesley was causing with his barque of frailty and her brood.

Agatha opened the first door and discovered a well-furnished nursery. The woman had the effrontery to steal Hammond House belongings for her baseborn brat! Agatha slammed the door and went across to the next room. Lesley's, obviously, with new dark blue hangings that Agatha estimated must have cost a pretty penny, money that should have stayed in the Hartleigh coffers. She slammed that door, too.

Carissa had been trying to take a nap. The children were in the back garden with Maisie and one of the footmen, where Cook could see them from the kitchen door. Aunt Mattie had gone to flaunt her good fortune at her old boardinghouse, taking her friends an enormous basket of food and a few candles, with Lesley's blessings. With his footman, too. The house was all in order, so Carissa had thrown a shawl over the canary's cage and a lavender-soaked towel over her eyes.

The new girls from the foundling home would never find decent positions if they didn't learn to go about their duties more quietly, Carissa thought. She'd discuss it with them later, when she woke up. Then her door crashed open.

"In bed in the afternoon, are you, you strumpet? I am not surprised."

Carissa was awake now. A tall, thin woman with an aquiline beak of a nose was standing in her doorway. The female had thick ringlets framing her narrow face and wore a magenta gown with a pink spencer. Her hat sported three feathers and a cascade of puce lace. She had rings on every finger, a rope of garnets around her scrawny neck, and ruby and diamond drops in ears that were almost as big as Gladiator's, and stuck out sideways.

"Who the deuce are you?"

"I am the one asking the questions, wench," Agatha insisted. "I have only one: Why are you trying to ruin my stepson's life?"

Ah, Carissa thought. Lady Hartleigh. Without getting up off the bed, she replied: "Your stepson's well-being is naturally of importance to me. I am making his life as pleasant and as comfortable as I know how, my lady, which is what I was hired to do. I do not consider that damaging."

"Hah! You admit you're being paid to pleasure the rake! And you do not think that is harmful? Who knows what diseases you bring, along with your bastards. But worse, you are destroying every opportunity the fool has of making an advantageous marriage. No one will join their family to such a scandal. No decent woman will accept his arm to cross the street, much less his hand in marriage! There is no way he can assure the succession, which means some corkbrained cousin will inherit. And it is all your doing, you jade. Lesley should be taking his rightful place in Society, not taking his pleasure in some hole-in-corner affair in Kensington. His name, *my* name, is becoming a byword for decadence. I can barely hold up my head in polite company."

That was likely because of the weight of the sugar-water paste keeping her curls in place, Carissa thought. Or her big ears. Carissa stood up and walked around to the other side of the bed. "Madam," she said, "you are talking moonshine. Your relative was on the path to perdition long before he met me, and likely at your instigation. Furthermore, no matter what you think, I have been hired to keep house for Lord Hartleigh and nothing else."

"Now who is talking fustian? I want you out of here, you and your brats."

"Do you know, I think it is you who should be leaving, Lady Hartleigh. I could not in good conscience throw my employer's kin out of his house, but this is my bedroom, and I do not believe Lord Hartleigh would expect me to be insulted in my private domain. Please leave."

"What, the rake's whore is telling me to get out? How dare you, you with your hair down around your shoulders in the middle of the afternoon, and your misbegotten brats littering the yard? I'll see you in hell, you doxy, whatever your name is."

Carissa had had enough. She folded her arms across her chest and said, "My name is Carissa Kane. I use Mrs. Kane out of respect for my dead husband, and to suit my current position, but you may call me *Lady* Carissa. And I am, *Lady* Hartleigh, more of a lady than you can ever hope to be, with your jewels and expensive clothes and polished airs. I would never think of demeaning myself by haranguing a servant like a Billingsgate fishwife, nor vilifying an innocent child. And you do not care for Lesley in the least. It is your reputation you are worried about, your coveted place in Society. Well, go find another rich husband to wed, Lady Hartleigh, another title to guarantee your access to the hallowed portals of the polite world. But remember this: Whatever you do, your father will still be a coal-heaver, while mine will still be an earl."

Chapter Twenty

Spite, that's what it was. Carissa now understood why Lord Hartleigh lived on the outskirts of London, sowing more than his fair share of wild oats. He'd been driven to it by that self-righteous, sanctimonious shrew, the same way Carissa was being driven to the opera. Of course she would ride in Hartleigh's elegant coach, if it could carry her weight with the chip Carissa held on her shoulder.

To . . . to the devil with all of them, she angrily thought once the viscountess had fled the house, claiming to be suffering an agitation of nerves that required the liveried footman—the large, handsome footman, Carissa noted—to carry her to her carriage.

Carissa had tried to live her life circumspectly, she reminded herself, as honorably as she possibly could. She'd gained nothing by it. No one believed in her virtue, not even Hartleigh himself, who should know better. At least he knew she was not his mistress, although he might have renewed expectations after that kiss she'd so brazenly shared with him. Virtue might be its own reward, but Carissa was reaping the wages of sin, without the enjoyment. That was going to change. Mrs. Kane decided she might as well please herself, since her behavior pleased no one else. She would go to the opera or Drury Lane or Vauxhall Gardens, and shame those high-nosed hypocrites with her presence.

For spite, too, she decided to buy a new gown, selling her wedding ring to finance the purchase. If that dastard Phillip Kane wanted to declare her his wife, let him provide her another. He hadn't provided her much else but aggravation.

Besides, the ring had likely been paid for with her own funds. Carissa was not going to worry about Phillip exposing her widowhood as a sham, not at the theater. What would he gain by that except a wife he did not want and a child he could not afford? The more she thought about his furtive behavior, his admitted "troubles" with the army, his needing funds so desperately, she realized that Phillip would not wish to be seen in public, any more than she wanted her deceased husband resurrected. He only wanted money from her, not a marriage. Well, she'd rather buy another gown for Aunt Mattie than give another groat to the man who'd already taken everything, including her future.

Pearl-gray was what she had in mind for her new gown, dignified, demure, and decorous. The inexpensive dressmaker her aunt knew of had an unclaimed gown, however, that she'd part with for half its worth. The frock was of burnt orange silk, with an ecru lace overskirt. It had three bands of darker ribbon at the hem, and matching trim at the low neckline and short, puffed sleeves. The gown fit perfectly, delineating both her slim hips and her bounteous bosom. There was nothing modest about the dress except its price, and Carissa loved it, from the whisper of the silk as she moved to the lace that barely concealed her breasts. With a matching ribbon at her throat and a coronet of orange rosebuds in her hair, Carissa felt she looked every inch the lady. Or a ladybird with good taste.

The entire household stood in the hallway to admire Mrs. Kane in her finery. Everyone except Sue, of course, who complained that she was not permitted to drool on the silk. Lesley was the most appreciative. He'd heard of Agatha's visit and could imagine what was said. He'd have words with his stepmother another time, and see that she never darkened this doorstep again with her venom. For now, though, he was thankful that the witch had convinced Carissa to show some starch of her own. Whatever it took to see her dressed to the hilt—and what a hilt—and out in Society where she belonged was fine with him.

Lesley knew he couldn't buy Carissa the dress, but he could purchase a pair of opera glasses or a filigree flower-holder for her, some impersonal item she could carry. He decided on a fan, the perfect thing in case she wished to avoid the inevitable stares, and he took only an entire afternoon to select the perfect one. It was silk, with laughing cherubim painted on it, and she adored it.

Carissa also adored how he'd invited Aunt Mattie's rooming-house cronies to share their box. Impoverished gentlewomen all, they gaily waved and called out to their prosperous relations, who could not, therefore, pretend they hadn't seen Hartleigh and his supposed housekeeper. He'd invited his stepmother first, as was proper, sending round a note saying that although he would be using the family box, she and her wards were welcome to share it with his other guests, including Mrs. Kane.

Agatha would sooner take tea with Attila the Hun. She would not sit with that woman, lending countenance to the disgraceful affair, as Lesley well knew. Unfortunately, even if she'd been willing to purchase tickets for herself and her stepsisters, all the other boxes were taken. Lady Hartleigh would *not* sit in the pit with the rabble, which meant she and her stepsisters had to be the only members of the ton not in attendance at such a major social event of the Season. Agatha would have gnashed her teeth, except that always gave her the headache.

The dowager would have had more than a migraine if she'd seen the widow—and her reception. Beyond the nods and half bows from the antique aunties' kin, a few of the viscount's gentlemen friends called at the box during intermissions. They were his friends, which meant they were neither trying to sniff out more scandal nor attempting to cut him out with the beautiful widow, at least not seriously enough to call forth a challenge. They were everything courteous, respectful, and appreciative. Lesley was thankful to his friends and proud of Carissa's gracious acceptance of their admiration. He was also careful to introduce Carissa to each gentleman using her title, her great-aunt's title, and her father's title. The highest sticklers might never accept her, but she was Macclesfield's daughter, by George, and now everyone knew it.

The Earl of Macclesfield was not quite so gratified. He

entered the box at the last intermission, when Lord Hartleigh had gone to fetch refreshments. With an angry jerk of his head, the earl cleared the box of the old ladies.

"It don't suit me to have m'daughter the *on dit* of the day," he declared by way of greeting to the child he hadn't seen in nearly five years.

It didn't suit him to *have* a daughter, Carissa thought. The earl had not seemed to mind her starving or going into service, so long as his friends did not see. She had no intention of brangling with him in public, however, so she merely inclined her head. "Good evening, Father, and how do you do?" He did as well as ever, she saw, somewhat grayer and somewhat more gone to fat, but with the same impatience for underlings, such as his wayward daughter.

"You'll never bring him up to scratch, you know. Hartleigh's not stupid enough to buy what he's been getting for free."

Carissa ignored the unveiled innuendo. "Not that it is any of your concern, Father, since you washed your hands of me long ago, but I would not think of trying to bring Lord Hartleigh up to scratch, as you so inelegantly put it." Again out of spite, and feeling good to so upset the old curmudgeon, Carissa waved her gloved hand at the surroundings, at herself. "I am quite enjoying my life as a fallen woman, don't you know. A box at the opera, a fancy gown, gifts. I am certain jewels will come soon, aren't you?"

Macclesfield glowered. "You always had an odd kick to your gallop, girl."

Acknowledging his opinion with a brief nod, she went on: "Besides, you know I cannot be thinking of remarrying. You've seen Phillip."

"That loose screw? He wants money, not you. Pay him off and he'll return to the rock he crawled out from. No one'll be the wiser. You ain't been dunderheaded enough to mention the bounder to Hartleigh, have you?"

"No, I would not bother Lesley with such trifles as a husband."

The earl was thinking. "You know, Heartless just might marry you after all. Be just like that randy young rip to hitch

146

himself to a whore, just to set the ton on its ears. If you nab him, I'll give you my blessings."

Carissa sat taller. "If I marry Lord Hartleigh, which is an impossibility as matters now stand, I shall not need your blessings, any more than I have needed them these past years to raise my daughter, your grandchild. Save your prayers for your shriveled soul, Father. You'll need them."

Aunt Mattie was enthusing over the lovely time they'd had, despite the somewhat uncomfortable circumstances, during the entire ride home. She was positive they'd laid all the gossip to rest, with Lord Hartleigh's contrivance. She must have thanked dear Lesley a hundred times, Carissa thought, well aware they hadn't changed a single mind.

Aunt Mattie kept praising the viscount to the skies, even as she undressed for bed, declaring the whole while that she was sure she wouldn't sleep a wink, so excited was she by the evening's entertainment.

She was snoring by the time her great-niece returned from checking on Philippa. Carissa was exhausted from the tension of the evening and the preparations beforehand, but she knew she couldn't fall asleep with such a strident symphony next to her pillow. She could not even join Pippa on her narrow cot, for when she checked, the dog had been stretched on one side of the child, the cat curled up on the other. And the dog snored as loudly as Aunt Mattie.

So she decided to share Lord Hartleigh's bed.

This was not a moment's decision, since she'd been thinking of nothing else for days, it seemed. She wanted him, he wanted her. What could be simpler? Carissa had only to smother her scruples, the way she covered the canary.

Her own father thought she was a whore. All of London thought she was Hartleigh's mistress, the mother of his backdoor baby. Even the old ladies had struggled to hide their titters as Lord Hartleigh leaned closer to Carissa during the performance, or held her hand overlong as he helped her into the carriage. Her own husband assumed she was having an adulterous affair—and thought to profit by it.

Well, Lord Hartleigh was paying her handsomely. He was acting the part of protector, provider, and particular friend. The only thing he was not was her bed-partner. Carissa was about to change that.

She was not ashamed of anything she'd done in the past, even if her actions had cost her reputation. She'd done what she had to, to care for her daughter. Carissa had not sacrificed her honor yet, not by marrying Sir Gilliam, not by dallying with the scores of men who had propositioned her, thinking her a lonely widow of easy virtue. Virtue wasn't easy and it wasn't very satisfying, either.

What she was about to do was wrong. Carissa would not try to delude herself into thinking the circumstances could justify her actions, although she did not think she had the power to stop, now that she'd decided to go to him. They were no star-crossed lovers, no innocents giving all for love. She was a fallen woman and he was a rake; that was the sum total of her excuses.

There was no future for them, she knew. Lord Heartless would move on to the next woman who caught his fancy, or the wife he would be forced to take. And Carissa's heart would go with him. She was going to suffer no matter what, and forever, she feared, so she might as well enjoy what she could of him now.

The decision made, Carissa was not merely going to fall from grace; she was going to leap before her good sense overcame her. Still in her evening finery, she raised her head, raised her candle, and raised her hand to knock on Hartleigh's door as soon as she heard Byrd leave.

His coat was off, as were his shoes and his neckcloth. Lud, she hadn't thought of what he'd be wearing, only that her own night rail was flannel, too faded and darned for an *affaire*. He looked up from the papers he was reading, expecting Byrd, perhaps. "What . . . ?"

"I couldn't sleep," was all she could say, not having thought about this part of the evening either.

"You couldn't sleep?" he repeated curiously as he rose to his stockinged feet. "And you thought I might have a book of sermons to make you drowsy? Or did you mistake my room for the kitchen, thinking to fetch some warm milk?"

"Don't be a nodcock, my lord. You know why I have come."

"Mrs. Kane, I have absolutely no idea what in heaven's name you are doing in my bedroom. I might have my fond hopes, but women bent on seduction do not go around calling their lovers by their titles. Women in a gentleman's employ do not keep reminding him of the canons he'd be breaking."

"Very well, *Lesley*, do not be a nodcock."

"Ah." He smiled, raised her hand to his mouth, and tenderly kissed the palm. "But I need to hear it from your own lips, my dear. There will be no recriminations in the morning?"

What was she supposed to say, that she did this all the time, that she never regretted a night's pleasure, or that she ached for his arms so badly that no amount of guilty feelings was going to sway her? She merely shook her head. No, she would not blame him, nor ask for more than he was willing to give.

"And your aunt Mattie won't come charging in here with a pistol and a special license?"

For answer she turned and locked the door, then handed him the key. "Ah," he said again, satisfied, dropping it to the floor. He took the pins out of her hair, letting roses also fall to the ground at their feet. Then he held out his arms and she stepped into his embrace, as if coming in from a long, cold journey. His lips on hers were everything she'd been dreaming of, fairy dust and fireworks and floating on air. Six senses did somersaults in her mind, in her insides. His hands were touching her everywhere, as if he'd memorize the feel of her, and she reached for him, too, to unbutton his shirt, to know his bare skin.

Lesley caught her trembling hands, brought them to his lips, and stepped back. "No. I am honored, I am moved, I am tempted beyond mortal man's frail resistance, but no, my dear. I cannot accept your charming offer."

Chapter Twenty-one

"No?" Carissa gasped. "No?" She'd humiliated herself, come panting after him like a mare in season, and he said no? "But I let you touch my—I let you touch me. And take down my hair, and oh, good heavens, my buttons are undone!"

He was smiling, the devil. "And delightful buttons they were. Here, turn around and I shall do them up for you again."

Carissa clutched the bodice of her dress, to maintain some shred of decency and dignity. "No, I would not bother you."

"Don't be foolish, you cannot go back to your room looking like that. What if your aunt awoke?"

"She would not be surprised. She already believes me to be your mistress. Everyone does." She added a bitter afterthought: "Except you."

Still smiling—no, grinning—Lesley told her, "It's not that I'm not attracted." He gestured vaguely to the snug fit of his satin knee breeches, bringing a furious blush to her cheeks. "But I simply do not need a mistress."

Of course. He had that opera dancer in keeping. Carissa wondered if they'd seen the woman performing tonight. Perhaps she was waiting for him even now in her rooms, or a hotel, or another love nest, since this one was overflowing with cuckoo birds. The viscount might, on the other hand, be waiting for some tonnish gentleman to retire for the night, so he could visit the man's wife. Carissa had seen the way every woman looked at him like a prize bull, assessing the strength and stamina. Any one of them would be willing to share his bed. He had no use for a dowdy housekeeper in her Cinderella-goes-to-the-ball togs. No, he did not need her at all, not even to run the household. Cook could manage, now that she and Byrd had come to an understanding. She'd have to, for Carissa did not think she could live under Lord Hartleigh's roof after this shame-filled night.

As if he could read her thoughts, Lesley reached out and gently touched her cheek. "You see, what I really need is a mother for my daughter."

Carissa brushed his hand away. If he was not going to be swayed by her presence in his bedroom, she was not about to be affected by his touch. "You said your man of business was looking into finding her a family."

Lesley took a deep breath and admitted, "The fact is, I don't think I can part with her anymore."

"Don't be ridiculous. That's the way people adopt puppies and kittens, not children. They come begging on your doorstep, looking adorable. Why do you think God made them so appealing and so helpless? That's how I got Cleopatra. There she was, a tiny scrap of black fur, mewing on the stoop. I thought, A bowl of milk and that's all. Then it rained, so I let her dry near the stove, thinking one night wasn't going to hurt. That was before Pippa was born, and she hasn't left me yet. But Sue? You have to think what is best for the child, not what your inclinations might be when you see her smiling at you."

"I have been thinking of little else since she came, Carissa. And I believe that I can make a good life for her, providing I find the right woman. I think you are the one."

Carissa loved the baby, as much as she'd tried not to become attached, knowing Sue would be leaving. And she could understand his thinking: If he set her up in a cottage somewhere, he could visit at his leisure. Carissa could give out that she was a more recent widow, which people would believe until he came to call. Continuing her reasoning, Carissa realized that if she were far enough away in the country, Phillip mightn't find her, mightn't be a constant sword hanging over her head. And Pippa would be happier there if she could bring her pony. Carissa would not have to be seeking position after position, uprooting them every time—and she'd get to see Lord

Hartleigh every now and again. "Yes, I think it could work. If Maisie can come, of course."

"Of course."

"And Aunt Mattie? I could not send her back to that boardinghouse, you know. And she would be good company for me."

"I wouldn't have it any other way. You can even bring Glad."

"Too generous, my lord. He stays here. The cottage will be too small for him."

"Cottage?"

"Why, yes, a cottage in the country. You didn't think we could go on here? Everyone knows Sue is not my daughter. Well, everyone who counts."

"I, ah, had something larger in mind. Larger and closer. Hammond House, in fact."

"Now, that is foolish beyond permission. We could never be welcomed at your family's home. Imagine the mare's nest you'd stir up bringing your housekeeper and your unblessed babe to Grosvenor Square."

"But if I brought my wife home, and my adopted ward?"

"No one will believe Sue is— Wife?"

"Wife." He nodded. "I am, my dear Mrs. Kane, asking you to marry me."

Carissa did not have time to find a seat; she collapsed onto the floor, amid the roses and hairpins. "Wife?"

Lesley sat beside her, picking up the rosebuds and placing them in her lap. "It won't be a bad bargain, I promise."

"You'd marry to acquire a mother for your child?"

"There are worse reasons, like marrying for money."

She was shredding the roses. "But to wed so Sue can have a mother?"

"Half the marriages in the ton are contracted for no other reason than to beget an heir. How is this so much different? I know you're fond of Sue and I dote on your daughter." He rubbed one soft bloom against the skin of her neck. "I would have to take a wife eventually anyway, to ensure the succession, and you know we are attracted to each other."

She knew that too well. Her head was spinning, even without his seductive stroking. Marriage. A father for Pippa, a home of her own. Respectability. And Lesley in her bed. Now there was a fairy-tale ending to put Cinderella's to shame.

"No."

It was Lesley's turn to be dumbfounded. This was the first marriage proposal he had ever made, and an impoverished widow with a dicey reputation was rejecting it. "No? You are turning me down? I would come down heavily on the settlements, you know, if that is your concern."

She shook her head, behind the veil of her fallen hair. She could not look him in the eyes for fear of giving in to this promise of heaven on earth.

"I see. You want tender words, a proper wooing. I thought I would appeal to your logical nature, lest you accuse me of turning you up sweet. But showing you my deep and sincere regard will be no hardship, I assure you. So many marriages offer much less. And in time . . . "

Carissa kept her head down, hiding her tears. "I cannot."

"It's my reputation, isn't it? I cannot swear to be a faithful husband, because I've never put it to the test, but I aim to try. And I would never be so indiscreet as to cause you embarrassment. I find I do not like being the center of gossip when my feelings are involved, and I daresay you feel the same."

"Gossip?" Carissa found her voice. "Your reputation? That is rich, my lord. I have no reputation! Marrying me would sink you beneath reproach. Your name would be dragged so deeply through the muck that you'd be ashamed to show your face in London. You'd have to rusticate, or else be constantly challenging all comers to duels. And you are so well known that even in the country you'd be the addlepated peer who was taken in by a scheming harpy of a housekeeper."

"Stop thinking of yourself as less than a lady, blast it!"

"I *am* less, I am a servant! It's you who will not recognize the truth. When you do, you will come to hate me. Let me take the children, Lesley, let me find a tiny cottage somewhere and make a life for them, while you go on with yours."

"Very well. We will not marry. Yet."

Perhaps because he could not imagine any woman of reasonable intelligence refusing such an advantageous offer of marriage, Lesley spent the rest of the night trying to make sense of Carissa's rejection. Pride was not the issue, not Lesley's at any rate. He knew she was fond of him. A woman like Carissa did not offer herself to a man otherwise. Therefore, he reasoned, she must have said no because of their unequal stations. He couldn't give up the viscountcy, but she could damn well give up being a housekeeper. Mrs. Kane wanted a little cottage somewhere? Too bad. Lesley was only so understanding. She'd just have to make do with Hammond House.

First he needed help.

One did not call on the dowager Duchess of Castleberry without an appointment or an invitation, unless one was Her Grace's favorite scapegrace godson.

"Well, jackanapes, what is all this rumgumption I am hearing? And what do you want me to do about it, for you wouldn't be calling on me else?"

There was no sense in wasting flummery on the downiest bird in London, so Lesley explained his problem.

Her Grace sipped her tea, deliberating before she issued her verdict: "There is no way you can bring that one into fashion, no, not even with my help, short of marrying her."

"I am trying, dash it. She won't have me."

"What, losing your touch, scamp?" The grande dame was enjoying his discomfort as much as her macaroons. "The father is a cabbagehead, of course. He practically pushed the chit into a runaway marriage by arranging an abysmal match for her. The rumor mill had it that Macclesfield gave his consent for Packword to pay his addresses."

"Packword? The man is close to sixty and pox-ridden!"

Her Grace shrugged her thin shoulders. "Was she better off with her handsome young soldier? I wonder. Still, the chit just might be the making of you. Turned you down, eh? If you are determined to have her, I'll talk to Macclesfield. The gel will need clothes and such, and our job will be that much easier if it's seen that her father approves. The rotter might as well be good for something."

No one refused the Duchess of Castleberry, Lesley knew. The Earl of Macclesfield might as well be sharpening his pen to write the cheques.

"Be warned, though, my lad, some doors will always be closed to your Mrs. Kane, no matter how many strings I pull."

As he kissed the old lady's parchment cheek, Lesley replied, "Some doors are not worth walking through."

One door that was important was the front door to Hammond House. When he opened the door to see Lord Hartleigh, the butler there looked as if he'd eaten something that disagreed with him.

"Cheer up, Wimberly," Lesley told the man. "I haven't come to take anything else away. In fact, I'll be bringing it all back, as soon as I speak to Lady Hartleigh."

"The mistress is not receiving. My lady has contracted a slight palsy of her left eyelid. The doctor recommends bed rest in a darkened room."

"Ah, then I shall have to rearrange the bedrooms myself, to prepare for our guests. And the nursery, of course. You do like children, don't you, Wimberly?"

"I'll fetch Lady Hartleigh."

Both of Agatha's eyelids started twitching when Lesley explained his mission. "Not even a rake like you would bring a loose woman into your own home, Hartleigh. You have more respect for your family name."

"Oh, I wouldn't and I do. That's why I am bringing Mrs. Kane here, and her aunt, of course. So everyone can see she is welcomed as an esteemed guest."

"Well, she won't be. The servants won't wait on her, I'm sure. They can always recognize Quality, you know."

"There are other servants. Ones who recognize a good position when they find it. You might pass that on to Wimberly. He cannot seem to recall who pays his wages."

"The devil take Wimberly. What about the child?" Agatha was blinking so hard, her sausage curls were flapping.

"Pippa? She'll be moving in too, naturally. Mrs. Kane would

never leave her behind, unlike those tonnish mothers who let nannies and governesses rear their children for them. I am sure you'll adore Pippa. She's a serious little thing, but her laughter is as sweet as birdsong."

"Why, you're smitten! With the baggage's brat."

He pulled a cat hair off his superfine sleeve. "Quite unfashionable of me, isn't it? I shudder to think what the fellows at White's will say."

Since he'd never given a rap for what anyone said about him, ever, Agatha was not deceived. "And the other child? The infant?"

"Sue comes too." He did not elaborate, he only stated the fact.

"Impossible. You might as well drape the bar sinister over our front door. It would sink my stepsisters' chances on the Marriage Mart to be living in the same house with your . . . your . . ."

"Ward," he supplied. "And since the Spillhammer sisters have been at Hammond House for their presentations, their debutante balls, and the past three Seasons, all at my expense, without receiving one offer between the two of them, I do not think Sue can be held responsible. If you think their reputations will be damaged, however, feel free to send your relatives packing. Make no mistake, Sue is coming. And Mrs. Kane is coming, with her child, her cat, and her aunt. And the aunt's canary, I suppose."

"If you bring that woman here," Agatha screeched, worse than Dickie Bird, "I am leaving."

The viscount struck his forehead. "Now why did I never think of that before? Lud, I could have brought Bijou LaBianca here and reclaimed my house years ago."

Chapter Twenty-two

Lesley's next call was to Bow Street, to see if his various inquiries had borne fruit. Thunderation, he wished that second will would come to light. If Carissa owned the Parkhurst house and the fortune that went with it, she would no longer consider herself a servant, an outcast of the elite. Hell, he'd purchase the blasted house from Parkhurst, if the cawker weren't too castaway to transact business nine hours out of ten. Then again, if Carissa became a woman of property, she'd never need Lesley's offer. He wouldn't think about that, that she might have another, more personal reason for rejecting him. She *did* like him. His years as a womanizer had taught him to recognize that much.

The officer handling his investigation was a wizened gnome of a man, small enough to have been a jockey in his prime, old enough to have ridden with the Normans. He tamped some tobacco into his pipe and riffled through a stack of papers on his desk.

The first report was on Mason. Parkhurst's butler was followed on numerous occasions to a local pub, a certain coffeehouse, and a particular emporium, where he seldom came out with packages. The barkeep, the waiters, and the shop owner had nothing good to say about the man, except that he paid cash. Most often, however, Mason's time away from his place of employment was spent at a set of rooms near the docks. Runners weren't too popular in that neighborhood, Inspector Nesbitt informed the viscount through a thick cloud of bluish smoke from his pipe.

"No one'll talk much to a Redbreast there, m'lord, so gathering information ain't so easy. Still, my man says no one answers his knock when Mason ain't there, and no one calls on him when he is. Solitary kind of bloke. Happens my fellow would have accidental-like found the door open, to have a look-see, but the man has three or four locks on his door. The landlord swears he ain't got the keys. Suspicious, I'd say."

"Deuced suspicious. I'd give a monkey to know what's in that room."

"For five hundred pounds, I'm sure we can get us a warrant. A'course, we ain't got nothing to charge the blighter with."

Lesley agreed they'd ought to wait a bit before taking such a drastic step as calling in a squad of officers. The Runners were as liable to be injured by the neighbors as they were to find anything incriminating. Nesbitt flipped another page. "In the pub they're saying how Mason's drinking heavier than normal, on account of the Parkhurst sprig. Don't improve his personality any, it seems. Staff is leaving like rats deserting a ship, between Mason's temper and young Parkhurst half the time not paying their wages. A regular Johnny Raw, that one, gambling away the blunt as fast as he can get it from the bank. And drinking hisself to death, if one of his bone-crunchers don't break his fool neck for him first."

Lesley wondered who would get the house then. Not Carissa, so the unprepossessing heir could go to hell in a handcart for all he cared. "About that other matter?" he prompted, eager to get out into the fresh air.

"The war records?" Nesbitt shuffled his papers some more. "Aye, here we go. There ain't any."

"What, no Phillip Kane on the casualty lists? The War Office is notoriously haphazard about its reporting, but there should be some record."

"Not on the casualty lists, not on the regimental rosters for the years you gave us. A'course, not every common soldier had his name spelled right, but you did say as how Kane was an officer, didn't you?"

"From the braid on his uniform in the miniature portrait, yes.

And my godmother recalled the gossip of the time naming him lieutenant."

"Aye, that's what I thought. Something havey-cavey there, so I set my man to a bit more digging. Had to part with more of your lordship's brass for access to the records."

Lesley waved away such minor concerns. "What did he find?"

"Well, nothing I'd swear to, but there was a Phillip Cantwell on the deserters list from about six years ago."

"A deserter?" He whistled. "But that was before Mrs. Kane wed him. She couldn't have known. She'd never have married a turncoat."

"No one could of known, what with him using another name, if Cantwell was Kane, in truth. You say you saw his likeness, eh? Happens the army puts out a description of its deserters, with a reward. Cantwell'd be about thirty now, medium build, medium brown hair. Just like you said the picture had. What color eyes did you say?"

"Hazel," Lesley promptly recalled, thinking that Pippa's brown eyes were just like her mother's, nothing like her father's.

"Says greenish here. Seems like a match to me. Too bad Mrs. Kane's a widow. The army'd still pay to get their hands on the dastard."

Lord Hartleigh was considering if Carissa had first found out that her husband was a deserter when she went to the army seeking a widow's pension after the craven died. Perhaps that was why she was so reluctant to speak of him, and why she was too ashamed to marry again. Damn, Pippa's father had been a coward.

Nesbitt poked at the bowl of his pipe with a nail, to get it going better. Lesley coughed, brought back to the matter at hand.

"What about the man I had you look for? I wouldn't be surprised if he was Cantwell's brother or something, come to extort money to keep mum about the bounder."

"Aye, you did say as how he 'peared sandy-haired and average height. No way of knowing, a'course, till we find the chap. But here's something else what I find interesting." Nesbitt found the appropriate paper and smoothed it on his desk, brushing ashes away. "I went to see the solicitor fellow, that Nigel Gordon, myself. Went to his room in Hans Town. Thought he might be willing to talk about that will you're so anxious to find if I invited him to take a wet with me, friendly-like, don't you know. He weren't there."

"That's not so surprising. The man likely came into a nice bit of change from Parkhurst and Mason. He was out spending it, I'd wager."

"I would've thought so m'self, but a fellow don't go off and leave his purse on the dresser. The landlady opened the door for me, you see, when I told her I was needing a will drawn up, quick-like, and wanted to leave the lawyer a message to call."

And Nesbitt had undoubtedly bribed the woman with more of Lesley's money, but he did not care. "And he hasn't been back?" he asked, knowing that the inspector was too thorough to leave such a stone unturned.

"Landlady ain't seen hide nor hair of him, and was helping herself to the rent money from his wallet. Only fair, I s'pose. Anyways, I took myself over to his office, an upstairs cubby over a print shop off Bond Street. The door was open."

Lesley wasn't surprised, he only wondered how much it was costing him. "And?"

"And Gordon wasn't there, but someone had been. The place was fair ransacked, papers everywhere, file drawers dumped out." The inspector tidied his own neat stacks. "Someone were looking for something real bad. Couldn't tell if they found it."

"There's no way of knowing if that has anything to do with Sir Gilliam's will, though. It tells us nothing."

"No, excepting here's where it gets interesting. I spoke to the clerk at the print shop and he hadn't seen Gordon since Monday, but on Wednesday a gent came calling. Asked Gordon's direction, he did. After the clerk said he didn't think Gordon was upstairs, the fellow allowed as how he'd leave a note. He was there long enough to write a book, but the clerk didn't think anything of it, till I showed him the office in shambles."

"And?" Lesley knew there was more.

"And the clerk remembered the caller had sandy hair, average height, and brownish-green eyes. Do you believe in coincidences, m'lord? I sure as Hades don't."

Lesley was more determined than ever to get Carissa to Hammond House. Who knew if the man who'd accosted her in the alley had done away with Gordon, or if he'd be back for more money, more threats? She was too vulnerable in Kensington. Now all he had to do was convince her to go, without intimidating her or frightening her.

Mice ought to do the trick.

"There are no mice in this house!" Carissa insisted, trying to see behind the stove and under the sink at the same time. She shivered, as if tiny, scaly mice feet were running up her spine.

"Yes, there are. Cook told me she saw two this very morning."

Carissa looked over at the table, where Cook was making piecrusts. "Two of the plaguey beasts," Cook agreed, as eager as the viscount to see Mrs. Kane returned to a proper way of life. "And their leavings in the flour."

"In the flour? That flour?" She might never eat one of Cook's pies again.

"Oh, I picked 'em out. I didn't want to upset you with them."

"Perhaps Cleo could catch them?" Carissa sounded dubious even to her own ears. Cleo wouldn't know a mouse from a muffin; at least Carissa didn't think so.

"I wouldn't want her to tangle with one of them," the viscount told her. "London's vermin are more often rats, half the cat's size, I'd wager. No, we'll do better to call in the rat-catcher. He'll try ferrets first. Have you ever seen them working?"

More furry fiends, Carissa was thinking, that sent rodents rushing in all directions. Wriggly, weaselly nasties that crawled under a woman's skirts and up her legs and— And she was tempted to leap atop the kitchen table.

Lesley was going on: "If the ferrets don't work, the rat-catcher will lay poison. Cleo would have to be locked in a room somewhere. No, much better to take her away. I thought to have the house painted at the same time. What do you think?"

She thought the walls should have had a fresh coat five years ago, but that did not mean she thought they should all pick up and move to Hammond House. She'd pick up a paintbrush her-self, rather than that. She'd pick up the ferret and dip its tail in the paint, rather than move to the viscount's grand house in Grosvenor Square. He was making it harder and harder to refuse, though.

"Paint fumes cannot be good for the children. They'd kill Aunt Mattie's canary for certain."

If the ferret or the rats didn't.

"Cook and Byrd will stay on here to oversee the workmen, to make sure the ferrets don't filch anything. Crafty little devils, don't you know. Most of the other servants you hired haven't been here long enough to earn paid vacations, and I'd hate to see them turned off if you and your aunt and the chil-dren put up at a hotel. If a decent inn would take you with the cat and the canary and Glad. I daren't leave Gladiator here where he might get into the poison."

Carissa agreed, but only because Glad wouldn't leave enough poison for the rats. The monstrous mongrel at a hotel? She could sooner imagine bald, barbaric Byrd butlering at Hammond House.

"And with the Season in midstride, I really do not wish to travel to Hart's Rest in Norfolk. No, it will have to be Ham-mond House."

"Pippa and I can go . . . go . . ." For the life of her, Carissa could not think of one place they could go, not without eating into her hoarded savings.

"And Lady Mathilda?"

She couldn't throw Aunt Mattie to the wolves, or the rodents. "But you cannot need a housekeeper there, my lord. We'll do better in a cottage somewhere, as I said."

"And I said I did not have time to find a suitable location. Besides, I am not asking you to work there. You'd be a guest, with no duties except for ensuring the children get all the care they need. You deserve the holiday after the wonders you've accomplished here. Oh, but my godmother might call on your assistance now and again, with her correspondence and such."

Now, that sounded more promising. Carissa had never considered becoming an old lady's companion because she doubted any would tolerate Pippa, but if his godmother took a liking to her daughter . . .

Then she remembered the perfect excuse for not taking up residence at the viscount's family home: the viscount's family. "You are forgetting Lady Hartleigh, my lord."

"I only wish I could," he muttered, but spoke up to say, "Agatha's health is uncertain, so she and her companions are leaving for Bath. Perhaps the waters there will improve her constitution." Or drown her.

The only uncertain thing about that woman's health, Carissa thought, was how she'd lived so long without being throttled. But if Lady Hartleigh was gone, so was her last chance of avoiding the move.

"Are you sure there are no mice at Hammond House?"

Chapter Twenty-three

*W*ere all men so stupidly stubborn? Were they born that way, or had a lifetime of authority made them think themselves invincible? Carissa had thought her father was intractable, but here was Lord Hartleigh, insisting she do precisely what she least wanted, because *he* decided she should be recognized by Society.

He was calling in every favor owed him, it seemed, to get her accepted, approved, even acclaimed for sacrificing herself for her daughter's sake. The retiring old lady Carissa had thought she was companioning turned out to be one of the leading doyennes of the Polite World. The viscount's godmother would be no less than a duchess, of course. And the few letters Mrs. Kane was supposed to be assisting with turned out to be hundreds of invitations to dinners, teas, and musicales—to introduce Carissa to the duchess's wide and lofty circle. If it wasn't miracle enough that anyone accepted the politely worded summonses, Her Grace of Castleberry had managed to convince Carissa's father to make her an allowance and to hand over a chest of her mother's jewelry. Macclesfield did not come in person—he wouldn't make that much of a concession—but he had added a note that Carissa's dressmaker's bills, modest ones, mind, should be sent to him. It wasn't seemly, he'd been persuaded in an uncomfortable interview with the duchess, for the viscount to be buying her shifts and stockings. It was seemly enough for her to starve, Carissa fumed, all the way to Bond Street to buy new wardrobes for herself, Pippa, and Aunt Mattie. Carissa did not suffer the least prick of conscience at spending the earl's money since she considered the expenditure to be her dowry that had never been paid out.

The earl's purse was one thing; the viscount's plotting was another. Carissa wanted to tell Lesley that his efforts would be in vain, that he should be looking about himself for a kind-hearted woman who would not mind mothering another fe-male's child, a woman from his own class, of impeccable reputation. Since Sue would not be cutting the rightful heir out of the succession or making the least dent in Hartleigh's deep coffers, many a wellborn miss would accept the baby if that was the price of a title and fortune. And how could anyone not love Sweet Sue? Or her father?

Carissa wanted to tell the viscount to stop thinking of her as that woman, to stop pushing her where she did not belong. He'd only be disappointed, although his suffering would not be deep inside, where Carissa was aching. No, he'd be dis-pleased, not devastated, to lose the mother he'd chosen for his child. Lord Hartleigh would not miss Carissa for any other reason, for he did not want her for any other purpose. That was a fact Carissa could not forget. Neither could she ever feel at-tractive or desirable again, no matter how many new gowns she had.

She wanted to tell him about Phillip so he would give up and let her go away before she was hurt worse, as she knew she'd be. But she never got the chance. Dress fittings and shopping took up hours of her time; socializing with the duchess's friends took up more, all to prove she was a well-behaved, proper female. It was not proper, the duchess informed her, for Carissa to be alone with Lord Hartleigh. She wanted no hint of misconduct, no tales for disloyal servants to carry. Therefore there were no private interviews. Aunt Mattie or the duchess was at Carissa's side, or Lesley was out of the house. She took tea with the dowagers; he took himself to White's. She was with the children; he was with his friends, for the duchess did not consider two youngsters, a nursemaid, and a footman ade-quate chaperonage. In fact, she decreed, any semblance of ap-pearing to be a family was to be thoroughly discouraged. Even

Pippa understood that was why Lord Hartleigh didn't take them riding anymore, having absorbed Her Grace's dictates.

Carissa knew they were all trying to restore her reputation, no matter how futile the effort. She also knew that she was seeing less and less of the viscount as she went out more in Society, where she'd never wanted to go. She was living in his house, missing him already, and he hadn't gone anywhere.

She had: to Lady Volsted's for tea, to Lady Quigley's for a poetry reading, to Lady Brockett's for silver loo. Like a raft without a rudder, she was being shoved, willy-nilly, into the sea of public scrutiny—right where Phillip Kane could find her.

She was in the park with the children that morning. The duchess never rose before midday, and for once Carissa was not required at the modiste's or the stationer's. There seemed to be fewer hours in the day than when she was working, so she was determined to enjoy this sunny morning with her daughter. She had no idea where the viscount was, since her elegant guest bedroom overlooked the rear gardens of Hammond House, not the bustling street. She would not dare inquire of Wimberly, the starchy butler, either. The man already thought she was an interloper, displacing his mistress. Carissa actually missed Byrd, and Cook's kitchen. Perhaps, if she ever got to speak to him, she could convince the viscount to let her return there shortly, as soon as the mice were gone.

Maisie was on a bench, rocking Sue's carriage and flirting with the young footman who was supposed to be holding Glad on a lead. The footman had eyes for no one but Maisie, and the dog, as usual, had his eyes on Pippa and the bread she had brought for the ducks.

Carissa was simply enjoying the sun, the relative privacy of the park in the morning, and her daughter's laughter, when she heard footsteps behind her. Hoping it was the viscount, for he often rode in the mornings, she turned around, a smile on her lips. The smile faded as she recognized her liveliest dread, her live husband.

"Landed in the clover this time, eh, darling?" He was boldly staring at her, assessing the value of her new sprigged muslin, the pearls at her neck, the ruched bonnet that could only have come from the hands of a master milliner. "Well, I forgive you for not meeting me the way you said you would, love, now that I see how you've been spending your hours and his lordship's blunt. I expect you'll have more than a pittance to give me this time, Carrie." Phillip reached out and fingered the strand of pearls.

His gloves were soiled, the edges of his coat were more frayed than when she'd seen him last, and he'd cut himself shaving. Carissa stepped back, her hand to her throat. "These are not mine. My father lent them to me from his estate, that's all. And he makes me a clothing allowance, nothing extravagant, I assure you."

Kane rubbed at the scabbed-over shaving cut. "So the old skint finally let loose the purse strings? Well, it ought to be mine, from your dowry, so I'll be having my share, a bit late is all. Hartleigh won't mind, not with his pots of gold." He reached for her fringed reticule.

Carissa pulled it away before he could grab the strings. "I have less money than before, since I cannot take wages from the viscount, not when I am a guest in his home. And my father pays my dressmaker bills, that's all. The pin money Macclesfield provides goes for everything else. I have no more to give you, Phillip, so you may as well stop asking. You are wasting your time."

"I don't believe you," he snarled. "Lord Heartless never let a mistress of his go without anything. That's why they all grovel at his feet. With enough blunt, a toff can have any woman he wants."

Carissa did not think that now was the time to mention that Lord Hartleigh's attraction had nothing to do with his wallet. She did say that she had decided not to give Kane any more money in any case. "If I had inherited a fortune from Sir Gilliam, perhaps I would have then, particularly if you were going to live with us, to make a proper home." She knew he wouldn't, which was the only reason she mentioned it, to placate him. Carissa did not think she could bear for him to touch her. Or to be near Pippa. For once she did not call her daughter back from the duck pond, no matter how near the edge she was. Better she get her feet wet than come face-to-face with this knave.

"I looked for that will, you know. Thought I could shake it out of that solicitor fellow, but he'd up and disappeared. Something rotten about that, I'd swear."

Carissa had thought so too, when Lesley related Bow Street's findings. "The constables have a description of the man who ransacked Gordon's office, you know. They wish to discuss the solicitor's absence with him."

"I didn't have anything to do with him taking a flit," Kane insisted. "He was involved with any number of unsavory deals, I heard. A lot of people might have wanted to see him unavailable for questioning, if you get my drift." He smiled, showing yellowed teeth. "And I bet they'll find Gordon's body adrifting in the Thames one of these days."

"In that case, perhaps you'd ought to go to Bow Street and tell them what you heard." Carissa wanted to see Phillip's reaction. An innocent man would volunteer the information to the authorities to clear himself from suspicion, unless he had worse to hide.

She was right: Phillip Kane was not getting within calling distance of a magistrate's office. He flicked his riding crop at a row of flowers, cutting the tops off. "And perhaps you're getting above yourself, Carrie. If I can't get that house in Kensington, I need a thousand pounds or so to find a new place, to set myself up in business."

"A thousand pounds?" Carissa had never seen that much money in her lifetime. "Where would I ever find that kind of fortune?"

"Lying around Hammond House, that's where. The pile is supposed to be filled with masterpieces and artifacts."

"Are you suggesting I steal something from Lord Hartleigh?"

"You don't have to steal. Smile pretty and ask your lover for it, or your father. Either one'd be happy to see the last of me."

168

But they never would see the last of him, once they'd given him a shilling. "No," she said. "I will not do that."

"Then I'll have to take the girl, I suppose. I hear certain men are willing to pay good money for an English chit."

Carissa was horrified. "What, you'd sell your own daughter into some kind of perverted bondage?"

"You can't deny she's mine to do with what I will, Carrie. And a fellow's got to live."

Why? Carissa was sure the rats at Lord Hartleigh's house felt they had a right to survive, too. "I will never let you take my daughter, Phillip. I'll have the magistrates after you faster than you can whistle."

"If they find me, and the lassie. They haven't in all these years. Keep moving, is the trick. Of course, I could have stayed put in the new gaming hell in Kensington, with a new name and all. I would have made my fortune. Damn you, Carrie, for letting that house slip through my hands!"

Carissa was beginning to think that perhaps Phillip Kane was not merely greedy and unscrupulous, but also unbalanced. She looked around nervously, but Sue was crying, and Maisie and the footman were walking the carriage up and down the path, farther away, trying to get the infant back to sleep. The privacy of a near-empty park was no longer so appealing to Mrs. Kane.

Then, right when she least wanted it, the dunderheaded dog lurched over to her to investigate the stranger, not out of any sense of protecting Carissa, of course, but to see if Phillip had any handouts. Wet from stealing the ducks' bread from the pond, Glad shook himself, spattering both Carissa and Phillip with feathers and fouled water.

"Damnation!" Phillip kicked out at Glad. He missed, but Gladiator was not one to suffer an insult. The hound growled and showed his teeth, then decided to help himself to a piece of Kane's boot, in lieu of a biscuit. Phillip was cursing and flailing at the dog with his riding whip, which incensed Glad further, so he moved his grip farther up Phillip's leg, getting a good jawful of trousers and flesh. Kane beat at the dog while Carissa tried to grab his arm, or Glad's collar, to drag the animal away to safety.

Then Pippa was there, with a handful of gingerbread she'd been saving. Glad released Kane's leg but stayed between the child and the man, snarling around a mouthful of cake.

Carissa's heart sank at having Pippa meet the man who'd fathered her. Or letting Kane near the child he thought of as chattel. Before she could think of how to separate them, though, Pippa looked up at Phillip and said, "You look like the picture of my papa. But he was a hero."

"Pippa, dear, take Glad over to Maisie," Carissa ordered before Phillip could say anything. "Tell her we are ready to leave."

Obedient as ever, Pippa held the dog's collar and led him away. Carissa turned to follow them.

"Not so fast, Carrie. How am I going to get my blunt?"

"Oh, go ask Broderick Parkhurst for it. Or Mason the butler. He'll know where Sir Gilliam's will is. Leave us alone."

"Why, so you can marry your swell? That's what all the finery is about, the gadding around Town, taking tea with duchesses. It's so no one can say he's marrying his whore. That's right, isn't it?"

"Go away, Phillip."

"Why should he have everything and I have nothing? No, I think I just might have to insist on my conjugal rights, unless I'm getting paid. Hartleigh won't want to share. He'll pay."

"You'd never go to him!"

"Oh, no? Then you'd better get the blunt." He had her by the arm, in a grip that would leave bruises. Carissa tried to get away, frightened in truth now, for Phillip Kane was not in his right senses. She did not want to scream lest she upset Pippa or bring her back to Kane's proximity. Nor did she want the young footman getting into a brawl in the park. So she struggled silently, digging her fingernails into the hand that gripped her arm.

Suddenly a rider tore up the path, leaped from his horse, and grabbed Kane by the back of his collar.

"Prepare to meet your maker, maggot," Lesley thundered, pulling back his right fist.

Chapter Twenty-four

*O*ne punch and the man was down. Instead of getting up to return the blow, Phillip put his hands to his bloody nose and cried, "No more!"

"What, you only fight women and dogs?" Lesley's heart was still pounding from seeing this dastard laying his hands on Carissa. He was ready to take on the entire French army, much less one sniveling skirter. "Get up and fight like a man, you lily-livered coward, you . . ." His eyes narrowed. "You're alive?"

Phillip mumbled that of course he was alive, but his nose was broken, no thanks to madmen attacking innocent strangers in the park.

"Cantwell? It is you, isn't it?"

Phillip's face drained of color, except for the claret pouring from his nose. He held a handkerchief over it and said, "I don't know what you're talking about."

Lesley hauled the man to his feet. "No? Well, I am sure the army will be more than happy to straighten things out, Lieutenant Cantwell."

"You are dicked in the nob, man. Tell him, Carrie. Tell your protector friend who I am."

Carissa's wits had gone begging. She looked from Lesley, who'd come hurtling out of nowhere, to her husband, who'd come back from the dead. She did not know what they were talking about, but Lud, this was not how she wanted to tell the viscount about Phillip.

"Tell him, Carrie," Phillip begged when he saw Hartleigh's fist clench again.

Looking as if he wanted to commit mayhem on her next, Lesley drawled, "Yes, *Carrie*, why don't you tell me who this useless scrap of offal is, so I can tell the army what to write on his grave after they hang him?"

"He is my husband, Phillip Kane. I don't know any Cantwells."

"And just when were you going to mention his existence, Widow Kane?"

Carissa waved to Pippa to stay near Maisie. "You have every right to be angry, but I was going to tell you, I swear. I just hadn't gotten around to it. You were gone so much, and we were never in private."

"We were deuced private when I asked you to marry me," he almost spit out while Kane was busy mopping at his nose. "You could have told me then, instead of letting me think it was myself you were rejecting!"

She'd file his hurt feelings away to examine later. "He said he was rejoining his regiment, but he never did. He abandoned me when I was increasing, and I was destitute. I had to give some excuse to people, so I said my husband was lost in the war. Phillip stayed gone, so I assumed he'd never come back. In a few years I could have had him declared dead, and no one would have known any different. Then he showed up in Kensington, that day you saw him. I swear I thought Phillip was dead until then. And I was too ashamed and too afraid to tell anybody."

"You weren't the only one he abandoned. The army has been looking to court-martial the dastard since before you met him, if they don't just shoot him out of hand."

"He's a deserter? I thought he'd invented his whole army career when the regimental office had no record of him."

"That's because he was using a different name. Phillip Cantwell left his comrades to die in battle."

Phillip had stopped the bleeding by now. "We were cannon fodder, nothing else, meant to hold the line until the blasted cavalry showed up. Should I have died along with the rest?"

"It would have saved the army the cost of a trial."

"If you hand me over to the authorities, you can be sure I'll tell them all about your little paramour, my loving wife. You won't like your dirty linen aired that way, Hartleigh."

"It will be worth it to see you hang, Cantwell. Then she'll be a widow in truth."

Phillip laughed. "Only till they put a noose around her neck for aiding and abetting a known criminal. I'll swear on my deathbed that Carrie knew I was wanted and knew I was alive the whole time."

"I never did!" Carissa cried. "I swear!"

"Why, you saw her give me the money yourself, Hartleigh. Helping me stay one jump ahead of the magistrates."

"I gave you the money to go away, nothing else."

He turned to her, curling his lip. "Who's going to be believed, darling? You saw a chance to snabble a title if you were a widow, so you paid me to disappear. I saved you from committing bigamy, is all."

"I saved myself because I always feared you'd be back. That's why I didn't marry Sir Gilliam, or accept your offer, Lesley." She turned back to Phillip. "And I don't care what you say or who you say it to. I hope they hang you!"

The footman had looped the reins of Hartleigh's horse around a bush, then returned to Maisie and the children, but he was keeping a careful watch. Careful enough to hear a word or two. So Lesley drew Carissa away a bit and asked, "Are you sure? If I hand him to the army, he will spew every drop of poison he can think of. I could have him impressed into the navy. He'd be gone long enough to be declared legally dead, if he survives at all. Many do not."

"No, he'd survive, and I would know he was alive. I'd never be free. Pippa would never be safe."

"You're right. I could, ah, dispatch him myself, though, before he spouts his filth. It would be a pleasure."

"What, become a murderer?" She pulled on his arm. "You must not! I would never forgive myself if you had that on your conscience the rest of your days. Besides, then you could go to jail, for everyone would know he wouldn't fight back. No, it is better for the army to handle this if he was a deserter. I will leave London before any of the ugliness lands on your doorstep, or Her Grace's. I only pray Pippa never finds out what her father was."

Lesley patted her hand, on his sleeve. "Very well, Carissa, he goes to the army. But you are not going anywhere."

"And neither are you, Hartleigh," Phillip shouted. While Lesley's back was turned, he'd pulled a pistol out of his pocket and now bashed the viscount over the head with it. Lesley went down and Carissa started to scream, until Phillip warned, "One more sound and I kill him. They can only hang me once." He snatched up the reins to Lesley's horse and jumped into the saddle. He called to her as he galloped past, "I'll be back for what's mine, darling."

Sue and Pippa were both crying, the footman was running after the armed madman on the stolen horse, so Maisie was shrieking, and Lesley lay on the ground with his head in Carissa's lap, bleeding all over her new gown, while the dog licked his face. It was a good thing the duchess had warned them there must be no hint of impropriety.

Tears were streaming down Carissa's cheeks until she saw the viscount's eyes open. The rogue had the nerve to smile at her, after frightening her nearly to death. She jumped up, letting his poor broken head fall back into the dirt, and shouted at him, "I told you I didn't belong in London!"

"Never turn your back on a jackal, Cap'n. How many times have I told you that?" Byrd shook his bald head, the seagull tattoo flying from side to side, he was that angry at missing the set-to. He should have been there, defending his master. For sure the viscount had made mincemeat of it. And his noggin. "You had to be the fine gentleman, expecting everyone else to play by the rules. You deserve to have your skull cracked."

Byrd was clipping the matted hair away from the wound on Hartleigh's head so he could clean it. Lesley was cringing with every snip of the shears. "Damn, go easy with the scissors. It'll never grow back."

Carissa had sent for Byrd the second they were back at Hammond House, figuring that the old sailor would know better than any sawbones what the viscount needed, having

174

been in so many brawls himself. She was standing by with clean towels and warm water. She knew her complexion was turning green as the water in the basin turned red, but Byrd nodded approvingly. "You've got bottom, at least, missus. Not like that silly chit Maisie. She set up such a screeching, 'twould be a wonder iffen the infant's milk don't curdle."

The duchess was prostrate with her smelling salts, and Aunt Mattie had swooned altogether at the first sight of Lord Hartleigh, as the footmen half carried him into the house.

The Bow Street investigators had been by, and the sergeant major of the local army barracks. Carissa had given them Phillip's portrait, telling Pippa that since the bad man in the park looked so much like her papa, the miniature would make their job that much easier.

"Don't worry, Mrs. Kane," Inspector Nesbitt had assured her. "We'll find Cantwell, by George."

Carissa was not convinced. She would not let Pippa leave the house, no matter how many extra guards and footmen Lesley hired, nor would she herself go out. The man was unsteady, but he was not stupid. After all, he'd avoided capture all these years, hadn't he? He could grow a moustache or wear a wig, and walk right past a watchman holding his picture. No, they were not safe, and neither was the viscount now.

"Besides," she told Lesley, trying to convince him to let her leave, "if they catch him, there will be a dreadful scandal. I would not bring such a disgrace on your house."

"There will be no scandal," he said through clenched teeth as Byrd poured spirits in the wound.

"No scandal? You must be concussed after all if you think this is a simple matter of some deb running off with her groom. The only way people will stop talking is if I am not here for them to dissect."

"Lassie's got a point, Cap'n."

"And no one asked your opinion, Byrd. Ouch! Dash it, Carissa, just where would you go, where you and Pippa could be protected, where a bumblebroth won't matter?"

"I have been thinking, and I've decided that my father will just have to take us in. Not here in London, of course, but at

Macclesfield Park in Somerset. The dower house is empty, so he wouldn't have to look at us. A groom or two with pistols would be enough of a guard in the country, where no stranger can go unremarked."

"He might not be unnoticed, but a bedlamite like Cantwell won't be stopped by a farmer with a pitchfork, either. And I'd wager that's where he'll look for you first, chickens returning to roost. That's why the fox is seldom hungry, Carissa. No, you'll stay right here until my head stops spinning and I can figure what's best to do."

"There is no reason for me to stay, I tell you. You've proved to the ton that I am a lady. That's what you wanted, isn't it? Now he'll prove you foisted an imposter on them, a liar and a cheat and a fortune hunter."

"Deuce take it, you are none of those things! You were a victim, by heaven. And I tell you, there will be no disgrace. You mightn't have been married to the rotter in the first place!"

Even Byrd stopped his patchwork to listen more carefully.

"That's right," Lesley explained. "Cantwell was the deserter; you married Kane. If it turns out that his real name was Cantwell, or something else entirely, then your marriage vows were invalid in the eyes of the law. And you weren't with him long enough to be considered a common-law wife, either. I have men checking on the legalities right now, along with parish records and Cantwell's enlistment papers. If you weren't married to him, you cannot be tarred with the same brush."

"Not married? You mean I was never legally wed?"

"Exactly. Phillip Kane never existed," he said with a pleased grin, until Byrd started stitching his scalp back together.

Carissa was horrified. Not that the big man was taking bigger stitches with her best sewing needle, but over the viscount's words. "But that makes Pippa illegitimate!"

"Only until I can change her name to mine."

"Change her name?"

"When we marry, Carissa. Haven't you been listening? I am the one with the battered brain box, not you. You are free to wed, or will be as soon as the legal chaps get the mess straightened out. We'll get a special license. My name will protect both of you from any gossip, and then I can make sure you're safe."

Free to wed? To wed Lesley? For a moment she caught a glimpse of heaven, then fell back to earth with a crash. "Safe on account of a special license? What makes you think that a scrap of paper will bother Phillip Kane? You are as cork-brained as he is. A marriage certificate did not keep him with me; it will not keep him away. Besides, no court can deny that Pippa is his child. What if he decides to claim her as his own?"

"He cannot claim anything, goose. He is a wanted man, a criminal. He'd be up on charges simply for striking a peer in the park."

"Yes, but I am not so certain I wish to declare my daughter born out of wedlock."

"My daughter was."

"But I am not a light-skirt, my lord."

He shook his head, then groaned. "No one said you were, dash it. Hell and damnation, I should have killed the cur when I had him."

"And what if he'd killed you? He was the one with the pistol, not you, Lesley. And you heard Byrd. Phillip would not have fought fair. I'd rather be his wife than have you dead."

"You are not that dastard's wife, blast it!"

Chaper Twenty-five

Carissa sank into despair. She'd never be free of the cloud that was Phillip Kane. Lesley sank back into depravity and debauchery. If Phillip Kane wished to find him, he'd be easy to spot at the clubs, the gaming hells, the low dives. Besides, the viscount had unfinished business.

He was not so lost to sanity that he went unarmed. Lesley did not carry a pistol, since, still seeing double occasionally, he feared shooting Wimberly the butler by accident. Then again . . . But he did take his sword stick, and he did take Byrd.

He also took a heavy purse. When he could not wager for what he wanted, he purchased it outright. In a matter of days the viscount had bought up a fortune in vowels signed by Broderick Parkhurst. The holders of the notes were pleased, for they never thought to see a ha'penny of their winnings else. No one knew how large Sir Gilliam's fortune had been, but young Broderick could have bankrupted Golden Ball.

When he had them all, or enough to purchase an abbey, Lesley and Byrd paid a call in Kensington. They went in the morning, without stopping to change their clothes, since that was the only time Parkhurst was liable to be home.

The schoolteachers next door were returning from their morning constitutional, little terrier in tow. They sneered. Leslie let Glad off his lead.

"Damn, Cap'n, I never seen a dog climb a tree that way."

"That isn't a dog, Byrd. It's a fur-ball with feet. Good boy, Glad."

He used the knob of his walking stick to rap on the door of Parkhurst's house, then waited.

"Seems like no one's to home, Cap'n."

"Nonsense." He rapped again. Carissa wanted this blasted house, and by Jupiter, she was going to get it. She'd never live there, no, and nowhere Lesley wasn't, for that matter, but she should have whatever her heart desired, as he fully intended to do. He no longer wanted a respectable woman to rear his daughter and his eventual heir, a responsible female he could install in the country and visit occasionally. The viscount had finally stopped fooling himself, and none too soon, as Byrd was the first to tell him.

He wanted Mrs. Kane. Not for his daughter, not for Carissa's demure dignity or her daughter, and not because he'd damaged her reputation. He wanted her for herself, for himself. And he wanted her badly enough to move heaven and earth, or that muckworm Mason, out of his way.

"Mr. Parkhurst is not at home," Mason told them when he got around to opening the door. There were no other servants and the place looked like Parkhurst had tried to ride his horse through it, with about as much success as he usually had atop a horse. The clunch would fall off Blackie, the viscount thought.

Mason was looking out of sorts, as well he might with the house going to rack and ruin after he'd lied and cheated to get it away from Mrs. Kane. Likely Parkhurst had reneged on their agreement about sharing the wealth too, the way he had reneged on paying his gambling debts.

"Oh, he'll be home to me," Lesley said, waving a sheaf of papers with Parkhurst's signature on them. Mason obviously recognized the writing, for his rat-black eyes narrowed. He opened the door and stood aside for Lesley and Byrd. He shut it again in Gladiator's face.

Broderick Parkhurst was not as inebriated as he wished to be, when Hartleigh entered his bedroom. Byrd stayed by the open door, arms crossed over his massive chest in case Parkhurst decided he'd rather not pay attention to what Lord Hartleigh was about to say, or in case Mason was paying too much attention.

Parkhurst might not have read a hand of cards right in a

179

month, but he could read trouble on Hartleigh's face. "I don't have your woman and I don't owe you anything. Go away."

"You are wrong, as usual." Lesley tossed the stack of gaming chits onto the bed. There were so many, Broderick's nose barely poked out of the mound. He pushed them away, holding one near his bloodshot eyes with the arm that was not in a plaster cast. "Oh."

"Oh indeed. How did you think you were going to pay all of these? And the tradesmen's bills, your account at Tattersall's, the stables for your breakdowns."

"I thought I'd come about. One big win is all it takes, you know. M'friends thought so, too. Kept finding new places for me to try, to change m'luck, don't you know."

"I know you've been fleeced royally, by every Captain Sharp and ivory tuner in town. That's who I purchased your vowels from."

"You mean they cheated?"

"The same way you cheated Mrs. Kane."

"The housekeeper? Uncle's convenient? Your doxy? What's she got to do with these?" Broderick ruffled some of the papers together.

"Nothing, you jackass, except it was her money you gambled away with your so-called friends. Now it is time to repay her for the wrong you've done. I would strongly suggest you not mention her name so disrespectfully again in my hearing."

Broderick held up his broken arm and looked toward Byrd, standing in the doorway still. "You might as well go ahead and get it over with, beat me to a pulp or whatever you have in mind, 'cause I couldn't afford to pay for candles, much less this king's ransom. Besides, if you don't kill me, the moneylenders will, or Mason."

"What, not paying your partner his share? No honor among thieves and all that, I suppose. And you've been to the usurers, besides? Lud, how did you survive this long with sawdust for brains? No, don't tell me. I have wasted enough time over this claptrap as is. I have a bargain for you, Parkhurst, so listen carefully. I will make good on your debts, on three conditions.

One, you sign over the deed to this house to Mrs. Kane. Two, you sign a statement that you were aware Sir Gilliam had another will. And three, you leave the country forever."

"I say, that's not much of a bargain!"

"On the other hand, I could have you thrown in debtors' prison for the rest of your short life, claim the house in lieu of my payment, and have you charged with any number of felonies, including the disappearance of your solicitor, Nigel Gordon. Or I could just hand you to Byrd."

None of those sounded too inviting either. "But . . . but how am I to live?"

Lesley didn't care. To expedite the transaction, however, he was willing to make a concession or two. "I'll arrange passage for you to America, where I have an interest in a stud farm in Virginia. They are always needing help with the horses." Lesley didn't say they needed assistance in the stables, shoveling manure, which was as close as this clunch was going to get to any decent horseflesh.

Parkhurst was wise enough to take the deal, after another look at Byrd. Lesley wrote out the documents and Broderick managed to sign them, with Byrd as witness. They left while Parkhurst was on his knees, trying to start a fire to burn the IOUs.

"You might want to help your employer with his packing," Lesley told Mason on their way out. "And ask him for a reference. I can guarantee Mrs. Kane will not be keeping you on." He'd made Parkhurst swear not to reveal the incriminating confession, so the magistrate could arrest the butler and search his rooms before he escaped.

Byrd wanted to make sure Cook was managing the painting crew, and Lesley wanted to send a message to Bow Street, telling them he had the proof they needed to get a warrant, so they headed toward Hartleigh's town house.

They could hear the shouting as they crossed the street.

Parkhurst came flying out of the house in his white nightshirt. Mason was close behind him, brandishing a stiletto in one hand, a pistol in the other. Parkhurst ran down the path and into the street, bumping into the Misses Applegate on their way back from the park, the trembling terrier looking both ways from its perch against the elder sister's bony chest. Parkhurst wove through carriages and wagons in the thoroughfare, Mason on his heels. Broderick, full white bedgown flapping against skinny, hairy legs, leaped in front of a passing horseman. The startled horse reared and the startled rider slid off its back, using words the Applegates had never heard, in all their years of teaching.

Parkhurst grabbed the reins with his one good arm and jumped aboard the crow-hopping horse. Mason stopped his mad pursuit and tried to take aim around the unhorsed rider, the walkers, the wagons, the girl selling violets on the corner, and the neighborhood brats throwing a ball. His first shot hit the streetlamp, which sent glass flying in every direction. The rider kept swearing, the girl tossed her flowers in the air, the children shrieked, one wagon overturned, the Applegates screamed, the terrier yapped—and Glad, covered in dirt, came bounding out of the bushes behind Parkhurst's house, right into the path of Parkhurst on his stolen steed.

The gudgeon's neck was not broken, Byrd declared, though he'd likely have a decided crick to it when he woke up, if he woke up. Mason was not among the crowd gathered around the inert body or huddled along the edge of the road. In all the confusion of the street, Mason had disappeared. Bow Street had his address, though, Lesley knew, so the murderous manservant could wait. Meanwhile, the viscount was checking to see who else was injured, who merely affronted. He sent for the watch, a physician, the magistrate, and someone to sweep up the glass, shouting to be heard over the melee.

Byrd picked up Parkhurst's unconscious body and was carrying him into Hartleigh's house. "Can't leave him lying in the street, Cap'n. Might cause another accident. Don't think he'd last long at his own place, either, with no help or Mason's. A' course, I don't blame that Mason for wanting to pop him none, public service, like."

So Hartleigh invited the others in for a restorative and for Cook to extract glass splinters until the sawbones arrived. Before following, Lesley bought up the violets—he offered a bunch to the Applegates and was refused—helped soothe the nervous horses, helped right the tinker's wagon, and chased off the ragamuffins who thought they could help themselves to the toppled tinware.

Finally pouring himself a drink, and incidentally noticing that his hand was cut, Lesley smelled smoke. This was not the usual coal smoke, nor wood-stove smoke, nor London's habitual stink. And it was thick enough to be casting a shadow on Hartleigh's newly painted walls.

He rushed outside again with Byrd right behind him, and Cook with her rolling pin. Everyone else poured out of the little house too, except for Parkhurst, of course, who hadn't regained consciousness.

Parkhurst's house was on fire, with black smoke billowing out the door. Either the nodcock had not placed his mounds of canceled debts in the hearth properly or he had not opened the damper. Or else Mason had decided that if he couldn't have the house, no one could. The antique carpets, the old wood paneling, the brocaded draperies, all went up like tinder while a crowd gathered on the lawn.

But where was Mason?

Lesley handed his coat to Byrd, who shouted, "You can't be thinking of risking your life for the likes of him, Cap'n! He ain't worth it. The bastard will roast now or in hell later, makes no never mind."

But it mattered to the viscount. Holding his handkerchief over his nose, he raced into the house while Byrd kept shouting and Cook cried.

The stair rail was starting to scorch, but the stairs appeared untouched so far. Lord Hartleigh found his way through the thick smoke up to the attics, calling Mason's name. He went down the service stairs to the kitchens, still shouting although his throat was raw. He could hardly breathe through the smoke, or see where he was going. The fire seemed to be spreading outward from three places, leaving Lesley with few escape routes. He could hear bells and whistles from the fire brigade, but they would not be on time to save anything but the brick shell.

Giving up, Lesley staggered out the back door, the one Mason had always thought he should use anyway. Coughing, wiping his eyes, he almost stumbled on Mason's body, half in a freshly dug hole, half in the pile of loose dirt with Gladiator's wide paw prints in it. A dug-up azalea bush lay next to Mason, and the pistol. He'd evidently gone out the back, tripped in one of Gladiator's holes, and accidentally pulled the trigger, killing himself.

Good dog, Glad.

"That's it. Pippa and I are leaving. London is too dangerous. Guns and fires and knives and madmen everywhere." And lots of violets in her lap.

Lesley had a cut on his hand, a burn on his cheek, and a cough. Byrd had a bruised jaw from urging the fire brigade— all fifteen members at once—to enter the house when he thought the viscount might still be inside. Cook was near hysterics, Parkhurst had been hauled away to hospital, and Glad needed another bath. They were in the kitchen of the viscount's Kensington property, where everything was spattered, sooted, and in disarray. One of the messengers had had enough sense to send for Mrs. Kane, along with the authorities.

"It's all my fault," she declared. "None of this would have happened if you hadn't tried to help me!"

"You?" Lesley lifted the damp towel off his aching eyes. "I was the one who let Mason and the muttonhead burn down your house. Can you forgive me?"

"It wasn't my house, you fool!" Carissa cried. "It wasn't my house."

"Yes, it was. Here's the deed." He fumbled in his coat, which Byrd had thrown around his shoulders. "I don't think it got near the fire or the water. I'm not sure about the glass or Parkhurst's blood."

Carissa looked at the piece of paper that gave her free and clear title to a burned-out shell of a building, a piece of paper that this impossible man could have died for. "You did that for me?"

He tried to give her the old rakish, raffish smile that had turned women up sweet since he was in short pants. She hit him with Cook's skillet.

Chapter Twenty-six

*Th*ey were going to Hart's Rest, the Hartleigh country seat in Norfolk. They were all going: Cook and Byrd and all the new maids and footmen, half of Bow Street's Runners (the half that wasn't searching for Cantwell in London), a bunch of youngsters from the foundling home, and two girl children big with child, with no husbands.

Pippa's pony was going, as was Blackie, Aunt Mattie and her canary, Carissa's vast new wardrobe, the baby's crib, cradle, and carriage, in case there was nothing suitable in all of Norfolk, and Lesley's dueling pistols.

They were a cavalcade of four carriages, three wagons, and scores of outriders. They might as well send Phillip Kane an invitation, Carissa crossly thought. She resented it all, especially how she had to ride in the stuffy, closed carriage with Aunt Mattie and her canary, who could not be subject to drafts. Cleo was furious at being kept in her basket, and Pippa was back to sucking her thumb. The baby was fussy and Maisie was getting motion sickness. Lord Hartleigh, meanwhile, got to ride in his shiny curricle, driving his shiny team, while everyone else followed in his dust. The viscount and his man got to be in the open air, happy as larks, with the loutish dog between them.

Carissa wanted to be going home to her father, not going to another of Lord Hartleigh's holdings. She knew it was foolish, to be wishing to return to the security of childhood, but she knew the neighborhood, knew the neighbors. Her father would have to let her stay.

Instead she was traveling into uncharted territory with an attics-to-let champion. With a misguided sense of honor, in her opinion, Lord Hartleigh had developed the nonsensical notion that he was responsible for her well-being. She knew Lesley could not wish to continue her acquaintance, not with the mess she'd landed him in, the scandal, the danger, the destruction. He could not wish to marry her, she was positive, not after she'd lied to him. Carissa knew she could never marry anyone she thought might be less than truthful, not a second time.

"If I were connected to that loose screw," he told her when she tried again at the first stop to convince him to let her go on alone, "I'd lie about it too. Why, if anyone asks me about Agatha and the Spillhammer sisters, I deny any relation. I do it all the time, without a bit of guilt." He touched her cheek with one gloved hand. "It's going to be all right, Carissa. You'll see."

"You wouldn't lie to me?" She was asking a lot.

He answered a little: "Why should I? You already know about Agatha."

When they arrived at the country house, which had twenty bedrooms in the guest wing, Carissa was too busy with today to worry about tomorrow. The house had been in the Hartleigh family for generations; so had the staff. The housekeeper wasn't the least offended by Carissa's offer to help, taking the opportunity instead to nurse her rheumatics. The equally ancient butler was happy to share his door-keeping duties with Byrd, what with all the comings and goings. The place had not seen so much activity since Lesley's father's funeral. After that solemn event, the new widow had taken herself to London and had never been back. Master Lesley had been away at school, then on his travels. The servants were not used to babies, children, or pets, to say nothing of armed guards. Three of the oldest, including the house steward and the cook, opted to accept their retirement pensions and moved into one of the numerous cottages scattered about the vast estate. The head gardener took one look at Gladiator and joined them.

Carissa had to find rooms for everyone, see that the children were settled comfortably, and divide up the work to be done among the old servants and the new. The house hadn't had a good cleaning in years, and the linens were in disrepair. She was so busy she did not have time to realize that she was a virtual prisoner at the estate, never allowed out of doors without a guard or the viscount at her side. She was also so busy that she never noticed that the kitchen cat was a tom. Cleopatra noticed.

Lesley, meanwhile, was organizing his troops to defend his castle, as it were. He also rode over the whole estate, visiting with the tenant families he'd grown up among, asking them to keep an eye out for strangers. Sometimes he took Carissa along in the curricle, sometimes he invited her and Pippa both to accompany him on his rounds on horseback. In all instances, Byrd or Nesbitt or another of the Bow Street gentlemen rode behind. Sometimes Jem, the head groom, followed too.

Pippa had the run of the kitchen garden, the knot garden, and the walled garden, when one of her guards was present. In no time she was berry-brown and her hair was sun-streaked. Aunt Mattie made the acquaintance of the vicar and his wife, who returned her calls. Soon other neighbors, the squire and his family, a retired general's widow, Lord Halbersham and his lady, who was breeding and so missing the Season, all started leaving cards and sending invitations. There were dinner parties, evenings of whist, dances at the local assembly, lawn picnics, and boating parties. Carissa was accepted as Lesley's guest. If anyone speculated further, they did it amongst themselves, not in her hearing. Everyone commended Hartleigh for taking in his "foundling" ward, so even the presence of his byblow was not dampening their welcome.

The tenants were pleased to see their landlord take up residence, for improvements got planned, investments got made in stock and tools, and problems were listened to, without waiting for the estate manager to contact his lordship in London. They would have been happy to see him if he'd brought his opera dancer to Norfolk. A well-bred, lovely lady had them hoping that Lord Heartless would settle at long last. Soon the farm wives were asking Carissa's opinions on recipes and roses, rearing children and reading lessons for their own daughters. With Lesley's approval and endowment, she set up a school for girls to match the boys' classes.

Everyone was kind, everything was blossoming. Life was good, better than Carissa felt she deserved, except for the ever-present threat of Phillip Kane. Like a nagging toothache, he could not be forgotten. There were no reports from Bow Street yet, no sightings, no arrests. Carissa watched Pippa exercise her pony on the front lawn, under Jem's tutelage, while Aunt Mattie napped on a chaise longue and Maisie rocked the baby in her carriage. She wished she could be as carefree as the others. Even her cat was getting fat and lazy.

Lesley had not mentioned marriage again. Carissa told herself he must have changed his mind, after reflection, choosing the much wiser course. Then she told herself he was merely waiting for the barristers to decide if she was a wife, a widow, or an unwed mother. She didn't want to hurry the verdict, wishing this idyll could go on forever.

It couldn't.

Sue was ill one day, feverish and fussing, and she would not eat. Carissa thought she was simply teething, but Lesley insisted the doctor be sent for. Until he arrived, they were taking turns walking with her, sponging her hot face, singing lullabies, both of them out of tune. Pippa was missing her ride with the viscount, her lesson with her mother, her walk with Maisie, so Aunt Mattie offered to take her along to play with the vicarage children. Jem would drive them in the carriage, naturally, and Pippa knew never to wander off by herself, so Carissa agreed.

The vicar and his wife had five children, one a little girl a year older than Pippa, the first young friend she had ever had. The rest were boys who had a wonderful collection of injured rabbits, broken-winged birds, frogs, and garden snakes in their old barn. They even had a pet hedgehog that would take seeds out of one's hand. After the animals were all picked up and petted, the children started a game of hide-and-go-seek around the barn. Only they never did find Pippa.

Every soul within miles was enlisted in the search, everyone who could ride and carry a weapon, that is, for Kane had to be desperate to steal his own daughter, and desperate men were the most dangerous. Riders were sent to outlying farms, abandoned cottages, and woodsman's shacks. Kane could not have gone so far, Lesley swore to Carissa, that they would not find him. Inspector Nesbitt assured her that Kane wasn't going to harm the child, that he undoubtedly only wanted to hold her for ransom. A note would arrive soon, he believed, and had his men hide in bushes near the house. Guilt-ridden that he'd taken the carriage horses to the blacksmith while Lady Mathilda had her visit, Jem was one of them, vowing to see the vermin hanged. Byrd sharpened his knife.

The note came a few hours later, before Carissa had time for full-blown hysterics, but via no messenger who could be questioned. A rock had been tossed through the schoolhouse window. One of the boys had lathered his pony riding to Hart's Rest to deliver the message tied to it.

Come alone, it said, *or the brat dies. Bring 2,000 pounds to the turnpike crossroads tomorrow at 9 A.M.*

"Good," Leslie said, "that means he is still in the neighborhood. We have all afternoon and night to find him."

"You cannot," Carissa protested. "He'll hurt Pippa!"

Lesley grasped her shoulders. "You'll have to trust me, Carissa. I would never do anything to jeopardize your daughter. You must know that by now."

She looked into his blue eyes and nodded. Besides, she did not need him or Nesbitt to warn her that Pippa's safety was not assured even if they did everything Kane wanted. The man was insane and had no sense of honor. "Very well, we'll try to find him. But where? You've sent riders in every direction, and none report anyone seeing him anywhere."

"I have an idea. Do not get your hopes up, but remember that I grew up in this neighborhood. Kane did not."

He left to give instructions for a squadron of armed men to spend the night at the crossroads, hiding behind bushes, up in trees if need be, to lay an ambush for Kane in the morning, in case they missed him this afternoon.

He returned with pistols in his pocket, sword buckled at his waist, and a fight on his hands. "No, you are not going. Nor you, Byrd. I need you here to coordinate all the other searchers and to get the best marksmen well hidden." Byrd merely told him to watch his back. Lesley assigned some of the others to stay to guard the house and the womenfolk. "I would not put it past that bastard to double back, intent on thievery while he thinks we are scouring the countryside. Come, Glad."

" 'Come, Glad'? You'd take the dog and not me?" Carissa was outraged. "The note was addressed to me. Pippa is my daughter."

It was his money, but Lesley didn't say so. He said it was too dangerous, instead. But he was telling it to her back, for Mrs. Kane was already outside, mounted.

Lesley hauled the dog onto his own saddle and mounted behind, calming the horse's fidgets at the unaccustomed weight. Glad sat like a maharaja on an elephant, long ears waving.

They rode back to the vicar's barn and dismounted. The viscount showed Glad one of Pippa's stockings that he'd had Carissa bring and told the dog to go find her.

"That's your plan?" Carissa wanted to know as they watched the dog circle the barn, nose to the ground, which wasn't all that far, considering his short legs. "To follow the hell-hound after hares? Gladiator could not find his tail if it weren't affixed to his rear end."

Lesley led his horse after the dog. "You have merely mistaken laziness for stupidity. Glad has an amazing nose. He can find a lamb chop two miles away; he'll find Pippa. Watch."

Soon enough, Glad had left the vicarage property and was heading up a deer path through a wooded region.

"Rabbits," Carissa scoffed, but followed.

Every few yards Glad would stop and sniff at the ground, then lick his lips. Lesley watched more carefully, then called back: "I was right! He's on their trail. Look, Carissa. Gingerbread crumbs. Pippa knew we'd be coming! What a brilliant child!"

Carissa could only think how frightened the little girl must be. She also vowed to have Cook keep a steady supply of steaks for the dog. As for the viscount, she could not imagine how she could make this up to him. He hadn't hesitated an instant to face down her demons, and pay for the privilege. She did not think she could ever love anyone more.

Lesley was pleased, for he thought he knew where the dog was heading. As he told Carissa, there was a decrepit shack hidden in the woods, where an old poacher, Mortimer, had settled. Lesley's father had permitted the encroachment because Mortimer had kept other trespassers away. He and the viscount had had a gentleman's agreement that Mortimer wouldn't use traps, interfere with Hartleigh's fox-hunting, or sell what he shot. In return, the viscount had pretended he did not know of Mortimer's existence. Both old men had been gone for years, and Lesley wondered if the place had stood empty since then or if some other hungry felon had discovered it. Perhaps a drifter had directed Kane to the rude shelter. It would be torn down before the week was out.

When they got nearer the area where he recalled the shack to be located, Lesley indicated they should tether the horses and proceed on foot, silently. Of course, Glad barged ahead, baying. Lesley shrugged and took Carissa's hand for comfort as they reached a small clearing. The remains of a rough stone cottage were in a heap, but the windowless wooden shed where old Mortimer must have kept a cow or a goat was still standing. And standing outside it was Phillip Kane, holding Pippa in front of him, with a pistol pressed against her temple. Lesley squeezed Carissa's hand, then slowly raised both of his above his head, away from the pistols or the sword.

"I knew you'd come," Kane said, ignoring Carissa. "Just the kind of mock heroics I'd expect from a prime goer like you, Hartleigh. Get in." He gestured them to go past him, into the thatched shed. Glad darted between them, trying to get to Pippa's pockets.

"Call him off, Hartleigh, or I'll shoot him."

Lesley whistled for Glad to come to him, but said, "Oh, I doubt that. Then your pistol would be useless, wouldn't it? You might have to fight me like a man."

Kane wasn't taking the gun away from Pippa's head. "Did you bring it, my two thousand pounds?"

Lesley nodded and slowly lowered one hand to his waistcoat

and withdrew a purse. "It's not the entire amount, just what I had in the house. But I've done better. I put in a letter for my yacht's crew. They'll take you anywhere you want to go." So long as it was down. "And we finally got the deed to Parkhurst's house. That's here, too."

"But the house is bur—" Carissa began.

"Being painted," Lesley quickly said. He tossed the purse wide, hoping to make Kane release Pippa to retrieve it, but the man stooped and told her to pick it up.

"You have what you wanted, Kane. Now let the girl go."

Kane was making his way to the doorway, his eyes on the viscount, his pistol on Pippa. "I let her go and I'm a dead man, Hartleigh. I'm not that big a fool. The chit is my safe passage."

"No!" Carissa screamed.

"Touching, *cara mia,* but the brat goes with me. Besides, she is my own flesh and blood. My darling daughter, isn't that right, Pippy?"

Pippa turned to look up at him. "My lord promised he'd be my papa," she said. "Not you."

"Well, then, to show there's no hard feelings, I'll make you a wedding present, Carrie. I'll leave the chit at the crossroads for you, like I said. The brat would only slow me down, anyway."

"It will be dark! You cannot leave her there."

He ignored her pleas. "And I'll even put some of my papers on a body somewhere when I get a chance, so the authorities can say I died. Clever, huh? You and your lover can thank me. For now you'll stay put here. Someone might come find you when the chit tells them. Then again, she might not remember the way or have any more bread crumbs." He shrugged. "That'll be too bad."

He backed out of the opening, holding Pippa like a shield, then slammed the door shut, barring it from the outside. Carissa rushed to the door and began pounding on it, crying, until Lesley pulled her away. "You've got to be brave, sweetheart."

"Oh, no, I don't, you clunch! I can be as frightened as I want! I simply have to do what is necessary to get my daughter back, but I do not have to be brave and you must not ask it of me! I refuse to try!"

"I believe you have just defined courage, my love. You'll do. Now let's figure a way out of here."

Chapter Twenty-seven

Lesley had his flint, and the old thatched roof would burn easily, but there was no guaranteeing that they wouldn't die before they could get out. He used his sword to poke at the lowest corner of the shed, where some of the thatch had fallen in. Two mice tumbled to the floor, and Carissa screamed and clutched his arm in a death grip. "Set the roof on fire! It's better than this!"

But Glad had chased the mice across the dirt floor to a hole that tunneled to the outside. He was digging furiously, trying to catch the escaping morsels. "That's the ticket, Glad," Lesley encouraged him. "Dig. We'll get that dastard yet." He used his sword to loosen the dirt and his hands to pull it away. He wasn't as fast as the dog, but he was more efficient.

"We'll be too late," Carissa mourned, trying to stand back from the flying dirt. "He has too much of a head start on us. At least we will get to Pippa before she can be stolen by Gypsies or eaten by wolves or—"

Lesley kept digging. "He has a lead, but I know the shortcuts." Soon the hole was big enough for the dog to squeeze through. Glad sat on the other side, barking his frustration that the mice were long gone. Lesley did a bit more digging, until the hole was larger still. "I'll go first, you follow."

"Me? There are worms there."

"What?" he shouted. "First mice and now worms? Dash it, woman, your daughter is on the other side of that tunnel!"

"Then let her come open the wretched door! Better yet, Mr. Know-It-All, you can crawl out and unbar the door. It does not take two of us to wriggle through worms. Besides, you forgot Glad."

Lesley was taking off his coat. "Dash it, Carissa, he can't open the door either!"

"No, you forgot that I'm afraid of dogs, too," she admitted. "I really am a coward, you know."

He kissed her quickly, dirt and all, before lowering himself to his stomach next to the tunnel. "As long as you're not afraid of me, you are perfect."

Once out of the shed, they raced for the horses. Lesley tossed her into the saddle, telling the dog he would have to stay behind until one of the men could come fetch him. They'd be riding too fast for his additional weight on the horse, too wildly for his balance. Carissa tossed Glad the loaf of bread she'd stuffed in her saddlebag, in case Pippa was hungry. Then she tossed him the cheese too.

Lesley did not know if his men would be at the crossroads when they got there, or if the ambush would be possible, he explained as they rode through the woods. He hoped to nab Cantwell as soon as he released the child. If not, he'd follow him to the antipodes.

As it turned out, Byrd and the others were at the intersection, picking likely hiding spots before it got too dark to see. Lesley had them disperse in a circle, out of sight, to cover all angles. Then he and Carissa stood by the side of the road Kane would be using, holding hands, waiting. They could hear a horse's labored breathing long before they could see Kane, hunched over the saddle, Pippa clutched in front of him. Lesley, Carissa, and Byrd stepped out into plain sight, drawing his attention.

"I'll kill the girl, Carrie. You know I will, so call them off." He had the pistol in his hand, ready.

"If you kill her, you are a dead man, Cantwell, and if you ride past us, you'll have a knife in your back before you've gone five meters. Put the girl down, now."

"And you'll let me go?"

Lesley aimed his own pistol at the ground. "Put her down."

Cantwell was wavering, casting nervous, hasty glances behind him. Lesley could not take a chance on him spotting the others and panicking, so he looked past Phillip and called out, "No, Glad, stay back. He has a gun."

Just as Phillip turned to look, Pippa stuck her thumb in his face. He had to release either the girl or the gun, to put his hand to his eye. He chose the girl. The second Pippa was on the ground, shots fired out, knives flew through the air. It was over. The deserter had met his firing squad a bit sooner, was all.

Carissa was hugging Pippa, dampening her with tears, begging her never to suck that particular thumb again, swearing the awful man would not bother them anymore. Then Lesley was there, holding both of them, vowing to keep both of them safe at every crossroad life put in front of them. Lord Heartless knew right where his heart was found.

Late that evening, Lesley scratched on Carissa's bedchamber door. He was wearing a velvet-edged robe, his tight-fitting trousers, and an open shirt. He carried a bottle of wine and a rose.

Carissa was dressed for bed, in a new pink gown and matching robe with falls of lace at the neck and sleeves. She'd been thinking he might come, hoping he'd come, fearing he would not. She couldn't go to his room, she knew, not again. There was not enough courage in the kingdom for her to take another chance on being rejected. His first words relieved most of her doubts.

"Well, Mrs. Kane, are you ready to become Mrs. Hammond at last?"

"I am ready, but are you sure, Lesley? There is still bound to be talk."

"Good grief, what do I care about talk? You are all I care about, Carissa. You have to know that."

His kiss relieved her of the remaining uncertainties. Then he said, "I hope you don't intend to go into mourning for the dastard?"

She eyed the bed behind them. "No, I did that ages ago."

Lesley tried to ignore the down-turned sheets, the soft pillows. While he poured them glasses of wine, he told her, "A rider came while we were out, with the results of the magistrate's investigation. Cantwell was his real name, not that it matters anymore. The messenger also brought a report from Bow Street about the search of Mason's rooms. They found this." He handed her Sir Gilliam's will, dated two years ago. In it he left his dearest friend and beloved honorary daughter his house and fortune, except for pensions for the servants and an allowance for his nephew Broderick. Carissa had to borrow Lesley's handkerchief to wipe her eyes.

"I'm afraid it's all gone, every shilling and then some, but I can offer you six houses, a horse farm in Virginia and a hunting box in Scotland. If none of those suit, I'll buy you six more."

So of course Carissa had to tell him that she'd live in a cottage with him, as long as there were no mice. And he had to kiss her again, mingling the taste of wine on their lips. Then he said, "The Runners also found two clothespresses full of women's gowns in Mason's rooms."

"Why, that sly dog had a woman friend all these years. I never would have supposed such a thing."

"The Runners don't think he had a lady friend, not exactly."

"Ah, a paid companion then. I am not surprised no woman would go with him without payment. That must be why he never brought her to Kensington."

"The neighbors told the men they'd never seen a woman go in the place, and it was empty when he leased it."

Carissa was confused. "There must be some explanation."

"Oh, there is. I'll explain it another time, after we are married, which had deuced better be soon. The messenger brought a special license also, my love, so we can be wed tomorrow, unless you want your father to be here."

"And the duchess would be insulted if we did not invite her."

"Hm." He was tasting her neck now. "We can decide about the wedding tomorrow, my love, but can we have the wedding night right now?"

Her kiss was answer enough.

So rapt in their awakening passion were they that Carissa forgot all about Pippa, asleep on a cot in the adjoining dressing room, in case she had bad dreams in the night.

Rubbing her eyes, Pippa wandered out of the dressing room. She saw her mother alone with Lord Hartleigh, in a lady's chamber, with no chaperon in sight. "I'm telling," she said.

Lesley did not bother releasing Carissa from his embrace. "You can go tell everyone, Pippin, because it is quite proper. I am to marry your mother and be your father, the way I promised. Now go to bed, your own bed. Sue will be missing you and I need to tell your mother how much I love her."

He locked the door behind her.

Sometime later, close to dawn, Lesley was rudely shaken awake. He opened his eyes to look into his beloved's brown ones, and smiled, a slow, satisfied, seductive smile. "It's been a long night, my love, but I'll try."

Blushing, Carissa shook him again. "Not that! It's Cleo. My cat is having kittens!"

Lesley rolled over, pulling her next to him. "Congratulations, Lady Hartleigh-to-be. You finally found something you cannot blame on the dog."

WINTERBOURNE

by Susan Carroll

In the harsh, turbulent Middle Ages, sweet,
timid Lady Melyssan is content to be alone. But
in a desperate move to resist the advances of the
dreaded king, she claims to be married to his
worst enemy, Lord Jaufre de Macy, the
legendary Dark Knight.

When she seeks temporary shelter in Jaufre's
abandoned castle, Winterbourne, she is
unprepared for the fierce, angry warrior who
arrives to confront her. He is a man as rough
and unforgiving as the Welsh borderlands he
rules. But neither Jaufre's dark heart nor
Melyssan's innocent one can resist the love
that is their destiny.

Now available in paperback!

BETRAYED

❧❧❧

Don't miss this breathtaking novel from
Bertrice Small, *the undisputed queen
of sensual romance.*

❧❧❧

When Fiona Hay offers Angus Gordon her
virtue in exchange for a dowry for her sisters,
she so intrigues the rogue that he demands
higher payment: She will be his mistress. Thus
begins a sensual battle of wills and carnal
delights that draws these ardent lovers into the
turbulent court of King James. Thrown into a
dangerous game of political intrigue, the
indomitable Fiona holds the key to a country's
future—a key that could destroy her one
chance at everlasting love. . . .

Passionate . . . compelling . . . powerful . . .

*Available in bookstores everywhere.
Published by Ballantine Books.*

ON SALE NOW

MIDNIGHT RIDER
By Diana Palmer
New York Times bestselling author of
The Long, Tall Texan series

To Bernadette Barron, Eduardo Cortes is the enemy.
A noble count with a sprawling ranch in the grand
state of Texas, Cortes challenges her with dark, pene-
trating eyes that seem to pierce her very soul. For
theirs is a marriage of convenience—he needs a rich
wife to save his land; she needs a titled husband. But
can't he see the burning truth: that she loves him?

It is a secret Bernadette vows to keep until desire
turns their marriage bargain into a passionate battle of
wills. For it is love's fiery initiation that will make
Bernadette aware of her own capacity for pleasure,
and it is the sheer force of her own love that will give
her newfound strength to battle against the odds to
claim a man she will not be denied. . . .

Published by Fawcett Books.
Available in bookstores everywhere.